COLD FEET

A warm and wicked sequel to Hot Breath.
She's free, fit and just under forty—so why does Harriet feel that life is slipping from her control? Life should be perfect, especially now that she has got rid of her staid husband. Yet complications arise on every front. Her determination to enjoy herself without male accessories is sorely put to the test when temptation is thrust under her nose in the form of a cold-eyed but hot-blooded magazine editor. Harriet's once-ordered world holds greater surprises than any of the plots she's dreamt up for her bestsellers!

COLD FEET

Cold Feet

by

Sarah Harrison

Black Satin Romance
Long Preston, North Yorkshire,
England.

British Library Cataloguing in Publication Data.

Harrison, Sarah
    Cold feet.

    A catalogue record for this book is
    available from the British Library

    ISBN 1-86110-004-3

First published in Great Britain by Macdonald & Co (Publishers)
Ltd., 1990

Published in Large Print October, 1996 by arrangement with Little,
Brown & Company (UK) Ltd.

Black Satin Romance is an imprint of
Library Magna Books Ltd.
Printed and bound in Great Britain by
T.J. Press (Padstow) Ltd., Cornwall, PL28 8RW.

For Jeremy, Laurence, Fan and Thea with love

CHAPTER 1

There were times when I felt awfully like one of my beleaguered historical heroines (of blessed memory) and this was one of them. At the end of my journey there before me was my very own latter-day equivalent of a Gothic pile, seething with bats and homicidal housekeepers.

Even the cab driver was sorry for me. 'Suppose everyone's got to live somewhere,' was how he put it, gazing glumly about him as he palmed my outsize tip.

'I have an idea it's becoming gentrified,' I said, unable to keep the tremor of doubt from my voice.

He very properly ignored this. 'What a bugger,' he remarked, awestruck. 'Journey's a bugger, place is a bugger. A real bugger,' he added, in case I hadn't caught his drift.

'Oh I don't know...but well done for finding it!' I said, bearing in mind that his might be the only cab in sight when I emerged later.

'All part of the service.' He executed a rapid three-point turn and cast a valedictory glance at the steep, blackened walls that surrounded me. 'Have fun.'

I stood in Clink Lane, buried in the hinterland of scuttling streets somewhere between Liverpool Street and the river, and wished I might be anywhere but here. I promised God, with whom

11

I had a friendly if interrupted relationship, that if he would spirit me back to Basset Magna I would not only change the sheets but also refrain from reprimanding the children for whatever I happened upon while doing so.

Not surprisingly, it was no dice. The dank, icy wind of early February scurried along the clogged gutters and nipped my ankles. Two winos on some nearby wasteground, their faces the only flashes of colour to be seen, raised their shared bottle of Strongbow in welcome. A three-legged cat cantered with gruesome agility across the road and into a derelict doorway.

This was where my similarity to my heroines ended. In these circumstances any one of them—plucky Maria, headstrong Kate or impulsive Anne—would have gathered her cloak about her and decided that any action was better than none.

Not so I. I'd probably still have been standing there as dusk and the winos closed in, had not a window high in the otherwise blind front wall beside me opened and a young man in red leaned out. The notion that he had spotted my plight and wished to help was quickly dispelled by the shower of crumbs that pattered round me on the narrow pavement.

'Goodness, how awful!' he exclaimed, hand to cheek, leaning out above me like a geranium in a window box. 'I'm truly sorry, I didn't expect anyone to be there!'

'That's all right,' I said, magnanimous with relief. I smiled up at him as I brushed fragments of carbonised toast from my shoulders. 'Perhaps

12

you could help me. I'm looking for the Hal Worship Studio.'

'Oh, but that's us!'

'Really? Are you Hal Worship?'

'Hardly, dear, a mere toiler in the vineyard. But this is the studio.' He folded his arms on the sill as if ready to gossip for hours. 'What can we do for you?'

My neck was beginning to lock. 'I'm supposed to be there. I'm Harriet Blair.'

'Welcome, Harriet.'

'I'm an author. Hal Worship's supposed to be taking my picture for the *Sunday News Review*.'

'That's right,' agreed my friend, 'I knew you rang a bell. We've been discussing how to take you.'

'Look,' I said. 'The thing is, where's your door?'

'You poor thing, I'm so sorry!' he cried. 'It *is* a bit tricky if you've not been here before. You go along towards the river and turn right, then along the snicket. You'll see Hal's sign, and the fearfully unpromising beige door is us. Just ring and we'll press the buzzer for you.'

'Thank you.' I lowered my head.

'I say...' I lifted it again. 'I say, isn't it a pity I don't have a lovely long plait of hair that I could let down for you to climb up?'

The way he'd indicated lead me into the teeth of a wind that carried with it a rancid alluvial odour. Litter of the kebab-and-war-comic variety bustled and pranced in the road. The appearance of thoughtful elegance so carefully cultivated by me before leaving Basset Magna began to feel less and less appropriate.

Ah, here was the sign, HAL WORSHIP PHOTOGRAPHIC STUDIOS, 2nd FLOOR, and here the unpromising beige door. I rang the bell and almost at once a voice bade me 'Push and enter'.

It was one of those curious buildings where nothing whatever seemed to happen on the lower levels. A narrow, echoing staircase led from the hall to a first-floor landing, on neither of which there was the least sign of human habitation. The second floor, however, more than made up for this. Here, a door stood wide open, there was a pleasing smell of toast and coffee. Vivaldi played, and a white, green-eyed kitten skittered away from me with its tail in the air, into a flat I sensed to be full of people.

I knocked and went in, calling 'Hallo...?' tentatively. I had the vague feeling that if my arrival were insufficiently advertised I might stumble upon some scene of domestic intimacy in which I had no place.

'Harriet, hooray, you found us!'

Hal Worship came to greet me with arms outstretched. He was tall, but tight-knit. Even his face looked as though it worked out with weights, and his bleached hair was short and slick like the coat of an otter. He wore a shiny outsize suit of pearlised grey, over a gleaming white vest. On his feet were snow-white trainers, their dainty soles innocent of any trace of the great outdoors, let alone the garbage of Clink Lane.

With his arm lightly around my waist he led me into the studio, in which were two young men and a plain girl. It was tough on the girl being plain because both men were staggeringly beautiful. At the far side of the studio, beyond what looked like a small dance floor, was an enormous screen covered with Bacofoil. In front of the screen stood a stuffed cheetah. I experienced another pang as to the suitability of my dress. Enormous lamps surrounded the dance-floor area, their cyclopean faces glaring relentlessly at the spot where I, presumably, was to be photographed. The white kitten scampered and played amid a tangle of wires.

As Hal entered, the young men drifted on to the set and stood with their backs to us, ostensibly conferring about the cheetah.

'Now then,' said Hal, 'we're not *quite* ready for you. Why don't you have a natter with Josie here while you wait?'

'Fine.'

'Hallo,' said Josie, 'I'm Art Editor of *News Review*. Just here on a watching brief,' she added, to disabuse me of any notion that she might be on my side. 'I'm new to the job and this feature was set up before my time.'

'So you don't know, sort of—how they're going to do it?'

'Not the faintest. But I've worked with Hal before and he's usually quite sound.'

Her choice of adjective struck me as curious. The studio's occupants appeared colourful, energetic, faintly threatening—but sound?

My friend in red came in, bearing mugs of

coffee on a '53 Coronation tray. The mugs were patterned with small fat X's and Y's which I took to be chromosomes.

'There we are, Harriet,' he said. 'I'm Paul, by the way. When you've sipped that and finished your chat with Josie I'll put a spot of make-up on you.'

'Right you are.' Now was not the time to tell him that I had spent a full half-hour gilding the lily before leaving the house.

Josie rummaged in her carpet bag, took out two small tins and began rolling herself a cigarette. I took a deep draught of the coffee which was very strong and had certainly filtered through fresh-roasted beans not long before. Hal was directing operations.

'Now then, Callum,' (fair, cleft-chin, outdoor type), 'we're going to want that foil *much* smoother across the back there. Could you...no, *no*, Callum, with the staple gun...that's it. No, hold it, could you go the other side, Zac,' (slim, dark, de Niroesque) 'pull it smooth, catch it there—that's lovely. Then, Zac, if you'll pop and fetch the statues,' *(statues?)* 'and I think we'll have that man-eating plant from the bedroom, just bring it through and we'll play about with it... Forward a bit with the moggy, Callum...' They were frightfully busy. Callum wore Levis and a Miami Dolphins sweatshirt, Zac was in black bondage trousers from which straps and chains depended at every conceivable point.

'Is that what you're wearing?' asked Josie.

I looked down at my discreet, well-cut navy suit. 'Well—yes.'

16

'Not to worry,' said Josie, 'they'll be able to do something with it. You'd be amazed.'

Zac had placed the plant on the set, where the kitten at once scrambled up its stem and swung upside down and ears flattened, from one of the branches. He now reappeared bearing two plaster cherubs. They were life-size and naked, their faces pouting and sly, their coyly positioned, dimpled hands failing to conceal their precocious little pricks. They filled me with a deep and awful dread.

I leaned across to Josie. 'What a lot of props! What can they be planning?'

She looked at me as if seeing me for the first time. 'You're an author.'

'Yes.'

'And it was Julia Pearcy who interviewed you, wasn't it?'

'Yes.'

'Well then. You know the score, surely.'

'Score?'

'The angle.'

'No. I mean, I thought it was just a profile. Sort of thing.' I added, modestly.

Josie, obviously realising the extent of my self-delusion, adopted a more careful tone.

'Well it is, in a way. But as I'm sure you know the *Review* is doing a whole issue about sexual fantasy—right?'

'I'm not clear...'

'You know, the fantasy and the reality, whether fantasies help your sex life, whether married women need them to relieve the boredom of domestic sex. All that.'

17

'Ah. Right.'

'See? And your bit—I'm sure Julia must have said—is about the fantasy-creator. I mean your body-strippers.'

'My what?'

'Your books—your books feed women's fantasies. Thousands of women read them and fall passionately in love with the heroes, and then pretend that their flabby unromantic husbands *are* those heroes...'

She prattled on, but I'd heard quite enough. A row of hideous suspicions had appeared on my mental skyline like an Apache raiding party sizing up a wagon train. I supposed I dimly remembered this fantasy business being mentioned during the course of a lengthy lunch at Julia Pearcy's expense, but I had at no time regarded it as the cornerstone of her thesis regarding me.

'The thing is,' I said, 'I'm no longer writing those kind of books.'

'Are you not...?' said Josie absent-mindedly, her attention on the set.

'No. I did actually make this point to Julia at the time, and she seemed interested.'

'I'm sure she was. She is a wonderful listener.'

I persevered. 'My latest book is totally different. It's contemporary, for one thing. It chronicles the changes in a relationship over many years.'

'Not to worry,' said Josie for the second time that morning, 'it's the other ones you're famous for.' I suddenly knew what she was going to say next. 'I haven't read them'—I was

18

right—'but I'm always seeing them in Smiths and whatnot.'

I stared in dismay at the set. The white kitten was sharpening its claws on the cheetah's already threadbare leg. Callum was spraying the triffid. Zac was draping one of the cherubs in a length of tulle. Hal looked on, arms akimbo, head a little on one side in the manner of a man who sees his vision taking shape.

'Right, Harriet.' It was Paul, standing before me with his hands together like a geisha. 'Shall we?'

As he worked, Paul explained that what in effect he was doing was blotting my face out and redesigning it from scratch.

'I mean,' he said, 'you and I both know you're the healthy, outdoor, bare-faced type, but we have to *create* that look for the camera. By the time I've finished with you, Harriet, you'll be the most natural-looking lady in town.' He placed well-manicured fingertips on my temples and gave a peek-a-boo smile to my reflection in the mirror. 'We are, however, going to dramatise those eyes.'

I was sitting draped in a black towel in Hal Worship's kitchen, which resembled one of the more elaborate sets from *The Empire Strikes Back*. It was a high-tech, low-effort, maximum-gloss monument to the designer's art. The cooker was a shiny black knob-less cube, and this and the other functional units merged into one another to form a horseshoe in the centre of the room, illuminated by concealed lighting and overhung by a gigantic

19

steel hood like a giant's candle-snuffer. Beyond the horseshoe a sleek black ledge ran round the outer wall, serving at various junctures as desk, bar, dressing table and a repository for TV and audio equipment. Surprisingly comfortable chairs of asymmetric moulded plastic stood by the ledge, and it was on one of these that I perched and submitted to Paul's ministrations. He dabbed, rubbed and stroked my face, and finally cupped it in his hands and pronounced me done. I wished Gareth and Clara could have seen me now. I looked as much like Cindy Brinkley as it was possible for an English housewife in her late thirties to look. My skin glowed, my eyes sparkled, my lips gleamed and my jawline seemed miraculously to have firmed up.

'Gosh,' I said.

'*Et maintenant,*' said Paul, '*les cheveux.*'

'I had it cut not long ago,' I pointed out.

Paul smiled brightly and soothingly at me. I remembered I used to smile like that at the children when they were very young and offering charming but naïve opinions on matters about which they knew nothing. It was clear Paul cared not a fig for my out-of-town trim.

'For the picture Hal has in mind,' he explained, 'we want a vibrant *mass* of hair. A stunning leonine mane.'

'Fair enough,' I said. I've never argued with a hairdresser in my life.

Paul flicked his fingers through my medium-length, medium-brown, lightly permed tresses.

'Hmmm...' he mused. 'Tina Turner it's not.'

'But she wears a wig!' I protested, stung.

'Precisely,' said Paul, and opened a drawer.

'Oh dear.'

He drew out a russet-coloured sunburst of shaggy locks and held it aloft. I felt as though a vulture was hovering over my head, about to perch there.

'No!' I moaned. 'I shall be unrecognisable!'

Though Paul was too polite to say so, it was obvious from his expression that this was the general idea. Still, he put the vulture back in its cage with a sigh and began to backcomb my hair with manic speed, his hands a blur like the feet of a dachshund digging a hole.

My imagination leapt ahead to the moment when I would have to emerge and make my way back, by taxi and train, to Basset Magna. I laughed nervously. 'You will go easy on the hairspray, won't you?'

But Paul had made enough concessions for one morning. 'Harriet,' he said, his face stern as he leaned round my hair, *'il faut souffrir pour être belle.'*

Like some alien lifeform beneath the unforgiving glare of the lights I gave myself up to Hal Worship's professional scrutiny. Hal, his acolytes and Josie were mere dark shapes in the safe obscurity behind the camera. They were murmuring together, discussing my appearance.

To remind them, and myself, that I was a sentient being capable of thought and speech, I called: 'Well? Will I do?'

21

'Just a tiny moment, Harriet,' Hal called back, and then inclined his head towards Zac, saying something *sotto voce.*

Zac came forward out of the shadows and stood a few feet away from me, his chin resting on his clasped hands, his expression roguish.

'Harriet, I wonder...would you mind removing your jacket?'

'No, not at all.'

He helped me off with the jacket and laid it neatly over his arm, looking over his shoulder at Hal.

'Yes? No?'

'Just a touch more,' said Hal.

Zac turned back to me. He had dense black curly hair and a tiny gold abacus on a chain round his neck. His skin was smooth and flawless. When he moved his chains made a soft tintinnabulation, like cowbells in an alpine pasture. He smiled confidingly at me, wrinkling his nose. He and I, he intimated, must accede to the thoroughly unreasonable requests of a higher authority. 'Could I possibly ask you, Harriet,' he said, 'to undo another button for us?'

I glanced down at the neck of my oyster-silk shirt, where only a chaste glimpse of collarbone was currently visible.

'What,' I said cloddishly, 'here?'

'If you wouldn't mind,' said Zac.

I didn't really know whether I minded or not. I was mesmerised. I undid a button. Zac studied me and then laid my jacket over the back of the cheetah. 'May I?' He stepped up to me with a little cuff-shooting gesture, like a conjurer showing an audience that he has not palmed any white mice, ping-pong balls or court cards. Then he took the two edges of my shirt in the finger and thumb of each hand and tweaked them apart. 'There.' He patted my shoulders reassuringly and then, to Hal: 'Yes?'

'Almost,' responded Hal.

Obedient to Zac's beseeching look I undid the next button, trying to remember what underwear I'd put on that morning. It was a perfectly unexceptionable white bra. Not exactly Linda Lusardi, but no disgrace either.

Zac gave my neckline another tweak, whispering: 'Hal likes his little flash of boobs.'

'Does he?' Only a very little flash, I imagined.

Hal stopped to peer at me through his camera and then emerged from the shadows looking, thank God, quite pleased.

'That's lovely, Paul's done us proud as usual. Don't think I'm going to ask you to do anything disgusting, Harriet, it's just that for the purposes of the feature we went you to look just a shade *exotic*. It's only a bit of fun.'

I thought sadly of the care I had lavished on appearing thoughtfully elegant. 'I wish someone had told me,' I said. 'I'd never have worn this suit.'

'Oh, nonsense!' cried Hal. 'We can hide the skirt, and now that we've got rid of the jacket'—he took it off the cheetah and held it out to Zac—'the little top is perfect. Now let me show you what I want.'

What he wanted was me kneeling on the floor with my elbows resting on the cheetah's back, and my chin in my hands. The cherubs and the triffid stood in close attendance. The cheetah smelled musty and the seam down its spine was coming unstitched, perhaps as a result of the kitten's depredations. I thought I detected another, fresher odour, also traceable to the kitten which had now been removed by Paul to frolic in the kitchen. One of the cherubs had a chipped prick.

'Yes,' said Hal, 'yes.' Zac hovered nearby, ready to make adjustments, but mercifully none were required.

'Right,' said Hal, 'I think we're ready for Callum.'

'He's just changing,' said Josie, anxious to be of service, 'I'll fetch him.'

'Relax for a moment,' Hal advised me, 'but try and remember that exact position.' I stayed put. In a minute Josie returned with Callum who had abandoned his all-American college-boy look for breeches, boots and a flowing white shirt. The metaphors seemed to be getting more mixed all the time, but his arrival was greeted with a chorus of the warmest admiration.

'Oh *great,* oh yes...'

'You know those boots are so soft, just like glove leather, really...'

'You suit that look, Callum, you should definitely wear it more often...'

'Did you see that old film *Tom Jones* when

24

it was on over Christmas...?'

I realised I was being severely upstaged, and pressed my arms closer together to deepen my cleavage. Pearls before swine, of course, but it was a gesture.

'You see what we're getting at now, Harriet, don't you,' said Hal, leading Callum to my side. 'You are this very erotic, very creative lady, this dreamer of dreams and weaver of fantasies. And this'—he slapped Callum's chest—'is the archetypal fantasy hero you have created for all your readers.'

'I see,' I said, rolling my eyes in Callum's direction. 'He looks very nice.'

'We thought so,' agree Hal. 'Now, Callum, stand alongside here, *so...*' he positioned Callum near the cheetah's motheaten rump, 'and stare straight out beyond the camera, into those wide open spaces...fold the arms, nice and Rhett Butler, that's the style.'

'Hang on,' exclaimed Josie, bustling forward, 'look what I found in the cupboard.'

'Well, *now,*' said Hal. 'Look, Callum, don't you think so?'

'Super,' agreed Callum. He took the furled bullwhip and slapped it speculatively against his thigh. There was a cheer. I didn't care for the direction things were taking.

'Try letting it drop,' suggested Hal. 'Let it trail on the ground as though you're just about to crack it.'

Callum let the black thong slither to the ground. Hal said to me: 'They give me the shivers, those things, don't they you?'

25

'Yes,' I agreed, though I was sure our reasons were diametrically different.

'Right, Harriet,' said Hal, tearing his eyes away from the moody and magnificent Callum, 'I want you to stare straight into the camera lens, a nice burning, predatory look, thinking all those naughty thoughts. And Callum, eyes on the distant horizon please—a sex object, no more no less.'

Hal walked back crabwise to his camera, making sure we didn't move. It seemed to me ironic that I was probably the only person in the room who was having trouble dredging up a naughty thought.

'Okay!' called Hal, his eyes to the camera, his hand aloft. 'Come on, Harriet, seduce the lens, very knowing, very sultry, I'm sure you can do it...and Callum, just let all those poor little housewives eat you up...'

What was this? What in the name of all that was literary was I doing here? Was it for this that I had made such a concerted effort to alter both my prose and my status? Why had I not simply refused to collude with Hal Worship and his merry men? Why was I not on the blower at this very moment giving Julia Pearcy a richly deserved piece of my mind? What deeply rooted, long-established habit of self-promotion had brought me to this unlovely pass? Goddammit, I—

'There you are!' cried Hal triumphantly, spreading his arms wide and addressing the world at large. 'What did I tell you? Harriet *can* do the look!'

CHAPTER 2

'Think Booker,' said Lew Mervin. 'It's the only way. Think Booker and fuck the lot of them.'

'You wouldn't say that if you'd seen them,' I replied gloomily.

Lew beamed benignly at me over his spritzer. 'One of the things I love about you, Harriet,' he said, 'is that rich vein of honest British vulgarity.'

One of the things I loved about Lew was his capacity for loving many things about *me*. I'd only given in and acquired an agent because I'd come across Lew. He was not by any standard the most brilliant or creative of his breed in London, nor did he have a track record studded with astronomical paperback deals and ten-hour Hollywood mini-series. His appeal was quite simple: once he had taken an author on to his list she ceased to be a humble writer of schlock prose and became, in Lew's eyes, one of the select, truly incandescent stars in the publishing firmament. All Lew's geese were swans, and his lame ducks soaring eagles. So a solid commercial success such as myself threw him into raptures. And that wasn't all. Where many agents might have advocated caution before throwing a proven formula to the winds in the quest for critical acclaim, he had taken it as further evidence of my brilliance, integrity and intellectual rigour. Visiting Lew was like easing aching limbs, battle-bruised and travel-weary, into a steaming hot bath redolent of fragrant oils. He thought all his writers wonderful, and me the most wonderful of all. I didn't much care whether he increased my value and standing in the marketplace: his usefulness lay in making me feel like a cross between Sue Lawley and Doris Lessing. So on leaving Clink Street with my morale in tatters I had dragged my battered pride and uneasy conscience round to Lew's flat in Kensington Church Street to wallow in his unconditional and undeserved approval.

I was admitted by his PA, Melissa, because Lew himself was on the telephone, but as soon as he saw me he said to his caller: 'Look, I shall have to go—the most sought-after novelist in London has just arrived!...yes...ah, that would be telling!'

It was midday when I arrived, and once we'd established that I would not be accompanying Lew and a cockney rock star to lunch at the Gadfly, he sat me down with a half pint of wine in his immaculate chintzy drawing-room, and began to draw me out. This was Lew's forte. He was a warm, soothing poultice, drawing out the poison and bringing comfort and relief.

I spread before him the horrors of the morning, the indignities of the cheetah, the bullwhip, the cherubs, the hairstyle.

'Actually,' said Lew, 'your hair looks great.'

'That's because I brushed it all out in the taxi.'

'You mustn't worry, Harriet,' he exhorted, up-ending the bottle over my glass and brandishing it at Melissa to indicate that she should fetch another. 'The thing is, it will be absolutely wonderful publicity.'

'But not the right sort!' I wailed.

'Any sort's the right sort. You, Harriet Blair, will look super-gorgeous, that's what people will remember. Most of the women who write serious novels are dogs'—Lew was master of the untenable assertion—'and besides, the more your popular success is underlined, the more remarkable your serious side will appear.'

'I wish I could believe you,' I was petulant, egging him on.

'You must,' said Lew, and then repeated the immortal line: 'Think Booker and fuck the lot of them.'

It wasn't long before I began to feel substantially better, and Lew leaned forward and patted my knee. 'There you are, you see, tea and sympathy.'

I drained my glass. 'Gimme drink and flattery every time.'

'Look, Harriet, why *don't* you come and have lunch? You can get properly acquainted with Mo, he's a great guy.'

'No thanks, Lew. Honestly, I can't.'

Lew was about to remonstrate with me when Melissa summoned him to the phone, and I was left to savour my narrow escape. The natural corollary of Lew's unstinting admiration for all his clients was that he expected you to join in, and to fall about in wonderment over any number of deadbeats, pseuds and posers to whom you would not normally have given the time of day. I knew Mo Townley to be all the aforementioned and a bore to boot. He was trying to escape from the cruel world of rock music (which had not afforded him a top-forty hit in ten years) by means of a board game he had devised, provisionally entitled *Hanging In.* It had to do with the players' ability to survive in the shark-infested waters of modern showbusiness (an ability which Mo himself signally lacked) and it stood not a snowball's chance in hell of catching on, labouring as it did under the double disadvantage of being both dull and complicated. Though I should quite have enjoyed a lunch spent basking in Lew's affections, the prospect of two hours listening to Mo grind on about the game in his glum monotone, interrupted only by Lew's effusions, was too ghastly to contemplate.

I looked around at Lew's drawing-room, almost as familiar to me as my own, though a great deal tidier and more elegant. On the table next to where I sat were photographs of his formidably beautiful ex-wife, now chief executive of advertising agency Whelan and Rowe, and his two cool, moth-eyed teenage daughters. Lew was an Anglophile New Yorker (his physical resemblance to Woody Allen was often remarked upon) who had somehow tricked the tallest, haughtiest, most glacial scion of a noble family into becoming his wife. That had been twenty years ago. It was now ten years since Lew and Marisa had divorced, and neither had married again. Marisa, I imagined, because she simply did not need the weight of a husband around her swanlike neck, and Lew because he still carried a torch for Marisa. There was no justice.

Lew returned. 'Reconsidered, Harriet?' he asked.

But by now I had regrouped my forces. 'I'd adore to, Lew, you know that,' I said, 'but I must get back to the homestead. I hadn't planned a whole day in town, I only came here so I could weep on your shoulder.'

'And it's very right that you should,' he agreed. 'What else am I here for but to take your part against these swinish media people? What do they know?' He patted my shoulder. 'This new book of yours is going to set them all back on their heels. I feel it in my water.'

'Is that really what you think?' I asked, from an ingrained habit of milking Lew for all he was worth.

'You know it is!' cried Lew. 'And the people over at Era feel the same! We all think you're so *clever,* Harriet!'

In the train on my way home I wondered whether that was really the Erans' opinion of me. My publishers were every bit as effusive as Lew, but only a fraction as sincere. In fact it would have been fair to say that the Erans were to sincerity what Lucretia Borgia was to home cooking. And after years of effortlessly coining in revenue from my shit-hot historicals—which had achieved a brand recognition as instant as

31

Guiness or Kelloggs—they would have had to be saints to welcome my conversion to Serious Writing. Though Lew's exhortation to 'think Booker' was, on the face of it, ludicrous, I knew that nothing short of a shortlisting for a prestigious literary prize would satisfy the Erans that I had done the right thing. And Lew's confidence notwithstanding, I could not see it happening. Events at the Hal Worship Studio were still fresh and raw in my mind. It seemed a cruel irony that just as I was making such an effort to reform in every area of my life, old dues should be exacted from me in the form of tasteless copy and salacious photographs. It was nearly three years now since the termination (a grim but apposite medical term) of my affair with Dr Constantine—Kostaki to me—Ghikas of Basset Parva, and the object of my ill-conceived lust had left the area. The trouble was he had left me feeling like a woman who has conquered a drink problem—officially cured, but knowing in my heart of hearts that the addiction was always there, waiting to pounce at the slightest opportunity. My brief fling had run its course and my husband George and I had had our first and last terrible row about it. In the end, in the face of my repeated and genuine protestations that it was all over, and being civilised people with an unblemished marital record thus far, we had settled back into the status quo—for a while.

When Kostaki was still around, running baby clinics, talking to the Young Wives about home hygiene, managing the Under Fourteens football team, he was a continual reminder of my fall from grace and how much I'd enjoyed it. Seeing him buzzing through the village in his little green Fiat, or across the room at cocktail parties, charming hapless females half to death, I was obliged to continue to tighten the rein on which I held myself. When he'd eventually gone I felt both relieved and saddened because that, after all, was that.

On his departure I wasted no time in finding outlets for my dangerous surplus energy. I embarked on my serious novel, *A Time to Reap*, I joined the local drama group, the Basset Arcadians, and I ran a marathon.

This last was my equivalent of the granddaddy of all cold showers. I entered for it the month that Kostaki left Parva, with no serious hope of being accepted, and to my astonishment the computer smiled on me. From that moment on I was bombarded with information about diet, footwear, mental attitude and training methods. I became familiar with such terms as 'carbo-loading', 'fartleks' and 'banking the miles'. On Sundays I left the house at seven a.m to describe an eighteen-mile circuit of Bassets Magna, Parva and Regis. Without fail George would come out in the car and cruise me at the halfway point, ostensibly offering orange barley water in a plastic bottle but actually, I knew, checking that I had not accepted lifts from any strange men. This discreet surveillance, carrying with it a maddening whiff of coffee, croissants and newsprint, played a crucial part in our eventual separation.

That, and the fact that I had so much time to think. Each of these runs was as much a mental as a physical journey. I passed through the phases of gloom, free association, boredom and elation, as I ran, and each moodswing had its corresponding landmark. The gloom would last a full seven or eight miles until the Little Chef on the Regis bypass hove in view. Not until I had left well behind those steamy, well-lit windows which framed the faces of motorists stuffing themselves with eggs, chips and maple-syrup pancakes could I settle down, switch on to automatic pilot and start dreaming of being a literary lioness. Sparkling, well-turned reviews in prestigious periodicals, searching but respectful interviews on *Kaleidoscope* and *Bookshelf*, residential seminars at four-star hotels in the Lake District—all whirled in my imagination, and as my pulses quickened, so did my pace. But by the time I reached the Bengali supermarket on the far side of town this phase would be ending, and as I struck out along the bleak 'A' road that constituted the section of my circuit furthest from home, I would enter a period of drab and terrible boredom. The shops, pubs, houses and filling stations were behind me, so there was nothing and no-one to divert a lone jogger except the occasional car whining smugly past at speed. The countryside was typical Barfordshire. Flat, bare and cheerless, the prevailing north-east wind whipping across it unimpeded, direct from the Siberian tundra. It was along this five-mile stretch that I most frequently asked myself the question: 'Why? Why was I doing this? What impelled me to pound the open road on a Sunday morning when sensible folk were snug indoors enjoying civilised pleasures? Why do a marathon? Unfortunately, hard on the heels of the question came the answer. As a displacement activity, that was why. To take my mind off Kostaki's departure, and the fact that George and I had not really succeeded in restoring the placid tenor of our pre-Kostaki marriage. We did our best, but nothing could conceal the fact that we were irritating the hell out of each other. Mutual resentment was our fellow traveller. I think I could have tolerated the marriage seeming merely dull, in the same way that I tolerated the tedium of my training runs. I could simply have thanked God for the peace and quiet, and sought my kicks in work and village activities. But the smooth, dull surface of our relationship was fretted with niggling doubts and suspicions.

And, of course, this was when George would zoom up with the orange barley water, cosy and warm behind the wheel of the BMW. Carly Simon on the tape deck, an Aran sweater over his pyjamas.

'Well,' he would say, consulting his watch, 'not so dusty. How are you feeling?'

How did he expect me to feel? 'Tired.'

'Never mind, you're half way.'

I'd finish the drink, hand back the paper cup and begin to run again, with George keeping pace, his pyjama legs tugging in the wind.

'See anyone you know?'

'No.'

'I'll expect you back in about an hour then!'

'Yes.'

He'd go back to the car and move gently, effortlessly past me, with a cheery wave and shout of: 'Keep up the good work!' which so enraged me that I'd manage the next mile in record time.

Yes, I may only have managed four hours forty in the marathon, but those long hours spent on my own, and out of the house, had enabled me to reach my moment of decision.

On the big day George was waiting for me in the family meeting place, the children having stayed at home to watch on TV.

'Well done!' he cried, and then couldn't wait to add: 'Get talking to anyone interesting on the way round?'

'George,' I said, as red and greasy as wrapped salami in my tinfoil cape. 'George—I think we should try living apart for a while.'

To do him justice, he behaved very well. I think he found it rather a relief. I certainly did. The children greeted the news with their usual phlegm, George took a compact but airy modern flat on the northern, smarter edge of Basset Regis, and we established an agreeable pattern of life pretty much like the old one except that for much of the time there was a safe distance between us.

When the organisers of the marathon sent me the standard photograph of myself breasting the tape, just behind a woman in her sixties, I saw that I wore an expression of calm satisfaction.

It looked rather impressive. Only I could have known that this expression was due to my having decided to turf my husband out of the matrimonial home.

I got back to Magna at two-thirty. The house had that slightly sinister calm of early afternoon. Noleen O'Connell, Declan's wife, had been in the morning, so hoovered, carpets and gleaming surfaces intensified the calm. When my previous domestic, Damon Prime, had moved on to higher things Declan had wasted no time in recommending his spouse for the position, and I must say I had never regretted employing her. I had once rather uncharitably likened her to a net curtain, pale, drab and limp, but against all likelihood she possessed a capacity for hard work that would have embarrassed the average shire horse. She was also, mercifully, silent. Very occasionally, in response to a question shouted directly at her when there was no-one else in the house, she would make a small, muted rustling sound, accompanied by a tremor of the head to indicate yes or no. While Declan, a verbal pugilist, fussed and fumed about the garden in a haze of misanthropic invective, Noleen went about her duties like a timid, threadbare ghost, leaving only a hint of furniture polish to mark her passage.

I breathed in the ordered tranquility and blessed Noleen. Even the dog and cat seemed disposed to display their best profiles. Fluffy sat by the boiler in the kitchen looking sleek and statesmanlike, a cat that would never so much as entertain the notion of wrestling the Sunday joint to the floor and chewing it all over before discarding it near the pedal bin. And Spot, lying curled in his basket beneath the stairs, resembled not at all the rapacious canine Lothario whose ever-growing band of ill-favoured puppies had blighted the lives of many a pedigree-bitch-owning family in the vicinity. I made myself a cup of coffee and sat down at the kitchen table.

At once the back door opened and Declan appeared, signal for the cat to exit and the dog to enter, both bristling.

'That pony!' he exclaimed, jabbing a corny finger in my direction.

'Hallo, Declan.'

'She needs showin' who's boss, so she does!'

'Shut the door, would you? It's rather chilly.'

Declan slammed the door. 'If she didn't nearly take my roddy hand off at the shoulder!' By this he meant that Stu's teeth had clacked shut a good metre or two from his arm.

'Bad luck.'

'Luck be boggered!' he spluttered, and began to describe in furious detail the events leading up to the attempted atrocity. I switched off and let him get on with it. This, after all, was one of the perks of his job.

At this time of the year, when there wasn't much for Declan to do in the garden, he earned his retainer by helping with Stu. Being Irish he laid claim to a preternatural understanding of horseflesh. In response to my asking whether he had ever actually worked with horses he had bellowed: 'How d'yer think I lost these teeth?', which effectively closed the discussion but left me wondering quite what point had been made.

'....lucky to have this hand!' he concluded. 'And me not insured!'

Spot snarled.

'Never mind,' I said. 'All's well that ends well.' I had finally learned that to gain ascendancy over Declan one had to deprive him of the oxygen of argument. These days, armed with a good supply of sturdy banalities and platitudes, I could contain his fires almost indefinitely. Now, his face was blackening nicely.

'Jesus!'

'Coffee, Declan?'

'No!'

'I wonder, would you thank Noleen for me? I wasn't in when she came this morning.'

'She has a cold!'

'Poor thing. How are Sean and Mary Rose?'

'Mary Rose has to have the grommets, so she does.'

'Oh well, it'll be a good job done.'

My choice of words had given Declan an opening, and he was swift to make use of it. 'And it'd be a good job if that pony was taken in hand!'

'I thought you were doing that for us, Declan.'

'She needs the bloody nonsense gallopin' out of her! Where's that girl of yours?'

'She's at school. She rides her when she can.'

39

Declan made a characteristic sound. It began with a click, went into a hiss and ended in an explosive snort. It conveyed rage, despair, and most of all, scorn. The finger came back into play. 'She needs sortin' out, or I shan't be responsible!' With this he stumped out, leaving me unsure whether he'd meant Stu or Clara. On balance, I felt that particular round had gone to Declan. Stu was not earning her keep at the moment, or at least not as far as I was concerned, though Clara was making a tidy profit out of hirings. Unwilling though I was to concede points to Declan, perhaps the time had come to take a firm line.

My coffee had gone cold, so I poured myself a fresh one. But my phone was programmed to ring at the first hint of steam rising from a mug, and it proved reliable as ever. I let it bleep a few times to demonstrate my independence, but was then overcome as usual by the idea that it might be David Puttnam calling about film rights, and hurled myself at it in panic.

'Hallo? Basset Mag—'

'Don't bother, Harriet, it's Lew!'

'Oh, hallo.' I tried unsuccessfully to keep the disappointment out of my voice, but I needn't have bothered. Lew was clearly in a ferment.

'Just listen, Harriet! I'm calling from the Gadfly because I've just heard some *very* interesting news. *Super* interesting news!'

'What's that?'

'It's all over this place, it's in this week's *Pub Talk,* apparently'—he referred to one of the many organs of the publishing world—'and as

40

soon as I heard about it I thought, "Harriet".'

'Go on then.'

'*Well*— have you heard of some people called Betabise? They're supermarkets.'

'I have as a matter of fact. I used to know someone who worked for them.'

'Really? Now that is interesting. Who would that be?'

'A chap called Stan Atkins, he lived in my village. But he was promoted and moved house. Look, Lew, what *is* this?'

'They're launching a literary prize, Harriet! I've made a note, here we are, the "Betabise Book of the Year Award".'

I felt a prickle of interest. 'Are they? What are the entry conditions?'

'No, no, wait—I'm going to tell you what it's worth, first.'

'Go on, then.'

'Twelve grand, Harriet.'

'Good Lord, they must be barmy.'

'Not at all. Just booming, and keen to promote a more upmarket image. By the way I checked and they are one of the chains that carry books.'

'Yes I know, we've got one here in Regis. They always carry a few Harriet Blairs. Old style, of course—.'

'No matter, no matter at all. The award is for any kind of book providing it's contemporary and deals with contemporary themes. A contextual book, in other words, Harriet. That's you, unless I'm very much mistaken!'

'I suppose it could be...'

41

'No question.'

'But mine isn't even published till the summer.'

'That's the beauty of it, they want *unpublished* works. Not necessarily first novels, but un-published. Now, do I ring Era right away and tell them to put your name forward?'

'When's the closing date?'

'Well now, I have to get hold of a copy of *PT* to check that out, but from what I gather there's plenty of time. The award itself will be made in early May.'

I cast about for a hitch, but there didn't seem to be one. 'I suppose we could try,' I said. It was what I'd been hoping for, but now that it had come along I felt unaccountably nervous.

'Try? Try?' Lew's voice rose to an affronted squeak. 'You're a cert for the shortlist at the very *least*, Harriet. *Reap* is just exactly what they're looking for!' The abbreviation of my book's title was one of Lew's most cherished affections. It was the means by which he managed to convince himself, sometimes me, and very occasionally his more gullible colleagues that my current novel was a household word, part of the *lingua franca* of those in the know.

'Okay,' I said. 'Let's give it a go. We've got nothing to lose.'

'Absolutely nothing to lose, Harriet, and just about everything to gain. You must excuse my vulgar little references to the money early on, because really that's the least important thing—'

'Oh, I don't know.'

'—it's the enhancement of your reputation that's the issue here. It's not as if you need the money, Harriet, I mean you're already one of the most successful authors around, but what I want to see for you now is the quality of your writing given the recognition it deserves.'

I heard the sound of cuckoos among the clouds.

Harriet?'

'Quite right,' I said. 'Go for it, Lew.'

As I replaced the receiver, I realised what it was that I feared: losing.

Gareth, 16, and Clara, 14 (as book jackets say), left Regis College at the same time and aboard the same bus, but arrived home ten minutes apart. This was due to a shared abhorrence of being seen together in public, or indeed of anything which might point to their common parentage.

Gareth came in first, his upturned blazer collar and loosened, abbreviated tie marking him out as a fifth year of some substance. He dropped his bag and headed for the breadbin, moving me pointedly aside as he did so. I continued with one of the few housewifely tasks I still retained, trying to match socks recently out of the wash with others from the odd-sock bag.

Only when Gareth had finished constructing a multi-layered sandwich of epic proportions, and consumed the first half of it, did he address me.

'Where've you been?'

'In London.'

'Where did you go for lunch?' Gareth had grasped only a few things about my work, and chief among them was that trips to the capital were generally for the purpose of lunch. It was my pleasure, on this occasion, to correct him.

'I didn't. I was having my photograph taken.'

'What for?'

'For *News Review*. They're running a piece on me.'

Gareth munched on peanut-butter, cheese and salad-cream, his eyes taking in my navy suit and tasteful silk blouse.

'Why were you trying to look like the Prime Minister?'

I did not stoop to take issue with him about this. When I walked off with the Betabise Award, time enough then to spurn my detractors beneath my heel. Clara came in. She, too, dropped her bag, and homed in on the breadbin.

'Hallo, Clara,' I said, 'good day?'

'Not bad.'

'She had a *very* good day,' said Gareth, in what even I could see was an extremely annoying tone of voice. 'A *very* good day, didn't you?'

'What are you on about?' Clara put uneven slices of white bread in the toaster, slammed them down and turned the dial to 6. Only smoke would convince her that her toast was done.

Gareth turned to me. 'She spent all afternoon break hanging around the staff car park with Colin Waller.'

'I was doing something for Mrs Chatterjee,' said Clara. 'So mind your own business.'

'You were doing something for Colin Waller too unless I'm much mistaken,' said Gareth. 'I've never seen him look so happy.'

'Who is Colin Waller?' I asked.

'No-one,' said Clara.

'Regis's answer to Bros,' said Gareth. 'Or he thinks he is.'

I pressed on. 'So what were you doing with him in the staff car park?'

'Oh for heaven's sake!' Clara yanked up her toast, disappearing into an acrid haze. 'I told you, Mrs Chatterjee asked me to fetch the overhead projector from the back of her car and said if I needed help I could take someone else with me.'

'Yes,' said Gareth, 'but I think she meant someone from school.'

'What?' I flung open the window to dispel the smoke. 'You mean he's not at school? How old is he?'

'No idea,' said Clara, coating her toast in marmalade.

'Eighteen,' said Gareth.

'And what does he do?'

'Works at the supermarket. Loading and unloading.' I saw Clara flash her brother a look of pure vitriol. He was certainly a mine of unwelcome information.

'Which supermarket?'

'Thing. You know. Betabise.'

Something must have shown on my face because Gareth, moving across to reclaim his

45

bag, put his hand on my shoulder and said soothingly: 'Don't get in a state. Waller's okay, wouldn't hurt a fly. That's his trouble!' Chuckling to himself, he left the kitchen and went upstairs.

Clara sat down with her toast, opened a newspaper which lay on the kitchen table and began to eat and read her horoscope at the same time. These activities, combined, were about the closest my daughter ever came to a religious experience.

'Clara...'

'Settle down, Mum. Just don't start.'

'He's much too old.'

'He's young for his age.'

This was probably true. And Clara was old for hers. She was the only Blair who displayed from time to time a core of real steel, and it was wellnigh impossible to deflect her from any course of action upon which she had embarked. It had been bad enough when, at the tender age of eleven, she had announced her intention of leaving school and running a mobile disco with my charperson, Damon. Only the threat of sanctions of the most punitive and draconian kind had persuaded her that this move would be unwise. Having quickly recovered from the injury to her pride she had moved on to cut a swathe through the first- and second-year youths at Regis College. She exuded the sullen allure of a banked-up coal fire, and the cool hostility with which she treated the wretched teaching staff only added to her appeal. George and I had all too frequently found ourselves in the invidious position of middlemen, deputed to encourage or rebuff according to instruction, to tell lies on her behalf of breathtaking and insulting transparency, and when she deigned to grant her swains an audience to make ourselves invisible and inaudible.

I stuffed all the renegade socks into the bag and sat down. 'You are absolutely not,' I said, 'to see this Kevin...'

'Colin.'

'...in school time. Is that understood?'

'Sure.'

'You know you can always bring him round here.'

'Okay.'

It all seemed a bit too easy. I remembered something else about which I was intending to do some plain speaking.

'And Clara...'

'Mm?' She closed the paper and gazed at me from beneath sooty lashes.

'About Stu.'

'Yes, I know. Perhaps we ought to sell her.'

Frankly, I was gobsmacked. I knew very well that over the past year Stu had represented for Clara not so much a means of healthy exercise as a useful power-base and source of regular revenue. So unscrupulous were her hiring arrangements that I had frequently received calls from hysterical parents whose little girls had been seen trotting briskly the wrong way along the dual carriageway, and who had been led to believe that the pony concerned was ours. The resulting shouting matches had got me nowhere. I had even, pocketing my pride, summoned George to discipline his daughter, but after a brief lull the hirings-out continued. So her apparent co-operation now was a most welcome development.

Nonetheless I was cautious. 'I think it would be sensible.'

'Mmm...' Clara licked her finger to mop toast crumbs. 'What do you reckon we'd get for her, with all her tack?'

I realised I had no idea. 'Well I imagine it would be silly to ask less than a hundred pounds.'

'A hundred pounds?' screeched Clara. 'God, that'd be giving her away.'

'It's not as if she's all that...'

'She's a really good pony! You want to ask at least four hundred for her.'

'*That's* daylight robbery.'

We squared up to each other, but I didn't feel like a row. 'We'll decide on something,' I said. 'But I'm glad you agree in principle. I was talking to Declan about it earlier.'

'Oh, *Declan,*' said Clara, getting up from the table. 'Silly old fart.'

With Gareth and Clara both upstairs I went into the sitting-room and sat down with a copy of the local paper. Turning to the classified section I found the section headed *Horses and Ponies* and checked to see what was on offer.

It seemed that you could describe the animal in every way possible except as a horse. One was designated a 'bomb-proof investment', another a 'schoolteacher'. Here was a 'friendly and willing ride-out', and here an 'elderly companion'. I spotted a comprehensible phrase, 'Excellent shoe, box, stable'. Would it be true to say that Stu was excellent to shoe? Terry had never complained, but he had now given up blacksmithing to be Damon's sidekick in various entrepreneurial ventures and I was not to know how great a part Stu's behaviour had played in his decision. As to a box, we didn't own one. Best not to mention box. 'Stable', what did that mean? The place or the character? She was sometimes a bit tricky to catch...best not to mention stable. Crestfallen, I set the paper aside.

The phone rang, but I didn't stir. At this time of day I stood no chance whatever of reaching it before Clara.

'Yeah?' I heard her say. 'Yeah...yeah. It's for you!'

I went out into the hall. 'Who is it?'

'Sloany Vanessa.' Her hand was not over the mouthpiece. I snatched the receiver from her.

'Hallo, Vanessa.'

'I've been called worse things.'

'I'm sorry.' I glared over my shoulder. 'She can be so childish.'

'Well, she *is* a child, after all,' said my editor indulgently, who obviously didn't know what fourteen looked like these days, 'but never mind that. I've just had Lew Mervin on the phone more or less insisting that we enter *A Time to Reap* for this Betabise thing. Of course Tristan and I had read about it in *PT* but I wasn't at all sure you'd want to get mixed up in a thing like that...' She made it sound like the white slave trade. 'I mean, you don't need any prizes, you are already an established and hugely successful author. If you enter and then—by some quirk of fate—or because of something the judges ate the night before—'

'You mean if I don't win I'll get egg on my face.'

'Well, I wouldn't have put it quite like that.'

'It doesn't matter.' The fact that she had voiced my most secret fear made me reckless. 'Nothing ventured, nothing gained.'

'Oh, splendid!' I could feel the warm torrent of relief gushing down the line. 'In that case we won't waste a second. You know we're all stunned by the book here. We have the most enormous faith in it.'

'Jolly good.' I was as breezy and cheerful with Vanessa as I had been gloomy and angst-ridden with Lew.

'Of course,' went on Vanessa, 'it's a little hard to say what de Myers will make of it.' She referred to my American publishers. 'The American market is such an unknown quantity at the moment. I'm not at all sure they know what they want themselves...'

She was bet-hedging and I would have none of it. 'Vanessa, you know what to do. You must bullshit them senseless. You must bang on about the themes and preoccupations of the novel, talk about life-enhancement and increased awareness. Say it's about the role of women, the role of men, the role of marriage

50

in modern society, the role of God in modern marriage—get in there and *talk* them into submission. You know you can do it, and so can Tristan.'

'Oh Harriet...!' Vanessa gave her silvery laugh, 'where would we all be without your sense of humour? You're quite right, we must go into overdrive.'

'You must.'

'I think there are grounds for describing this novel as apocalyptic.'

'I'm sure there are,' I said, 'and if there aren't you make some.' There was a brief pause. I wondered if I had inadvertently achieved the impossible and offended Vanessa. But when she spoke she sounded reflective rather than incensed.

'I hope you won't mind my saying this, Harriet, but you've become a lot more outspoken lately.'

'Have I?'

'Oh yes,' said Vanessa. 'And it's so refreshing!'

CHAPTER 3

The following evening the Basset Arcadians assembled to rehearse their spring production, *Trick of Hearts*. Bernice Potter and I, in the respective roles of Diana (a loose woman) and Yvonne (the voice of wisdom), sat in our overcoats on the stage of the village hall, our breath smoking in the chilly half-light. Half-way down the hall, snugly consulting his script by the fan heater he had brought along for our greater comfort, stood our producer Percy Norton. The rest of the cast were huddled in the brightly-lit kitchen at the far end, sipping coffee and munching chocolate digestives.

'Sod this for a game of soldiers,' Bernice spoke in a venomous undertone.

'Never mind,' I said, 'if we get this scene out of the way it'll be their turn to work and our turn at the refreshments.'

'Right, Diana and Yvonne!' called Percy, 'from the top of page thirty-two.'

Bernice rose to her feet, her French's acting copy in one hand, and began: ' "When I hear you talking, Yvonne, it all sounds very reasonable. God knows, you may even be right, but—" '

Percy lifted his hand, 'I say, Diana!'

'The name is Bernice.'

'Bernice, I'm sorry'. Percy hastened to the foot of the stage, lowering his voice as if to protect our reputations. 'I'm sorry, but it's books down tonight, remember?'

Percy was an ex-Royal Marine in his early fifties, who now ran the delicatessen in Basset Parva. He misguidedly thought of himself as a ladies' man, and this evening wore bounder's togs—cavalry twills, a yellow pullover and shoes that he undoubtedly referred to as brothel-creepers.

Bernice treated him to her very best look of blank astonishment. 'Come again?'

Percy's smile became crocodilian as he advanced up the steps. 'Books down, love.'

'Out of the question, petal.'

Percy came and stood so close to Bernice that his primrose jumper actually brushed her opulently filled overcoat. A lesser woman might have given ground, but Bernice held fast. Her face was a study in polite attentiveness. Poor old Percy, he had absolutely no idea what he was taking on.

'I know it's difficult,' he said, 'but we all have to escape the tyranny of the book some time, and it might as well be now.'

'But I don't know any of the lines,' explained Bernice, as if to a mentally deficient foreigner, 'so what good would it do?'

Percy smiled indulgently. 'You probably know far more of them than you think.'

Bernice put her face towards his so that he had to step backwards. 'Watch my lips: No Lines.'

'I see, fine, okay. But why don't you give it a try, Bernice? For me.'

'Oh well, if you put it like that—' Bernice held her script above her head and gave it a flourish. 'God for Percy, England and St George!' She laid the book open near the front of the stage.

'Good girl.' Percy gave her cheek a kiss and thankfully turned away in time to miss her wiping it with her coat sleeve. As he trotted down the steps and returned to his place near the heater her eyes followed him, twin beams of withering contempt.

'Jesus H Christ,' she muttered to me from the

side of her mouth. 'What a prize waste of time. You know this bit, I take it?'

'Some—the gist of it.'

'Goody two-shoes!'

'You should be damn grateful!'

'Okay girls, hush now,' called Percy. 'Take it away.'

We stood in silence. Somebody out in the kitchen dropped a cup in the sink.

To break the silence, I said: ' "When I..." ' and then nodded encouragingly like Muffin the Mule.

'What's the matter?' asked Bernice.

'Come *on*, girls,' moaned Percy. 'Hit it!'

Bernice bit back the obvious retort with a visible effort. 'Harriet's saying something.'

Percy sighed gustily. 'We should have the prompt. Dilly!' Dilly Chittenden scuttled out of the kitchen. 'When it's books down, we need the prompt.'

'Sorry. Hang on—sorry. Now where are you?'

'Top of page thirty-two,' Percy told her.

Bernice stood at the front of the stage, bent forward from the waist, scanning her copy.

I tried again. 'Bernice—"When I hear you talking..." '

She flapped a hand at me. 'Hold your horses, Harriet, you will in a moment.'

Dilly gave a little cry of satisfaction and placed her finger at the top of page thirty-two. 'I've got it! Diana—Bernice—"When I hear you talking..." '

Bernice straightened up, smiling glassily.

'Should I be saying something? I don't recognise a word of this.'

'It's your line,' I pleaded with her. 'Page thirty-two.'

'Oh, *thirty*-two!' She picked up the copy, turned a few pages and replaced it. 'They must have flipped over. Now then.' She bent over. 'When I hear you talking, Yvonne, it all sounds very reasonable. God knows you may even...'

So it went. Bernice was being appallingly childish and obstructive and she was a new member. As her sponsor I felt deeply embarrassed. The trouble was that for the fourteen years of her marriage to Arundel Potter D.Litt, Bernice had been accustomed to get her own way, mainly by foul means. Arundel disapproved of almost everything about his wife except her body, by which he was enslaved. Bernice had learned to fight dirty. The Potters were without issue, so she had not even had to contend with the daily ego-crunching meted out by children. Her idea of teamwork was on a par with Mussolini's, as the Arcadians were about to find out. She had joined them quite cynically as an escape from Arundel and because, since my affair with Kostaki, she cherished the hope of finding a lusty local bachelor for her own diversion. In this she was entirely shameless, and yet she was curiously innocent in community matters, never having been part of a community. She assumed because she saw the Arcadians engaging in backbiting, scandal-mongering and rank duplicity that this was their received *modus operandi*. She had not, like the rest of us, drunk long and deep at the well of the double standard.

We continued with our scene, with Bernice reading her lines from the book on the floor and I struggling through my dollops of homespun philosophy with considerable assistance from Dilly. I was conscious of Percy jingling his change and bouncing on his heels. The group in the kitchen, aware of an atmosphere, gathered in the doorway so as not to miss anything good. My embarrassment finally got the better of me.

'I say, Percy,' I said. 'Isn't this rather a waste of time?'

'You tell him, girl,' breathed Bernice.

'I should have thought so,' replied Percy in a pained tone, 'but you two must be the judge of that.'

I turned to Bernice. 'Well?'

Bernice put her hand to her breast. 'You know me—I'll just fit in with whatever's happening.'

'May God forgive you,' I hissed. I turned to Percy who had advanced to the edge of the stage. I noticed that his well-brushed and anointed silver-grey hair lay in exactly even corrugations across the top of his head as if it had been set in a waffle-maker.

'Why don't we just read?' I suggested, 'then at least we can put some feeling into it. It's perfectly obvious we need another week or so to get familiar with these lines.'

'A week?' shrilled Bernice. 'You jest, Harriet.'

'Let's discuss it,' said Percy, coming on to the stage. He took a packet of cigarettes from the breast pocket of his checked Viyella shirt, offered one to Bernice, took one himself and lit both with a Dunhill lighter, shielding the operation with his cupped hand. You're never alone with a Strand... I was sure Percy could, and did, blow smoke rings.

'All right, team, take five,' he called down the hall to the group in the kitchen who had already taken six times that. Then he took Bernice by the wrist and guided her to one of the chairs, pulling up the other one and sitting astride it, back to front. His corniness was absolutely mesmerising. Even chocolate digestives could not have lured me away at that moment.

'Now then, Bernice,' he began in the oh-so-confidential, nasal voice in which he sold hummus and rollmops to the ladies of Basset Parva. 'What I'm asking myself is this. I'm wondering whether in your heart of hearts you would rather be relieved of this part.' His voice sank lower so I had to strain to catch it. 'Believe me when I say that you are absolutely perfect for it, I could hardly believe my luck when you happened along just as we were casting this play...it needs someone with real physical presence...genuine earthiness...' Bernice stared back at him, unmoved. I knew that if Percy had interested her even the tiniest bit she would long since have vamped him into quivering submission. As it was she was playing him on the line with the nonchalant ease of an expert.

Percy shunted his chair a few inches further forward. 'But I have a theory,' he said. 'Want to hear what it is?'

Bernice flicked ash on to the stage. 'Fire away.'

'It's this. A happy company is the best company.' He paused for the full effect of this to sink in.

Bernice exhaled. 'Yes?'

'God knows I don't want to lose you, but if you're having real difficulty with these lines...'

'I didn't say I was having difficulty, I said I hadn't learned them.'

'M-hm, you'd be amazed how many people, even professional actors, experience this self-same difficulty.'

'I dare say I would, but I'm not one of them.'

'What I'm trying in my clumsy way to say is...'

'You're giving me the elbow.'

'Now, Bernice...'

'The push. The old heave-ho.'

'Good God, no!' Up till now it had been like watching two monolingual foreigners conversing in their respective languages. Not any more. Percy's face was a study. 'You have entirely misunderstood me, Bernice, you simply couldn't be more wrong.'

Bernice dropped her cigarette-end and crushed it beneath her boot. 'Show me.'

This was the moment to go for coffee and bikkies. Within five minutes, I knew, Bernice would be setting out the terms under which she would be prepared to continue gracing the boards with the Arcadians, and Percy would be outlining the ways in which she could be made to feel more at ease and at home. The rest of the cast greeted me as an emissary from the battle zone.

'Are we likely to go on late this evening?' asked Dilly Chittenden. 'Only if we are I'll give Ricky a ring and tell him not to come straight here after Young Wives' Bright Hour.'

'I should do that,' I said. 'I'll run you home if he doesn't want to turn out a second time.'

'Oh, thanks!' As Dilly went into the lobby to use the payphone, Barry Langley, who played my uxorious husband, passed me a coffee.

'There you go, Harriet. I must say she's a great girl, your Bernice. Where d'you find her?'

I explained that we had known each other for years and that she was my oldest and dearest friend.

'I like her style,' said Barry with a chuckle.

Glynis Makepeace hrrumphed. 'She's got a thing or two to learn about ensemble playing.' I forebore to point out that this was a bit rich coming from Glynis, an Akela who ruled over her little troop with the iron fist of a dictator. Trevor Tunnell, like Barry a refugee from a less than idyllic marriage, and therefore disposed to appreciate Bernice's talents, said: 'That may be so, Glynis, but I've got a pound that says she turns in a really good performance on the night.' No-one took up the bet, so he turned to Brian and Delia Arnold. 'What do you think, as the experts?'

This was tricky for Brian and Delia, who had not long ago moved to Basset Magna and were consequently anxious to please. They were youngish, keen, had belonged to a drama group when they lived in Godalming, and were mad about what they insisted on calling 'theatre' wherever it was to be found. They both worked for the BBC which lent them a certain lustre, but they were at pains to behave like humble postulants, willing to perform the meanest tasks for the good of the whole. Delia was a natural for the daffy *ingénue* and Brian, being only about thirty-three with a good head of hair, had been ushered into the juvenile lead (male). Their youthful appearance was enhanced by those with whom they had to share the stage, notably Glynis (Phyllis, a kindly old card) and Trevor (Pargiter, the loathly blackmailer). It was obvious from Brian's style and delivery that he was actually terribly good and should, were there any justice, have been accorded star status forthwith. But if he nursed any such aspirations he should have been disabused. In the Arcadians, any male who could pass for twenty-five at a safe distance with the light behind him was doomed to play juveniles in *saeculo saeculorum,* or until another came to take his place.

Brian gave Trevor's question careful consideration. 'It's obvious,' he said, 'that she's a very lively lady with a lot to give. She just needs sensible direction, that's all. And I'm sure Percy's the man to give it to her,' he added diplomatically.

'I agree,' said Trevor. 'Delia? You got four penn'orth to put in here?'

60

'Not me,' said Delia in her breathy little voice. 'I simply admire anyone who can direct a play.' We fell silent in the face of this assertion. Delia carried on. 'And as for learning lines, *what* a nightmare!' (She was word perfect.) 'fortunately most of mine are the same, as long as I say "It's all too horrible!" or something like that, I'll get by!'

Dilly returned from the phone. 'That's fixed. We're not still all out here, what on earth's going on?'

'Sensible direction,' suggested Barry.

'It's really not good enough,' grumbled Glynis. 'I've been here over an hour and done nothing so far but stand around. And,' she added grimly, 'I took the trouble to learn my lines.'

'We all have our methods,' said Trevor. 'I put mine on tape and play them over and over in the car, it's surprising how they gradually sink in. Mind you, you get a few funny looks at the traffic lights, chatting away to yourself.'

'What a good idea,' said Brian. 'Thanks, Trevor, I'll try that.'

Barry Langley took the last digestive. 'I think we're in real danger of taking ourselves too seriously. For God's sake, we'd be lost without the usual quota of fluffed lines and falling scenery.'

Brian laughed immoderately at this, but there was a steely glint in his eyes which suggested that Barry would get short shrift if he took that attitude in any play that he was producing.

'Yes, it's the banding together to overcome the problems that makes it all so enjoyable,'

61

volunteered Dilly. 'The spirit of the blitz, in a way.'

We could all agree with this, and stood in silence for a moment, gazing at the stage. Percy's voice had now sunk so low that it was completely inaudible, and his hand was on Bernice's shoulder.

'Percy's very good, isn't he,' whispered Trevor in my ear, 'very patient.' He raised his voice a little to address all of us: 'We're in good hands here. Percy's got such a wealth of experience.'

Everyone nodded and those of us in a position to do so reflected on the body of Percy's work: *Mother Goose, Godspell, a Gang Show* or two, a notably disastrous production of *The House of Bernarda Alba* and *Blithe Spirits* without number.

Suddenly, the tête-à-tête was at an end. Percy pushed back his chair and shouted: 'Okay, everyone, just give me time to pour myself a cup of something hot and wet and then it's straight into Act Three.'

We filed out of the kitchen, passing Percy on his way in. Brian turned to Barry. 'Are we blocking tonight, do you know?'

'Blocking?'

'I checked the schedule, but it didn't say.'

'Haven't a clue, squire.'

I could tell from Barry's expression that he was about to make some crass remark about technical terms, so I intervened. 'Percy likes to get books down first,' I told Brian.

'He does?' Brian slipped his own copy into the pocket of his flying jacket. 'Suits me, I've got nothing against unorthodox working methods.

Don't we need a table down right for Act Three?'

'Search me,' said Barry. 'Need a hand?'

They struggled with the table, and Percy came alongside me, carrying his coffee. 'All's well that ends well,' he confided. 'Time spent on talking things through is never wasted in my experience. Jaw-jaw is better than war-war, and I say that in spite of my service background.'

'Quite,' I said, 'well done.' I was not above getting my nose brown in the interests of harmony.

'All right, Bernice, you can have a coffee, you're not needed for a while!' When Bernice had got her coffee she came and sat next to me at the back of the hall.

'Poor Harriet,' she said unrepentantly, 'did I let you down?'

'Nothing I haven't learned to cope with.'

'I say, straight out of the knife box.'

'Just the truth.'

'May I say something, Harriet?'

'It's a free country.'

'Exactly. And you're getting very censorious.'

'Just because I speak my mind for once.'

'Let me finish.' Percy glanced over his shoulder with a glare which he swiftly changed to a quizzical smile, and Bernice lowered her voice. 'If there's anyone who shouldn't go round criticising her fellow woman, it's you.'

'What can you mean?' I just wanted her to say it, just say it, that was all. And being Bernice, she did.

'When I think of what you were up to in the

not-so-recent past...'

'Bernice, that was *three* years ago!'

'...I'm astonished you dare cavort on a public stage, let alone get all tight-arsed and prim-lipped with me over a few unlearned lines!'

'Now who's being censorious!'

Percy looked round at us again this time not bothering to alter the glare. We sat silently eyeballing each other like a couple of mongrels in a park.

'Good evening, ladies, how goes it?' It was the Rector, Eric Chittenden. Bernice beamed lasciviously and suddenly decided to take her coat off. She was the bitter end, it was why I loved her so.

'Evening, Ricky,' I said. 'Slowly. We thought you were with the Young Wives.'

'They were decimated by a virus, so we called it off. I thought I might as well come here and check developments.'

'Are you involved in this shambles?' asked Bernice.

'Front-of-house manager.' Eric waved his hands in front of his face to show what a minor cog he was in the mighty Arcadians machine. 'I shall have to get my dinner-jacket out of mothballs. Oh, good evening, Jimmy!'

With the arrival of our stage manager and lighting director Jimmy Jardine it was as though we had been transported into a mediaeval morality play in which the representatives of Good and Evil are set to slog it out. Though Eric had received the call late in life, after eighteen years in industry, he was full of missionary zeal, keen at all times and in all places to spread the good news by example. Jimmy Jardine, on the other hand, was Basset Magna's answer to the Amityville Horror. The irony of his association with the forces of light was impossible to ignore. Jimmy was a Prince of Darkness, a cold-eyed, shock-headed perfectionist who stalked the perimeter of the hall during rehearsals with his flies absent-mindedly gaping and a bad word for everyone. Now he made a sound which might have been 'Evening' through barely opened lips and stood staring furiously in the direction of the stage. He had come straight from his work at the nearby Ministry of Defence establishment, and wore a suit and tie, but his shirt was incorrectly buttoned and his chin was blue.

Eric leaned over Bernice's shoulder. 'Jimmy's our stage manager.'

'Well!' said Bernice. 'Should I get my prayer mat out now or later?'

Without taking his eyes off the stage Jimmy burst out: 'I wish someone would tell me what's going on! I've seen no fucking script, no set requirements, nothing!'

Bernice raised her eyebrows. Percy looked at us and tapped his forefinger to his lips.

'The man's an idiot!' snarled Jimmy.

'It's early days yet,' said Eric. 'I'm quite sure Percy's experience and your formidable expertise will ensure that all's well on the night.'

Jimmy looked at Eric as if seeing him for the first time. 'If you say so, Vicar. Miracles are your territory.'

Bernice and I buried the hatchet over a Bailey's at my house. No matter what liberties she took I knew life would be intolerable without her self-interested friendship, and Bernice would have been lost without the entertainment I unconsciously afforded her.

'Your vicar's quite nice,' she said. 'There's something titillating about priests.'

'Bernice,' I warned, 'don't even think of it. He's a happily married man.'

'Oh yes, to that middle-aged Carroll Baker.'

'If you must seduce someone do at least be realistic.'

'Like you were, I suppose...?'

'Don't start that again. Learn from my experience.'

'I'm trying to. That Jimmy person's got a sexy little bum, is he spoken for?'

'No.' I tried to wrap my mind around the idea of Bernice with Jimmy Jardine. 'And for very good reasons.'

'I could see he was a maniac of some sort, but that might be rather fun.'

I decided it was time to change the subject. 'Guess what?' I said. 'My new book's being entered for a literary prize.'

'No! Really? What sort of prize?'

'Twelve thousand pounds.'

'Harriet! You *have* to win, then you can take the two of us on one of those single people's holidays and we can have a real blast!'

'That's not very likely,' I said modestly, 'I'll be happy if I make the shortlist.'

'Which one is it? Whitbread, W H Smith?'

'It's newly launched. The Betabise Book of the Year Award.'

'Betabise Book of the—Harriet, you don't say!'

'Yes. Why?'

Bernice shriekd with laughter. 'You don't know about Arundel then?'

Liquid ice crept through my veins. 'Is he entered for it?'

'Oh, far worse than that,' burbled Bernice gleefully. 'He's one of the judges!'

It was a long night, and a black one. The sheer unfairness of it was breathtaking. I had made a genuine and sustained effort to raise my game, to engage with serious issues, to write more spare, muscular and thoughtful prose. And what happened? My path up Mount Parnassus was blocked by Arundel Potter, the one man on earth who would without hesitation have thrown me into a quicksand with my typewriter tied round my neck.

CHAPTER 4

I awoke next morning in combative mood. Was I downhearted? Well, yes, but I was buggered if I was going to let Arundel Potter dampen my spirits for long. After all, who was he? Only a distinguished media-don with a string of letters after his name and an even bigger list of acclaimed academic works to his credit... I stopped thinking about who Arundel was and, as soon as the children had left for school, I embarked on a massive desk-clearing exercise, which I generally found as therapeutic as a good evacuation after prolonged constipation.

I sharpened pencils, cleaned rubbers, weeded out defunct biros, salvaged paperclips, threw away letters now too embarrassingly old to answer and stowed mounds of loose paper in box files. Since delivering the typescript of *Time to Reap* I had not embarked on another novel, and the nice clean, tidy desk seemed to invite some show of industry so I stuck a piece of A4 in the typewriter. I then turned to the noticeboard, where the forms, notes, memos and invitations hung thick and overlapping as the leaves on a Virginia creeper. Here were all manner of events that I had either been to, thought I might go to, or forgotten about completely. Regis College had apparently coped without me at their disturbingly named soiree 'Sex Education for Parents', and I'd also managed to overlook their all-day workshop on 'Craft and the Family'. However, I had attended a play for which Gareth had painted Doric columns and in which Clara had taken no part whatsoever (my daughter being to interpersonal meshing what the Vikings were to etiquette). I had been to community halls without number to address assorted women's organisations, on My Life as a Writer, had my teeth and eyes checked, made a cake for Dilly's Bring and Buy and been to two cocktail parties and a fork supper. Finally, it appeared that I had bought enough raffle tickets to paper a fair-sized rumpus room and not won a damn thing. I threw most of it away.

So that was it. Desk clear, noticeboard clear—there seemed to be nothing else I could place between myself and the exercise of the creative imagination. Besides, Noleen O'Connell had arrived and was going spectrally about her duties so I couldn't sit down and read the paper with a clear conscience. I crept like a snail unwillingly to work.

It was then that I remembered about selling Stu. It was obviously of paramount importance that I compile an advertisement for the local paper. Clara was in agreement, and the animal had battened on us for long enough, merely adding to our already excessive burden of useless mouths. There was no time like the present.

I fetched the paper and opened it at the relevant section. The trouble with all those friendly schoolmistresses was that they smacked of the sort of ads one saw in newsagents' windows in Paddington. I decided to go for more straightforward wording.

'13 hh grey mare,' I wrote, 'sadly outgrown' (might I be forgiven) '14 yrs. Suit small adult or keen young rider. Good ride-out, jump, gymkhana.' I hesitated, and then put: £400, includes tack, NZ rug.' I sat back gasping at my own cheek. Still, it wasn't all lies and I was pleased with the 'keen young rider' touch.

69

Wimps need not apply. Nice one, Harriet, the training is paying off.

Just for the hell of it I wrote beneath this the strictly factual advertisement which would never see the light of day.

'13 hh grey mare, longstanding liability. Equine Manson. Hippophobe's nightmare. Eventful ride once caught. Full complement of vices. Suit keen masochist. Pay £150 collection and haulage.'

Without more ado I phoned the first version through to the *Barford Echo* and the *Regis Gazette,* and went to make myself a cup of coffee.

Noleen was sitting at the kitchen table nibbling at a packet of crisps. 'I'm putting the kettle on, Noleen,' I said, 'can I make you a cup of something?'

She indicated her small, tartan-patterned thermos and twitched her head.

I filled the kettle noisily. 'Not at all a bad day so far, is it?' I asked, but when I turned back she had gone.

I went back to my desk. Since transferring my centre of operations from upstairs to downstairs I had the advantage of being closer to the phone, the door and the jar of instant coffee, but I no longer had the pleasant view over the garden. In fact nothing to stare at at all except the unforgiving paper. This I now did, and prayed for a miracle.

My prayers were answered. Ah, the phone, the writer's friend! I sped with winged feet into the hall.

'Hallo?'

70

'Would that be Mrs Blair?' It was a man's voice. Plump, middle-aged, London.

'Yes.'

'Gareth's mum?'

'Yes.'

'My name's Reg Legge. Chief Scout, Barford United.'

My mind was a perfect blank. 'Oh yes.'

'I thought it was about time I contacted you, Mrs Blair, because I've had my eye on your Gareth for some time now.'

'Have you?'

'I have, and my colleagues and I really like the look of him.'

'Do you?'

'Listen, Mrs Blair. That boy's got all the skills and all the speed, plus he's a big lad for his age. With his ability and his height he could be a new Terry Butcher.'

I racked my brains to remember the old one. Still, the conversation was beginning to move into focus. I experienced a great flush of maternal pride. 'Do you really think so?'

'I know so. Heading ability in the air like your Gareth's got is worth twenty-five grand a year to any decent club.'

'Tw—how much?'

'A very considerable amount. I've worked in football for thirty-five years so I can safely say that I'm a judge of these things.'

We both, for our separate reasons, allowed a meaningful pause to elapse. I sensed that the ball was in my court. 'So what exactly,' I asked, 'are you saying?'

71

'What I am saying,' said Reg Legge, 'is that we're very interested in Gareth.' He announced this in the self-satisfied manner of one accustomed to meeting with delirious enthusiasm.

It would have been stylish to disappoint him just for once, but I couldn't manage it. 'Golly!' I squawked. And then took a firm hold of myself. 'Now Mr Legge—'

'Reg.'

'—Reg. You're going to have to be a little more specific.' It was like a seduction, the fencing and feinting, the veiled promises and coy questions.

'I can be a great deal more specific,' said Reg. 'We may very well want him to sign some forms in the not too distant future.'

'I see...' My imagination was going into overdrive.

'But first we'd like to bring him up here for a few days, get him to put in some training with the other lads, see how he copes in a friendly with the youth team. Put him through his paces a bit.'

'I understand. Mind you,' I demurred faintly, not really wanting Reg Legge to take much notice, 'he has exams in the summer.' But far from brushing my feeble protest aside he pounced on it and lifted it shoulder high, going into an absolute paroxysm of agreement.

'Of course, of course, Mrs Blair. Of course he has, and schoolwork comes first every time, as I say to all my parents. There's no way Barford United is going to stand between a lad and his

72

academic studies, no way.'

'Jolly good,' I murmured, trying to sound really pleased.

'Now then,' went on Reg, 'would I be right in assuming that Gareth's exams are still a few months off?'

'In the summer, yes.'

'Then I'd also be right in thinking that as regards his visit to us it's a case of the sooner the better?'

'I suppose so, yes.'

'But I expect you'd like a little family chat about the whole thing before we fix anything...?'

I could suddenly picture the kind of domestic set-up which Reg imagined he was discussing. In Gareth's interests it might be as well to go along with it.

'I'd like to talk about it to my husband. And to Gareth, of course. He has a mind of his own,' I added, backing a hunch.

The hunch proved correct. 'He certainly does! You can tell that from the way he plays. Football's all about feet, of course, but your boy plays with his head,' said Reg confusingly. 'It's the kind of extra something I look for in a young player.'

I was beginning to get the hang of things. I realised it could only be to my advantage to put up a last show of reluctance. 'Gareth has always intended to stay on at school and do "A" levels,' I said, 'I don't think he's ever considered football as a career.'

'All to the good, Mrs Blair. A boy with a wider outlook on life, and who makes a positive decision to go for a future in the game, that's a boy with one hundred per cent commitment.'

It was all quite fascinating. I was getting a taste of what it must be like to be an agent. And Reg Legge was a worthy sparring partner, since he of all people must be aware that any youth offered a place by a first division soccer club was not going to need prising away from his desk.

'So shall I ring you when we've talked?' I asked.

'I'd prefer to save you the trouble and expense.' He very properly didn't trust me.

Yet again I toyed with him. 'Um, let's see...we're a bit tied up for the next few days. In a week or so?'

We fixed an evening, and then Reg said: 'By the way, Mrs Blair...'

'Yes?'

'Please, I don't want you or the boy to get too excited. We like the look of him, but it's early days, and these are only schoolboy forms we're talking about here.'

I gulped back a gobstopper of resentment, and said airily. 'I realise that.'

'It's a long, hard road, and it takes a heck of a lot of graft and guts to make it to the top in this game,' went on Reg, pressing home his advantage. 'Gareth's got talent, but that's just the beginning. I've seen more talent bite the dust than Lineker's scored goals.'

'Of course,' I smarted.

'So long as we understand each other.' It occurred to me that Reg Legge's script seemed to have been provided for him by Euston Films.

'I'll be in touch then, Mrs Blair. And thank you for giving me so much of your time.'

After he had rung off I sat there in the hall for a moment or two, stunned. In spirit I was in the Royal Box at Wembley on Cup Final day...plucky little Barford versus the Liverpool giants...my profile proud but tremulous beneath the brim of a fetching hat as *Abide With Me* swelled around the terraces—the roar of the supporters as the teams ran on to the pitch... Gareth as I had never seen him before, clear-eyed and fresh-faced as Roy of the Rovers in Barford's distinctive ice-blue strip... And then the grief, the glory, the unbearable tension of the game itself. Two-all after extra time (both Barford goals from diving headers by new boy Blair)...then the final triumph, victory to Barford in a penalty shoot-out...me shaking hands with the Barford lads, my smile tear-stained but radiant... Gareth lifting the Cup aloft, blue ribbons a-flutter, for a lap of honour...by God I was going to tear Gareth away from his books if it was the last thing I did.

I rushed back to the study, sat down at the desk and switched on the typewriter. At the top of the sheet of paper I typed the words: *Abide With Me, A Novel, by Harriet Blair,* and then had to pause to blow my nose. This was about as much creative endeavour as I could manage in my emotionally overheated condition. I decided to go for a run, which, since the marathon, had become less of a daily routine and more of an event.

I went upstairs and put on my newest red

tracksuit. As I laced my trainers Spot sat and watched me with a martyred expression—he no longer cared for jogging. Today he was in luck, for I'd already decided against taking him with me. I couldn't trust myself to notice if he bit babies, chased sheep or disappeared beneath the wheels of a juggernaut.

Noleen was sluicing the wall tiles in the bathroom as I emerged from my room and she blinked at me as though the red of my tracksuit hurt her eyes. 'Cheerio, Noleen—just going to get a bit of exercise.' She blinked again and wrung out her cloth. As I went downstairs I wondered idly if Declan mistreated her, she was such a bleached, timorous creature. On the other hand she was strong as an ox so perhaps the only punishment he meted out was the free-firing verbal sort.

I was on a high. In fact I'd gone a mile and a half before I even noticed I was moving. I kept picturing the faces of the Tomahawks YFC supremos when they heard the news. It was a measure of my glee that I even rather regretted not having gone along to the football club's AGM and landed a sinecure on the committee. My connection with the Toms was now purely parental, but it would have been fun to get all the bigwigs together in one place for my announcement.

Of course, I reminded myself, there was still Gareth himself, whose reaction I had hardly considered at all. But surely he would be, well, over the moon. Of George I was a little less certain. He would certainly have to be consulted, and unlike me he would consider school work of paramount importance... I did so hope he wouldn't choose this moment to play the heavy father. And then of course there was the issue of the Dominant Male. Not that George, as far as I knew, had harboured any longstanding ambitions to be a professional footballer—he was more of a squash and rugger man himself, and regarded the intrusion of soccer into our lives as a kind of creeping proletarian blight. But Gareth's sporting advancement might well bring with it the rustle and creak of time's winged chariot about to overtake on the inside... I took the road that skirted the nearside of Parva, and was jogging along pretty happily when a vehicle zoomed up behind me, swished past and braked about twenty metres in front. As I approached, the driver leaned out of his window and flagged me down. It was Damon Prime—once my home help, now purveyor of Christmas trees, fast food and dubious videos to the inhabitants of Basset Magna—in a white Mitsubishi jeep and a chainlink bracelet.

'Morning,' he called, 'still keeping it up then?'

'Yes,' I answered, drawing up alongside. 'Though not as often as I used to.'

'As the bishop said to the barmaid,' responded Damon without a flicker of humour. It was both chilling and part of his curious charm, the way money had coated him in a kind of teak-look veneer, which entirely failed to disguise the chipboard beneath.

'Hey,' he said, 'you thinking of doing another marathon this year?'

77

'No. Not for another ten.'

' 'Cos if you are,' went on Damon, 'I could offer you the services of Prime Enterprises.'

'Services of...'

'...transport, refreshments, toilet facilities. For the supporters.'

'No, Damon, I shan't be doing a marathon,' I said more firmly. But the word 'supporters' had activated my urgent need to tell someone about Gareth. I wouldn't normally have selected Damon as the first person to hear such momentous news, but...

'Speaking of supporters,' I said casually, 'I've had some rather interesting news. About Gareth.'

'Oh yeah?' Damon took a properly crumpled packet of Marlboros from the pocket of his black ciré blouson. 'What's the old boy been up to?' Since fortune had smiled on Damon it pleased him to refer to Gareth in a slightly avuncular manner.

'I had a call this morning from the chief scout of Barford United,' I told him, as he inhaled and squinted at me through the smoke.

'Is that right?' Damon had perfected a whole battery of these constipated mid-Atlantic clichés. I was going to have to get to the punchline if I wished to spare myself any more of them.

'Yes. They want to sign Gareth,' I said, leaving out the 'up' in the approved manner.

It was worth it. Damon's jaw—on which the zits peeped like harvest mice through the designer stubble—actually dropped, and his eyes goggled.

'Meg-a!' he breathed. 'Wick-ed!'

I realised that this might well be the very best reaction I was going to get. I no longer regretted telling Damon before anyone else. His whole demeanour of awestruck admiration was most gratifying. For all I knew his tenuous connection with Gareth might qualify Damon as a local hero back where he came from. 'Solid gold!' he exclaimed now. 'United's in the first division these days, innit?'

'It certainly is.'

'Good for Gareth! A-mazing. When's he going up there, then?'

'I don't know. Gareth doesn't even know about this himself yet. Mr Legge's going to...'

'Reg Legge?'

'That's right. Why, Damon, do you know him?'

'Know of.' An indefinable expression fled across Damon's small features like the shadow of a cloud.

'The idea is,' I went on, 'that Gareth should go up there, to United, for a few days' training, and perhaps play in a match.'

'A match?' Damon threw his half-smoked Marlboro out of the window like a dart and picked up a dog-eared personal organiser from the seat next to him. 'When?'

'As I said, I don't know yet. We have to talk about all this, and then Reg Legge is going to ring back.'

'Local boy in big game...' Damon's voice became dreamy. I felt some stirrings of unease.

'Just a youth match,' I explained.

'Yeah...curtain raiser. Great stuff. Look here.' Damon handed me a card which indicated that the administrative hub of Prime Enterprises was at 12 Scargill Cuttings, Basset Regis. 'When you hear when it's going to be, give me a bell, eh? I could organise a coach, banners, the lot. A great day out for the whole family. Fantastic.'

'Well—all right.'

'I know where your husband is these days, I could get him a booking slip 'n all.'

'That's a kind thought.' I could not in a million years envisage George availing himself of Damon's charabanc, six-packs and return journey singalong, but I didn't want to hurt his feelings when he'd been so unstinting with the enthusiasm.

'All I need,' said Damon, 'is the date and time, and you can leave the rest to me.'

'Thank you,' I said humbly.

'It's cool,' Damon assured me.

'Well,' I executed a few brisk running steps on the spot, 'I'd better be on my way.'

'Gotcher,' said Damon.

As I jogged on my way I reflected that it was rather touching, really, the way all the trappings of his small wealth had not robbed Damon of his unique and special naffness.

In the event, the news of Reg Legge's phone call brought unforeseen reactions all round.

'Oh yeah?' said Gareth. 'About time.'

'How do you mean?'

'I mean,' said Gareth, folding bread around a

cold sausage, 'he's been hanging round for long enough.'

'So you knew who he was?'

'Come on, Mum, wise up, they're like Plods, you can tell them a mile off.'

'How?' I was curious.

'I dunno...the walk, the mac.'

'You make them sound like flashers.'

'Well...!' said Gareth, and gave a short laugh before introducing the banger buttie into his mouth. Both the syllable and the laugh contained, for their size, an absolute wealth of ponderous irony.

'What's that for?'

'Nothing.'

'Gareth, that is so irritating!'

'Forget it.'

'Forget what, though? What were you implying?'

'Nothing! You're always looking for hidden meanings.'

'It wasn't hidden, or I wouldn't ask. Gareth.'

'Blimey...'

'It was my saying they were like flashers...'

'All right, all right! They're not flashers.'

'So what are they?'

Gareth sighed heavily. 'It's just that one or two of them are gay.'

'I see.' It was my oh-is-that-all tone of voice, employed by me at moments of the acutest anxiety. Having forced open this particular can of worms I should have liked time to think, but Gareth was now determined to tell me a lot more than I wanted to know.

'It's a joke, really,' he said. 'I mean, the bloke

from City just signs up anyone who'll let him...'

'I don't want to hear, Gareth.'

'You were dead keen a moment ago.'

'I was not dead keen about anything, I simply dislike innuendo. What goes on at Barford City is their problem. I assume you're not implying that Mr Legge...'

'Cool it, Ma. Legge's not a shirtlifter.'

'Don't use that horrible expression!'

'Okay, okay, no need to get out of your pram.'

I took a few deep breaths, while Gareth hovered in the kitchen doorway as if waiting to be dismissed. The conversation was not going as I'd hoped or planned. I made a last-ditch attempt to steer it back into more conventional channels.

'The main thing is, it's a wonderful opportunity. Assuming you're in favour, we'll have to discuss it with your father.'

'Sure.'

'He's going to want plenty of assurance that schoolwork won't suffer.'

'Yeah.'

'*Yes*. Reg Legge was very emphatic that it wouldn't.'

'Well, he would say that, wouldn't he? He's not daft.'

I couldn't help it, I felt crestfallen. 'I somehow thought you'd be more excited about it all.'

'It's okay,' said Gareth. 'It's fine. It's just that he's been hanging about for a couple of seasons on and off so, you know, you get used to the idea.'

'I suppose so.'

'Better go and do my homework.' Gareth edged further out of the door. 'Mustn't let all this get in the way of my studies.'

'No.'

Brave and calm, I told myself. I mean, I hope I'm as enlightened as the next woman, but somehow the tabloid headlines kept shrieking in my head: 'SEX SECRETS OF THE SOCCER SCOUTS SIGNING HAD NOTHING TO DO WITH SKILLS, SAYS BARFORD NEW BOY.'

That evening I rang George. To my utter astonishment his reaction was as enthusiastic as Gareth's had been tepid.

'Fantastic! That's really terrific. He'll be able to keep us in our twilight years yet!'

'You're pleased?'

'Yes! Why, aren't you?'

I remembered that I was, I really was, that I had already decided on the type of hat I'd wear to Wembley...

'Yes, I am. I just didn't think you'd be so keen.'

'Whyever not? Life is short, Harriet, and these days the young need every leg up—no joke intended—they can get. If he's got that much talent he should capitalise on it. Unequivocally.'

'I agree.'

'But?'

'But nothing.'

'How's our hero taking it, anyway—on cloud nine?'

'Not exactly. Phlegmatic, actually. He's seen

it coming for months, apparently.'

'Good for him, a good balanced attitude.'

'You're not concerned about—about his schoolwork, for instance?'

'Not particularly. If these clubs wrecked people's exam chances they'd have gone out of business long ago. Besides, these days everyone takes more "A" levels, and does OU and whatnot, whenever they feel like it. They go back into the education system. Life is a lot less rigid than when we were young, Harriet.'

I gritted my teeth—I would *not* point out how old that made me feel. 'It's a very short career.'

'A short one but a gay one,' replied George, casually reactiviating all the panic buttons. 'And lucrative too. By the time he's thirty he'll be out to grass in some nice Tudabethan pub on the Regis bypass, flogging his autograph for a fiver a throw. Maybe we could charge stud fees, what do you think?'

When I'd put the phone down I poured myself a large g and t. It was odd the way just as I was getting serious the whole of the rest of the world was getting sillier and sillier.

CHAPTER 5

The Erans took me out to a fat lunch to celebrate my book's official entry for the Betabise Award. We went to the Gadfly, a media persons' club which had only been open a few months, but whose decor and furnishings had been artfully distressed to give an appearance of age and decadence.

'You're going to have to join, Harriet,' said Vanessa in the taxi en route. *'We've* all been made members willy-nilly. The GM put money into it, so all his management have a sacred duty to use it at least once a week.'

'It's not that bad, actually,' put in Tristan. 'otherwise we wouldn't dream of taking our most successful author there.'

'That's right,' agreed Vanessa. 'It's definitely the place to see and be seen at the moment.'

She was probably right about this, but when we arrived I didn't give much for my chances of being spotted in the chattering throng of aspiring personalities and low-wattage stars. Because the Gadfly prided itself on being unstuffy most of its patrons felt it incumbent upon them to dress as much like riff-raff as was possible on incomes ranging upward of thirty thousand a year. In the case of pop singers, A&R men and photographers this came naturally and could be carried off. The TV crowd had scarcely changed their pink shirt and pullover look in twenty years. The women journalists were draped and swathed, the men dressed like fugitives from an Irish wake. Only the publishers failed utterly to strike the proper note of creative disarray.

Tristan had never been a slave to fashion, and was impeccably turned out in navy chalk-striped three-piece suiting with a pale blue Turnbull and Asser shirt and a Liberty handkerchief and tie. He had always been slightly rounded and was now definitely overweight by the stringbean standards of the day, but his avoirdupois managed to convey gravitas, like those Maori chieftains who regard fat as a sign of wealth.

Vanessa, now that she was Managing Editor of Era Books and reputedly sharing Tristan's humble flat in Regent's Park, had set aside street style in favour of designer casuals of stunning plainness. Today she wore a black angora shift, thick black tights with a suggestion of wrinkle at the knee and black suede ballet slippers. Her hair was cut so short that it resembled reddish fur. In all they made a handsome couple, and I was glad we were meeting up with Lew or I should have felt something of a gooseberry.

We entered the bar, where everyone was behaving in a fairly unfettered manner. Great cacophonous assemblies of Levis, baseball boots, pea-jackets and peroxide-whitened hair filled the corrals formed by the maroon and bottle-green velvet armchairs. Handsome girls, far too well-bred and highly qualified for the job, patrolled disdainfully among the clientele, wearing black trousers and wing-collar shirts. Behind the bar were a couple of slender, consumptive-looking youths who would certainly have caught the eye of the Barford City scout had he been present. On the edges of the vivacious throng were a few solitary souls, busy making it perfectly clear that they didn't give a toss about being on their own. The loners' chief weapon was reading matter—each of them had his or her nose buried in a book, paper, magazine or, in the case of one woman who must have been the

86

envy of all the others, a blue folder containing a typed TV script.

The one behind *Pub Talk* turned out be Lew. He had consulted the *Miami Vice* fashion look and wore a pale pink suit with an oversized jacket, a grey T-shirt and loafers without socks. 'There he is,' I said. 'Lew, we're here!'

He sprang to his feet as we approached and we greeted each other in the customary shower of kisses. With Lew at the vertical it was possible to confirm what at a distance I had only suspected, that Lew was no Don Johnson. He'd obviously tried repeatedly and without success to push the jacket sleeves up his stick-thin arms, so that now they hung like twin concertinas to the first joint of his fingers. However, he had managed to conserve two-thirds of a burgundy chesterfield for Vanessa and me. Tristan, who attracted service as a flypaper collects flies, perched on the arm, placed an order for drinks and our little party was underway.

'To the glittering prizes!' pronounced Tristan, raising aloft his Bloody Mary.

'To Harriet!' responded Lew.

'To *Reap,*' added Vanessa.

I felt I should contribute something, but couldn't think of any toast that wouldn't sound either vain or self-serving, so contented myself with my famous (though these days less frequent) modest smile.

Our glasses clinked and Lew slopped most of his spritzer over the table. There followed a characteristic charade as he tried unsuccessfully

87

to catch the eye of the ineffable waitress, and finally produced a handypack of tissues from his briefcase and began to mop up the mess himself. To dissociate himself from all this Tristan asked: 'Now then, who knows the judges?'

'They don't seem all that notable,' said Vanessa (how I wished Arundel Potter could have heard her) 'except for R.N Morell, of course.'

'Oh, I don't count her,' said Tristan. 'Old R.N is so far beyond reproach she's practically invisible.' They referred to one of the Grand Old Bags of English letters, a writer of the sort of thrillers read by cabinet ministers and dons. 'No,' went on Tristan. 'I mean susceptible to nobbling.'

'Let's think...' Vanessa tapped her glass against her lips. 'There's Lawrence Bennett of Sallow and Windrush.'

'God in heaven,' said Tristan, 'they might as well have asked me.'

'Surely there's someone from Betabise,' I offered.

At this, Lew held up his index finger to indicate that he was about to rejoin the conversation. 'No judge, but the organiser's a woman,' he said, closing his eyes and snapping his fingers in the air like someone about to render *That Old Black Magic.* 'Betabise's head of...er...' We gazed expectedly at him. His eyes flew open and he gave a final mighty click. 'Betabise's head of Concept Analysis!'

'My fault for asking,' said Tristan.

'Whatever is that?' asked Vanessa.

'Silly darling,' Tristan patted her arm. 'It means having a shit-hot money-making idea and checking to make sure it won't land you in court.'

'Good heavens,' said Vanessa, 'I think Era could do with one of those.'

Lew nodded. 'She's one of their high-fliers. Welsh, I believe, though you'd never know, Rhiannon Parsons, I met her not all that long ago.'

Tristan brightened. 'Now that is interesting. Where was that?'

Lew blushed. 'At the launch of Filofood, a brilliant new cookbook by a client of mine. We invited people from all the top supermarket chains. Parsons was especially interested. She's a very bright woman.'

'But can she be bought?' persisted Tristan. I glanced nervously about. We were used to Tristan's little ways, but anyone overhearing could have gained quite the wrong impression.

Vanessa tinkled with laughter. 'Tristan, really —we're going to win this competition fair and square, aren't we, Harriet?'

'We can try.'

'There is another judge,' said Lew, 'another man...'

'That's right,' I said gloomily, 'Arundel Potter.'

'Who's he?' asked Tristan.

'An academic.'

'Ah. Media prof?'

'Latterly.'

'And you know him?'

'Unfortunately.'

'Oh dear...' Vanessa furrowed her brow. *'Non simpatico?'*

'No.'

'I don't think I've come across him,' said Lew. 'What exactly is his line?'

'Sweeping value judgements based on intellectual snobbery and rampant misogyny,' I answered, congratulating myself on my restraint.

'Can't be helped,' said Tristan, taking a menu from the cocktail waitress. 'We'll just have to concentrate on the others. Now then, what's everyone having?'

The Gadfly menu was a nicely calculated blend of cuisines nouvelle and Anglaise. It was perfectly possible for Vanessa and Lew to have spinach roulade and the chef's warm salad with mange-tout and endive, and for Tristan and me to tuck into liver and bacon with fried onions and bubble and squeak, without either pair feeling conspicuous. Tristan ordered champagne.

'There's all sorts in here today,' he explained as we sat round our table in the upstairs restaurant, 'and they'll be wondering what we're talking about. Drop of fizz'll give them something to get their teeth into.'

By the time we reached the thin mints we'd got through a second bottle of bubbly, the brandies were on their way, and our vivacious discourse and immoderate laughter had probably convinced our fellow diners that we were celebrating film rights with firm commitments from Streep and Nicholson.

From time to time Tristan raised his eyebrows or his glass to mystified colleagues in other parts of the room and Vanessa, off to the loos, did a great deal of bobbing and peering (to use the police phrase) to assure that her presence was registered.

Lew, usually a modest drinker, was becoming deeply emotional, and put his arm round my shoulders. 'This is quite a day, Harriet,' he said. 'Quite a watershed for you. A sea change. The tide is turning.'

I clenched my bottom. All those watery metaphors reminded me that I should soon have to follow Vanessa. 'Let's hope so,' I replied. 'Though I think it's going to take more than this for me to shake off the schlock tag.'

'Who wants to shake it off?' put in Tristan, who no matter how much he drank retained a firm grasp of the salient issues. 'Not me. Far better to be a good schlock novelist who can be literary when she chooses, than some pot-hunting bluestocking that nobody's read.'

'I'll drink to that,' said Lew.

'It would be nice to be taken seriously for a while,' I said. I was still unable to shake off the memory of my exploitation at the hands of Hal Worship.

'But what does that mean, "seriously"...?' mused Lew, tilting his chair back on two legs. 'What do we really mean when we use that word?'

'Well, I know what I mean,' I said a bit testily. 'I mean being seen as a writer who addresses issues and explores notions and investigates perceptions.'

'Tosh,' said Tristan, weighing in somewhat surprisingly on Lew's side. 'You've been listening to too many book programmes. Your average consumer would far rather read some ripsnorting rogering than issues being addressed, take my word for it.'

I bridled. 'That's like saying a paper should contain nothing but tits and tips because that's what people like.'

Tristan shook his head. 'Good lord, Harriet, your self-esteem is in a state if you're honestly comparing those super books of yours with the smutter press—'

'But I'm not!' My voice rose and a few heads turned. Tristan beamed approvingly. 'I'm not! You were, by implication.'

Lew nodded. 'She's got a point there, Tristan.'

'No she bloody hasn't,' said Tristan comfortably. 'She's talking balls and she knows it, don't you, Harriet?' He must have seen my veins beginning to stand out, because he carried on seamlessly: 'The point is that your readers *do* take you seriously, and you would agree, I know, that they come first, last and always.'

Skilfully Tristan had steered the conversation back on to safe territory. It was my cue to do my unaffected, good-sport, real-trouper number, so perhaps it was just as well that we were interrupted.

'Lew, old son, how you doing?'

It was Mo Townley. He gave Lew's startled face a chummy slap. Lew grabbed his hand and wrung it.

'Great to see you, Mo! Great, I really mean it! Why don't you join us?'

'Vanessa's coming back,' Tristan warned.

'Sorry, I'm with someone,' said Mo.

'Too bad. Do you know Tristan Whirley-Birch?'

'Don't think so. Hi.'

Tristan gave Mo his most cobra-like smile. 'How do you do.'

'Harriet you've met of course,' went on Lew, presenting me with an upturned palm like a waiter serving the soup of the day.

'Hallo again,' I said.

Lew, having faffed around to find a spare chair, stood up to keep Mo company, his napkin still tucked into the waistband of his trousers. 'Harriet was really disappointed that she couldn't join us for lunch the other day,' he said. 'She dropped by the office and I invited her along.'

'Did you?'

'But sadly she had to get back to her family.'

'Too bad,' agreed Mo.

'How's the game?' I asked. 'Any luck yet?'

'There's still a bit of fine tuning to do,' Mo told me, 'but a couple of manufacturers are, you know, nibbling, and I reckon come summer I'll have myself a deal.'

'Which would be perfect for a pre-Christmas launch!' explained Lew, beaming happily, and went on to outline his plans. I glanced at Tristan. He looked quite petrified with irritation. There was no doubt that Lew's adulation for all his clients was self-defeating when two or more of them were gathered together in one place. If Mo hung around much longer with his lank ringlets, his BO and his constipated conversation, my own status was going to be in serious jeopardy.

'I've got a few other projects in the pipeline,' promised Mo. 'I aim to diversify.'

'That's right,' said Lew, 'in fact Harriet here's doing the self-same thing, aren't you, Harriet?'

At this juncture Vanessa belatedly returned, pregnant with gossip culled along the return route. She cast Mo a nod, cursory as only she could make it, and began to whisper intensely to Tristan. Mo took this as his cue to leave.

'Do you have to?' pleaded Lew. 'I can ask for another chair.'

'No, really, people are waiting for me.'

'Who are you lunching with?' I asked. I could afford to be civil now that he was going.

'OTT with Phoebe Delore,' said Mo. 'The band,' he added helpfully.

'Marvellous.'

Mo bade us farewell and sloped off.

'That's my kind of people,' said Lew, his eyes glistening with emotion as he sat down. I watched Mo return to his table. OTT were a couple of dull-eyed youths with flat-tops, plus a sleek black boy of dazzling androgynous beauty. Phoebe Delore was of a certain age, painted, hennaed, and dressed for a Black Mass. I entertained a diverting picture of the four of them in bed together, mixing and matching as the mood took them.

'...*Harriet!*'

Vanessa was tapping me frantically on the arms as if trying to get ketchup out of my elbow.

'Sorry...'

'News, Harriet, news!'

'Yes?'

'Guess who I met downstairs?'

'I couldn't possibly.'

'Terry Wogan?' suggested Lew.

'Better than that!' While Lew attempted this mental leap, Vanessa kept her eyes glued to my face, and asked again: 'Go on. Guess.'

'Honestly, I've no idea.'

Vanessa sat back. '*Only* Persephone Marriott.'

'Oh yes?'

'She hasn't a clue,' said Tristan indulgently. 'Go on, Nessa, put Harriet out of her misery.'

'No, hang on!' cried Lew, going into another paroxysm of finger-clicking. 'It's coming—it's coming—' We watched with varying degrees of patience till it came. 'I've got it! Persephone Marriott, producer of *Considered Opinion*, BBC TV, presented by Hugh Lorimer—am I right?'

'Very good,' said Vanessa. 'Take a gold star. But Harriet, she is just *such* an impressive lady. Did you know that show is entirely her idea and she's made it into the flagship current-affairs programme at the Beeb?'

'She's pretty formidable,' agreed Tristan. 'Doesn't suffer fools gladly. I understand that

Labour front-bencher who bared her breasts in the Commons wrote to La Marriott about a dozen times just begging to be considered and *still* hasn't been asked on.'

'Excuse me for being slow,' I said, 'but what has this to do with us?'

Vanessa leaned forward. 'She knows about you, Harriet.'

A tingle of anxiety ran up and down my spine. 'Knows about me? Knows what?'

'About your coke habit and your string of toy boys—about your *books,* Harriet, what else? She's a fan, apparently. You are the author she reads for relaxation.'

'Goodness, am I?' I wasn't quite sure how to take this. The touchy part of me wished to be something more than the author Persephone Marriott slipped between the cocoa butter and the Tampax when she went to her Tuscan farmhouse. The realistic part knew I should consider myself lucky to be in the case at all, and viewed with respect a woman who had at her disposal a whole hour of top-people's television, an hour which would be reckoned an adornment to the most distinguished CV's in the land.

While I sat there cloddishly considering the implications, Tristan took me on the inside and left me for dead. '...would be simply tremendous, and just what we need at this moment!' he was saying. His business ardour, temporarily doused by the clammy hand of Mo Townley, had been fanned back into a healthy blaze by the thought of Persephone Marriott and her guest list. 'What exactly was she doing?'

'Just having a drink at the bar.'

'With anyone?'

'Yes, a man, she did introduce him but I'm afraid I didn't take it in.'

'No matter.' Tristan turned to me. 'I take it you've never met Persephone Marriott?'

'No, never.'

Lew craned forward, craving a piece of the action. 'I see where you're coming from, Tristan. And I think I can make a pretty shrewd guess where you're going to.'

Tristan went on as though Lew hadn't spoken. 'I suggest we mosey down to the bar for a last brandy, stumble across Persephone and her gentleman friend, and Nessa can effect the relevant introductions.'

'I think she'd be most receptive,' said Vanessa. 'She spoke so warmly of Harriet's books.'

'I say,' I said, 'we're not—what are we trying to achieve?'

Lew's eyes glistened fondly. 'We're all thinking what an asset you'd be to *Considered Opinion*,' he explained gently.

They were unbelievable. 'You don't honestly think she's going to pollute her highbrow panel with someone like me, do you?'

'False modesty,' said Tristan, rising from the table and tweaking the points of his waistcoat, 'will get you nowhere. Do you need to powder your nose before we go into action?'

'No thank you,' I replied ungraciously. 'It's my mind she's after, she'll have to put up with my distended bladder and greasy cheeks.'

'You look marvellous,' Lew whispered, squeezing my arm. Or perhaps he was catching his balance, we were none of us that steady on our feet.

'Doesn't she?' agreed Vanessa. 'Gorgeous as always.' She flashed me the special smile she used to stifle retaliation, like someone throwing a cloth over a parrot's cage. Basically, excuse would not be brooked. It was get out there and work the audience time.

We weaved down the stairs into the bar and approached Persephone Marriott with all the nonchalance of wild dogs closing on a wounded wildebeest, I led the way, trying to look as though I were making for the door, but alert at all times to Vanessa's summons. I could hear Lew's heavy breathing behind my right shoulder.

'Hold hard, Harriet!' I stopped and spun round as if we were playing Grandmother's Footsteps. 'There's someone here who'd like to meet you,' said Vanessa. Obediently I returned and my backing group closed around me. Vanessa introduced me to Persephone Marriott. My hand was all but guided into hers. I spoke of a long and sincere admiration for her programme, and she admitted that there were times when she didn't know where she'd be without a Harriet Blair book. She presented her companion, the lofty editor of an even loftier right-wing weekly who murmured something restrained about it being a pleasure. I retained an impression of dark hair, good cheekbones, frosty eyes and a long, disdainful nose. Also elegantly sloping shoulders, a cool, tight handshake and finely chiselled lips—

'Why don't we have a drink together?' carolled Vanessa, and Tristan and Lew chimed in with their yeah-yeah's.

'Why not?' said Persephone, glancing at her companion, who was expressionless.

'Splendid,' said Tristan, 'what will everyone have?'

'I must be off,' said the magazine editor. He was definitely pissed off about our arrival, and not trying too hard to conceal it.

'Oh, must you?' Vanessa held out her hand. 'It's been super meeting you.'

'Bye bye, Edward,' said Persephone, and they bumped cheeks. It was a kiss that was not so much chaste as the shorthand for something else. He then raised his eyebrows at the rest of us by way of farewell, and left.

'I hope we didn't interrupt anything,' said Lew, as Tristan got the drinks in.

It seemed a bit late to be worrying about that, but Persephone said by no means. 'We go back a long way,' she explained. 'Edward and I stool perch here once a week and then I have a late lunch at the members' table.'

While Vanessa described exactly what *we* had been doing here, I studied Persephone. She was undoubtedly a woman for whom the members' table at the Gadfly—and those of other, more distinguished clubs for all I knew—was home from home. She was a striking, debonair woman in her mid-forties with an easy but enquiring manner and wonderful legs. She must have known about the legs, because whereas the rest of her was clad in not unfetching bluestocking drag, the gams were resplendent in sheer black seamed stockings (I was willing to bet they were stockings) and black suede courts with five-inch heels. It was a winning combination, that energetic intelligence and those sleek, shapely legs.

'So, Harriet, you're changing tack,' she said to me. As she turned in my direction I could feel the brainpower emanating from her in waves. 'Truthfully I don't know whether to be pleased or dismayed—not that it's any of my business. Does this mean we are to have no more glorious Blair heroines?'

'Good heavens, no, there'll be plenty more.' Was I mistaken or was there an audible exhalation of relief from the Erans? 'But there are other kinds of novel that I want to write and one has to try these things.'

'I must say I do think it's awfully courageous of you to do that when you're so brilliantly successful in another genre,' said Persephone. God but she was a nice woman.

'She's going to be successful in this one too, I can assure you of that,' said Lew. 'Really, no writer has the right to be so darned versatile.'

Persephone smiled, revealing slightly crooked teeth. I wondered what she made of us.

'The new book's a winner?'

It was Tristan's turn. 'Artistically, without a doubt. We were all utterly stunned when we read it.' Lew and Vanessa nodded energetically. 'And in fact we have such faith in it that it's entered for the new Betabise Award, have you heard of it?'

'I haven't, but then I know nothing about publishing.'

'It's only recently launched. We think *A Time to Reap* stands an excellent chance.'

'Wouldn't that be marvellous?' said Persephone. 'Think of the publicity.' She said she didn't know about publishing but this remark indicated a fiendishly accurate intuition.

'Tell me,' I said, 'when does the new series of *Considered Opinion* start?'

She went on to speak with surprising freedom about the organisation of the programme, the way ministers trod on each other's faces to appear, her own policy of never putting anyone above the selection process and of using as many women as possible. She was interesting, amusing, a woman in command of her subject and herself. It was a full half-hour before she finally begged to be excused, and went to take her place at the members' table, and not a moment of it had dragged.

'Formidable,' remarked Lew as we waited for our coats in the lobby, 'and from a titled family, I gather.'

'Oh, they're not all that,' said Tristan breezily. 'I used to go to her younger brother's birthday parties at their house in Hans Crescent and there was generally a fair sprinkling of oiks.'

'Doesn't the real aristocracy have a pretty high tolerance of oiks?' I said, which shut Tristan up briefly as he tried to decide where this left him.

'I liked her a lot,' said Vanessa. 'But with what she earns she really ought to get those front teeth fixed.'

Lew agreed that dental work, or the lack of it, was what let the British down, and went on to say that he'd even gone as far as insisting Marisa take the girls to a New York orthodontist rather than entrust their choppers to an amateur. Not waiting for Lew to finish, Tristan put his face close to mine and murmured: 'It's been one of those magic lunches, Harriet.'

As we emerged into the chilly Soho afternoon I could feel the magic ebbing away. Our mild drunkenness, which had made us so mellow and amusing in the Gadfly, rebounded on us sharply. The traffic seemed awfully loud, the pavement awfully crowded, our fellow Londoners awfully unlikeable. That was the trouble with lunches: they gave way, inevitably, to afternoons. There was only one thing which post-lunch afternoons were good for and it was seldom available when you needed it.

'I'll say goodbye, then.' I began to sidle away. The others moved with me as if unwilling to let me out of their sight. 'Thank you for lunch.'

'No, thank *you*, Harriet,' said Tristan, 'for writing such a super novel, and for charming Persephone as only you know how. I shouldn't be a bit surprised to see that meeting bear fruit.'

'Oh, for sure,' said Lew, kissing me. He looked frozen in the pink suit. 'Give me a ring when you're ready to talk about the new one, won't you?'

Vanessa laughed. 'You'll be lucky, Lew! Harriet is so secretive about her writing—that's why she's full of lovely surprises.'

It was with their gales of merriment ringing in my ears that I finally made a break for it and headed for the underground.

CHAPTER 6

Prevailing excitements on the publishing and football fronts were in danger of driving *Trick of Hearts* right out of my mind. With rehearsals now twice a week I realised I'd better perfect my lines and most of Bernice's if a crisis was to be avoided. I knew this might be seen as unsporting, as crises of every denomination were meat and drink to the Arcadians, but I did not wish to be instrumental in Bernice's walking out.

I decided to take a leaf out of Trevor Tunnel's book and put my cues and speeches on tape so that I could learn them while driving or jogging, and not let them intrude into valuable working time. Mind you, it was actually some weeks since I'd done any work. The page headed *Abide With Me* had not been troubled further. I loitered in the fool's paradise of planning and making notes, and even these were sketchy.

So many matters vied for attention in my head, trampling my concentration underfoot. Apart from the Betabise Award and the meeting with Persephone Marriott from which the Erans expected so much, it was over a week since Reg Legge had rung, and I expected his second call daily. Could it be that he was toying with me as I had toyed with him? It was like being a lovelorn teenager again, I had developed an unwholesome obsession with the telephone, and it was taking all my self-control not to ring Barford United (whose number I had taken the precaution of looking up) and demand to speak to Legge. The strain was telling on me. I had even taken the major step of having a phone point installed in the study so that I could keep the machine under close surveillance the whole time.

Of course it never stopped ringing, and it was never Legge. Nor, it must be said, was it Persephone Marrioott, nor R.N Morell, chairman of the Betabise judges. It was mainly people enquiring about Stu.

Since placing the advertisement I had been astonished at the number of families desperate to take on the expense and responsibility of a large, dangerous animal. This was Monday morning, and over the weekend Clara and I had done our best to show Stu off to advantage to four groups of prospective buyers. It had not been a success. Stu had bitten one child's bottom, refused to break out of a walk for another, and continually put her head down to chomp grass with a third. The parents had shaken their heads sadly. Sorry, but it wouldn't do. Prior to the arrival of the fourth group I had sent Clara to the field an hour in advance to catch Stu and exercise her vigorously so that she would be relatively malleable when the strange child climbed aboard. But as I escorted mother and daughter to the gate there was Clara, scarlet in the face and swearing like a trooper, still pursuing Stu with the headcollar.

It had not so far been an auspicious start to my spell in horse dealing. The last mother had confirmed my darkest fears by taking me aside when she had ushered her weeping child into the car, and saying: 'Forgive my saying so, Mrs Blair, but would I be right in thinking you're not all that experienced with horses?'

'Well, it depends what you mean. I...'

'Only you ought to know that you're asking far too much for that animal. It may be a nice enough pony but it's totally unschooled.'

'I wouldn't say that.'

'I would. That is not a child's riding pony. I certainly wouldn't let any child of mine get on it—and that's assuming I could catch it! Good-bye, Mrs Blair.'

Watching the woman's Volvo zoom away I fumed. I was mortified. I also suspected she was right. Stu was a monster, and an expensive one at that. But Clara had furiously opposed any lowering of the price and we had finally agreed to take the advertisement out of the papers for a week or two and replace it when people had had time to forget.

This morning I made this my first task, and then spent three quarters of an hour (to poor Noleen's consternation) putting my lines on tape. After this it appeared that there was nothing for it but to get on with *Abide With Me*. When the phone rang my heart leapt. This was more than just a reprieve. This, surely, must be the first of the many calls I was so eagerly awaiting.

'Harriet? It's Nick.'

'Nick!'

'Long time no see. Or hear. Since before Christmas unless I'm much mistaken.'

'I think it must be.'

'At any rate it's been far too long. D'you fancy coming in to do the programme on Wednesday?'

No, it wasn't any of the people I'd expected to hear from, but nor was a call from Nick Daniels of Metropolitan Sound wholly unwelcome. He was the producer of a radio chat show called *Time for Talk* which was recorded midweek to go out on a Friday. Over the past eighteen months I had become part of the regular squad for this programme, and the frequent and remunerative trips to London for the purposes of recording it provided, as George was wont to say, 'movement and colour' in my otherwise humdrum rural existence. Though the summons was always phrased as an invitation, I had never been known to say no.

'Yes, of course.'

'Nothing much to talk about...' This was another constant factor. 'At the moment I'm kicking around Dialect, and Hemlines...'

'Mhm. They both have possibilities,' I said dutifully.

'I thought so. I'm just, you know, having a

106

ring round, sounding people out...but bear those two in mind.'

'I will.'

'See you Wednesday, then. Same time same place. 'Bye, Harriet.'

I had often wondered what radio producers actually did. Once, under the influence of Metropolitan Sound's Japanese bubbly, I had asked Nick how he would describe his role and quick as a flash he had replied: 'I am an animator.' And then gone on to speak of catalysts and something he referred to as 'people management'. Actually I suspected that his effectiveness consisted in only partially briefing his guests so that they arrived for the recording in a state of nervous anxiety, ready to sound off like free-firing cannons rather than remain shamefully, ignorantly, silent.

Since I'd recently been much occupied with horses, an equine analogy sprang readily to mind. Of course, Nick was the teaser, getting us mares all worked up for the stallion in the shape of our chairman, David Doubtfire. I entered *Time for Talk* in my diary, scribbled 'Dialect, Hems' on a piece of paper and went to the kitchen to make coffee. There in the garden was Declan, glaring affrontedly at the timorous green spikes of the daffodils I'd planted in the lee of the hedge. The hedge itself was one of the many areas which Declan liked to keep shorn to within an inch of its life. Nature may have abhorred a straight line, but Declan worshipped them. My expected hundred or so frilly golden trumpets, bobbing and fluttering in springlike profusion, were going to wreck his scheme to turn my back garden into a municipal park.

Not wanting a confrontation I stepped back, but Declan, with that sixth sense he had, looked up, spotted me, and beckoned me out in a manner which did not encourage refusal.

Shivering, I went out and joined him. He greeted me with a hail of abuse.

'What are these boggers doing here?' Anyone would think they'd staged an overnight coup instead of pushing their way modestly through the earth over a ten-day period.

'Oh yes,' I said, bending down to study them. 'They're the ones I put in in the autumn. Special offer in Regis market. They're going to be lovely.'

'You can't expect anything to grow up against this hedge, woman!' snarled Declan, ignoring the evidence to the contrary.

'But they seem to be doing quite nicely.'

'There's going to be hell to pay when I cut the grass, so there is!'

'I'm sure it'll go quietly, Declan.'

'And what about keeping this hedge tidy?'

'The daffodils will be over by the summer, and anyway it doesn't matter if it's not all that tidy. I like things to look natural.'

'Natural's one thing. Jongle's another.'

'Noleen will be having her tea in a moment,' I said, 'would you like to join us?'

'I got work to do!'

'Oh yes, so have we all, but everyone needs a break. Even you, Declan.'

'I'll have something out here.'

I wondered not for the first time how the O'Connells had ever managed to get together long enough to conceive offspring.

'How is Mary Rose,' I asked, 'and the grommets?'

'She goes in at the end of the month.'

'Oh well, that'll be a good job done,' I said soothingly. For one who actually accepted money from Metropolitan Sound for my sparkling discourse it was staggering how banal and platitudinous I could be. And it worked. I fought Declan with tea and unwanted sympathy.

Of course, I also had good old blackmail up my sleeve. I, and I alone, knew of Declan's carnal liaison with my neighbour Brenda Tunnel. I had actually observed them in the act, and heard Brenda, borne on waves of desire, apostrophise her lover as 'Cecil'. Though so far as I knew the affair had long since run its course it was a warm and wonderful feeling to have so much dry powder available should the need arise.

When I'd furnished Declan with half a pint of treacly Darjeeling and a flapjack which would play havoc with his plate, I put *Trick of Hearts* in my Walkman and set off for a run.

That evening George came round. He tended to call unexpectedly like this, and I sometimes wondered if he was checking up on us. If so, he must have been gratified on this occasion. We supplied the cast-iron proof that without him standards flew straight out of the window. Gareth, still in his school uniform, was sitting in front of the TV with a 7-Up in his paw. Clara and I were in the kitchen. Clara, in an acid house T-shirt and tanga briefs, was reading about schoolgirl mothers in *Sweet Sixteen,* and I was finishing off the shepherd's pie direct from the dish with a serving spoon. As pretty a picture of domestic decadence as you could hope to find. At times like this I wished I had not agreed to George retaining his key. What had seemed enlightened and sensible at the time now seemed rank folly.

The kids managed a 'Hallo, Dad!' and then scuttled off to their lairs like rats up a drainpipe, leaving me with grease on my chin and the nice crunchy bits round the edge still uneaten.

'Hallo, George.'

'Harriet...' He kissed me, as he always did. And as always I was relieved to find that he presented neither threat nor temptation. The kiss engendered only a kind of familiar, affectionate resentment.

He put down his briefcase and coat and glanced about him. 'Everything all right?'

'Yes, fine.'

'Have you been out somewhere?'

'No, not today. Just the usual round.'

I watched as he fought the temptation to brush the seat of a chair before sitting on it—and lost.

I too, weakened. 'Sorry about the mess.'

'Don't apologise to me. It's not me that's got to clear it up.'

'That's true.'

'I hope I wasn't disturbing your supper.'

110

'No, no! We'd finished.' I turned on the hot tap with such force that the jet of water spurted out of the shepherd's pie dish, soaking my shirt and the sleeve of George's suit. 'Oh, God, I'm so sorry—here.' I squeezed out the J-cloth under the tap, but George leapt out of his seat. 'Don't worry, I've got something.' He would have, of course. Out of his briefcase he took one of those nifty little spot-removing cloths in a sealed sachet and applied it vigorously to the splash marks.

'How are the children?' he asked, putting the used cloth in the pedal bin and hanging his jacket over the back of the chair. 'They didn't seem very eager to talk.'

'They're not. It's a condition, not a reaction. Nothing personal.'

'Clara seems to be—growing up.'

'Yes.'

'We'll need to keep an eye on her.'

I thought of Colin Waller. 'Yes.'

'You must let me know what goes on, Harriet. Keep me posted. Just because we've embarked on this trial separation doesn't mean you've suddenly become a one-parent family. I want to be properly involved with their upbringing.'

'Of course.' He had a point, and I felt guilty, a sort of closet child-spoiler.

'How are you, anyway?' he asked. 'Work going well?'

'It is, as a matter of fact.' I told him about the Betabise Award.

'I say, how simply splendid. Congratulations.'

'I haven't won anything yet.'

111

'No, but you've achieved your objective—to write a book that people take seriously.'

'If they do.'

'Of course they will!'

'Maybe.'

'I'm looking forward to reading it. Will you let me have one of those proof copy things when you get them?'

'Sure.' For once I wished George wouldn't show such a flattering interest in my work. He'd have been better off not reading *A Time to Reap*. 'How about a glass of wine? Have you eaten?'

'Nothing to eat, but wine would be nice.' I milked the wine box in the fridge for its last two glasses. 'Thanks.'

He took a sip. 'This stuff's fine, actually, so long as it's well chilled.' I could just picture George sitting down on an evening in his tidy, tasteful flat, with a plate of Marks and Spencer pasta salad and a glass of irreproachable white burgundy. It was quite wearing being with someone you felt sorry for, envious of, and irritated by all at the same time.

The phone rang, the sound drowned almost instantly by the crashing open of bedroom doors and the thunder of feet on the stairs.

'Hey!' shouted George, 'for heaven's sake!'

'It won't be for me,' I explained. 'Not my time of day.'

We listened as Gareth answered and then said: 'Oh, Hi.'

'Sounds as if you were right,' said George. The door of Clara's room banged shut again.

We continued to listen to Gareth, not out of

curiosity but as a kind of displacement activity to obviate the need for conversation.

'Yeah...yeah...yeah, she told me. I am, yeah. Sure. Any time...sounds okay to me. Do you want to talk to her? My dad's here too as a matter of fact...yeah. I'll get her, hang on.' Gareth appeared in the kitchen doorway. 'Okay, so who wants to talk to Reg Legge?'

'At last! I thought he'd forgotten about us!'

'Reg Legge...?' asked George.

'The Barford United scout, remember?'

'Of course, great stuff, Gareth, I hope you told him you won't step out the door for under a ton.'

Gareth gave a tolerant smile as I rushed by. 'Nice one, Dad.'

I picked up the receiver. 'Mr Legge?'

'Reg.'

'Reg. Nice to hear from you. You just caught me, I was going out.'

'Good. Well, I won't keep you long, Mrs Blair. I wondered what the result was of your family conference. Can we firm up Gareth?'

I flinched. 'Well, he's keen, and my husband has no objection provided schoolwork isn't disrupted.'

'Well, you've already had my assurances on that one, and I can only repeat them. Would you like me to have a word with your husband?'

I glanced at George and made interrogative gestures at the phone. 'Carry on,' he mouthed, 'you're working well.'

'It's all right,' I said to Reg, 'he's quite satisfied.'

113

'Good. It's a shame to waste talent in the family, isn't it?'

'Yes!' I flapped at Gareth who was looming over my shoulder in order to hear both ends of the conversation.

'So when would it be convenient for Gareth to come up to the club for a few days' training?'

'It's half term at the end of this month.'

'Fine. Ideal. That's a whole week, is it?'

'That's right.'

'Then why don't you bring him up here midweek? We have a youth team match before the big game on the Saturday so we could give him an outing then, see how he copes, and you could take him home Saturday evening.'

'Right, yes.'

'And if all goes well I'll be sending you and your husband some forms for you and Gareth to sign. Let's hope this is the start of a long and successful relationship.'

'Indeed.'

Reg's parting shot was: 'We take our youth policy very seriously at Barford. After all, these lads are not just the players but the citizens of tomorrow. Football's a wonderful game, and it needs great ambassadors. When we take a lad on it's the whole lad we're interested in.'

That, I didn't like to tell him, was what I was afraid of.

Gareth slapped me on the shoulder. 'Autographs later, fans.'

'I shall expect to get mine free,' said George. 'Harriet, you realise you're going to have to write a book about all this.'

114

We were five on *Time for Talk*, of whom the only constant was our chairman, David Doubtfire. He was a New Zealander who had first infuriated and then enslaved the British listening public by being too clever by half. The received view was that you either loved David or you loathed him, so I kept my own shameful indifference a secret. He was said to have a lovely wife, mewed up in an Oxfordshire farmhouse like something out of the *Ancrene Wisse*, but her existence had not prevented him from acquiring a reputation as a womaniser. No female, it was rumoured, was safe from his attentions or immune to his charm, so it was something of a shock to realise that I was both.

David must quickly have sensed my entirely unforced apathy, for he never gave me any trouble and treated me just like his male guests—as dull but necessary make-weights.

As usual, I knew who else was to be on. There was Nemone Shadbolt, conductor of the Eastern Chamber Orchestra, for one. She was a slender, tremulous, soft-spoken woman with untidily pinned-up hair and long, expressive hands. Nemone was so sensitive that she actually seemed to vibrate like a delicately plucked violin string. Her role was to provide a sort of ethereal descant on whatever mundane little theme the rest of us were pursuing. I was her polar opposite, the resident blunt instrument. Only when Nemone was away, touring mob-handed in Italy or Yugoslavia, could anyone else attempt anything approaching subtlety without sounding crass.

Philip Butterworth wrote a facetious and opinionated column for the London *Evening Mercury*. He was generally regarded as a poisonous, self-serving creep who used his vast portmanteau of anecdotes to come across on air as a darn nice bloke with whom one would gladly sink a pint.

Fifth in this week's group would be Lowther Berry, Professor of Applied Economics at Wakefield College, London. I liked Lowther, a dandyish sixty-five-year-old with a rakish line in Borsalinos and an irreverent attitude to broadcasting.

The recording was always at five-thirty, which meant struggling into the West End against the rush-hour traffic like a salmon forging its way upstream. Metropolitan Sound was in a back street of Holborn Kingsway. From outside it was nothing but a plate glass door and some Art Deco lettering, but beyond the door was a network of richly carpeted stairways, corridors and green rooms, and a warren of studios large and small. An impressive testimony, in fact, to the human urge to communicate.

Everyone at Metropolitan Sound was absolutely convinced of the existence of a huge and enthusiastic listening public for their programmes. I had never met a group of people—unless perhaps it was the Erans—so confident of their usefulness and popularity. They seemed unfazed by the existence of dozens of other radio stations in the capital alone, all catering for a finite number of listeners with an equally finite number of viable presenters and contributors. But who was complaining? Not me, certainly. Their money was as good as anyone else's and considerably better than some.

'Afternoon,' said Ozzie the doorman. 'And who is it for?'

'Harriet Blair for *Time to Talk*, Ozzie.'

Ozzie ran a huge, gnarled finger down his ledger. The fact that I visited the studios once a week for thirty-five weeks of the year did not deter him from going through this ponderous ritual. He wore his uniform with the particular care and pride of one who has spent the greater part of his adult life in the plain blue shirt and trousers of Her Majesty's Prisons. His hair was stiff, straight and so naturally wayward that it could be only partly brilliantined into submission. He smelt of nicotine and boiled sweets, the one evidence of his addiction to snout, the other of his unsuccessful efforts to give up. 'Oh *Ozzie!*' the young women of Metropolitan Sound would cry as they breezed out to lunch. 'Oh Ozzie, that is a filthy habit, think what you're *doing* to yourself, and where would we all be without you?' Now Ozzie looked me up in his ledger like a somewhat lived-in St Peter at the gates of heaven, sucking and sniffing glutinously.

'Here we are,' he said eventually. 'H. Blair. Know where you're going?'

'Yes, thank you. Studio A13.'

'All right for getting there?'

'Yes. I do it quite often.'

117

'A lot of people come in and out these doors,' said Ozzie reprovingly. Lips parted in concentration he peeled off one of the round black and white stickers which would proclaim me as a bona fide visitor. This he pressed to the lapel of my coat, and I was then free to go up the flight of steps into the reception area, and the lift.

The welcome board, I observed in passing, had only one name on it: E Lethbridge. A lean day, obviously, when Metropolitan Sound could only rustle up one name, and that not even remotely famous. I had an idea I'd heard it *somewhere*, but where, and in connection with what, I couldn't remember.

In Studio A13 Nick was on the phone in the control room and his PA, Sarah, was pouring the champagne. David and Nemone were already there, deep in conversation. Sarah looked round at my arrival, her pearl stud earrings gleaming.

'Hallo, Harriet, good journey? Come and be refreshed.' I took a glass. Nick caught sight of me and raised a hand beyond the glass.

David swung his chair in my direction. 'Harriet, I've been talking to Nick and we think we should take it fairly easy on the death of dialect.'

'Suits me. Hallo, Nemone.' Nemone fluttered her pale frond of a hand.

'Yes,' went on David, 'it smacks of a serious subject which, as you know, we've so far managed to avoid on this show. But when it comes to the politics of the hemline we can

118

let rip. I'm sure you girls will have plenty to say in that area.' It occurred to me that like many a Romeo before him, David was just an old-fashioned unreconstructed chauvinist who screwed women to keep them in their place. 'The musical interlude deals with fashion, too,' he added. 'Fashion in speech, fashion in clothes, the Oddfellows have done a neat *segue.*'

I glanced round apprehensively. 'Are they still here?'

'No,' said Sarah, 'but they said they'd join you all at the pub afterwards.'

Nemone sighed. 'I'm afraid I'll have to dash off today. We're at the Barbican tomorrow.'

Sarah began to quiz her about this as Lowther and Philip arrived, and Nick came through from the control room.

I poured the drinks this time, and Nick and Philip fell on each other for a concentrated session of mutual ego-grooming. As I handed Lowther his glass he kissed my cheek and said: 'Thank you, Harriet, you know just what a tired old man needs.' He could be just as chauvinistic as David, but with three times the charm.

'Someone for Christ's sake tell me what we're talking about!' said Philip, to remind us what a hectically busy, free-wheeling chap he was.

'Come and sit by me, old friend,' said David, 'and I'll point you in the right direction. I much enjoyed your piece about Burns Night, by the way.'

'Christ, but that was funny!' said Philip. Nick, David and Lowther gravitated towards him to listen to one of the famous anecdotes. Sarah

119

began bustling about with sheets of paper. That left Nemone and me to each other.

'Do you have much on hems?' I asked.

'Do you know,' she replied, steepling those elegant hands beneath her chin, 'strange as it may seem I feel there's quite a lot to be said...don't you?'

It got no better. It was not to be my day. On dialects I found myself set up as the archetypally English butt of David's antipodean prejudices, and when I tried to redress the balance by telling a joke against myself nobody laughed and a stage-managed laugh had to be recorded. After the music—the taped Oddfellows sounding mellifluous and urbane, which goes to show you can't judge people by their voices—we moved on to hemlines, which Philip commandeered with a string of stories about mini-skirts. David's acid put-downs, Lowther's sociological line and Nemone's delicate interjections harmonised well with this, but somehow I couldn't find a way in. My brand of jocund, let's-not-mince-our-words comment was entirely *de trop*. And when I weighed in with an astringent dash of feminism I could hear myself becoming shrill and humourless.

When we finished Nick came into the studio rubbing his hands. 'Energy, that's what I like. Terrific.'

'Not bad, was it ?' agreed David, 'and only three minutes over by my watch. When we've skimmed off the fat we'll have a good one there.'

Lowther chuckled. He was one of the last great chucklers. 'We certainly made a volcano out of a molehill on those hemlines, Philip, you were incorrigible.'

Philip tipped the last of the champagne into his glass, 'I gave you all something to fire at, though, didn't I?'

'I'm sorry,' I said to Nick, 'I was awful today.'

'No, you weren't. There wasn't quite enough of you, that's all.'

'It's so difficult when one's had a break, I find,' soothed Nemone. 'If one doesn't exercise the muscle, it wastes.'

'I keep telling my wife that!' said Philip and laughed heartily.

Nemone said she must go, and she and Lowther agreed to share a taxi. David, Philip and I set off for the Cap and Bells, leaving Sarah and Nick to crack the last bottle of bubbly and skim off the fat in peace. 'You know,' said David as we went down in the lift, 'when I look at our Nemone I continue to be amazed that she does that job.'

'Christ, yes,' agreed Philip. 'Orchestras are widely recognised to be among the most bloody-minded and contentious bastards on earth, If they don't like a conductor they can crucify him. If Nemone can win the respect of that mob she has my undying admiration.'

David nodded to Ozzie and we emerged into the street. 'Now if it was Harriet who was bossing up forty-odd hard-boiled scrapers and pluckers, I shouldn't be a bit surprised!'

121

'Is that intended as a compliment?' I asked.

'An observation.'

'I couldn't do it,' I said. 'People management's not my drop.'

David didn't pick up on this, because we'd arrived at the pub and he wanted to know what we were going to drink. Then he and Philip disappeared inside, leaving me out on the pavement in charge of their briefcases. Drinking on the pavement in all except blizzard conditions was one of David's less endearing foibles. He didn't care to be jostled or, he said, to be recognised and pestered, though there was at least as much chance of this outside as in. I knew they wouldn't hurry back. The few minutes at the bar where they could engage in showy but harmless verbal horn-locking was vital to them. I stood there in the lurid, noisy darkness, my hands in my pockets, the two briefcases between my ankles as though I'd just given birth to them. The drivers of cars slowing down at the adjacent traffic lights stared dully from their windows. A little old lady in Salvation Army uniform elicited a pound from me. It seemed to be getting colder.

Just then I became conscious of one of those currents which alert you to the approach of someone you know, a sort of vibration in the air like that which is said to precede a typhoon in the topics. I glanced along the street and saw, rounding the corner beneath a streetlamp, the Singing Gynaecologists. That was how I thought of them, thought it wasn't how they styled themselves. They were introduced on

Time for Talk as the Oddfellows, and this was the name which appeared on their record labels and in the programmes of the concerts which they gave in good venues all over the country, affording innocent pleasure to many thousands of sober citizens.

I could only think how glad St Zavier's Hospital must have been to wave them off on their numerous concert engagements, for Fergal and Dominic were mavericks, the Quantrill's Raiders of both the medical and musical words. This evening there was someone else with them as they bore down on me. 'Thar she blows!' bellowed Fergal, vocalist. 'How's the thrush these days, my darling? Still dying to be rogered by a red-hot poker?' The rules of confidentiality were as nought to Fergal.

'It's all right, thank you,' I muttered.

He loomed over me in his sheepskin coat, hipflask in one hand, cigar in the other, his taut corporation thrust into my solar plexus. 'Good girl. Where are the rest of those rats?'

'Getting the drinks in.'

'That's for me!'

Fergal bounded off. Dominic, pianist, his long thinning hair in a pony tail, snatched up my hand and kissed the palm uninhibitedly. What was it about doctors?

'Hallo, Dominic.'

'We've brought someone with us. Do you know Edward Lethbridge?'

For a moment I wondered which mauler of the uterine tract they had recruited. But then, in the streetlamps' glow (as I was wont to write) I

123

took in frosty eyes, dark hair, the bone structure of an Apache chief—

'Actually,' I said, 'we have met. You won't remember...'

'I remember,' he said. 'Nice to meet you again, Mrs Blair.'

'Call her Harriet for fuck's sake,' said Dominic. 'Anyone would think you were in fine company.'

'I will if I'm invited to,' said Edward Lethbridge.

'Please,' I said. 'Do.' He gave a little bow of his head with his eyes closed. His mouth might accurately have been described by the Old Me as cruel but sensuous...a hint of repression, of banked up fires...

'Didn't I see your name on the notice-board at Metropolitan Sound?' I asked.

'That's him,' said Dominic. 'Under all that bespoke tailoring he's just an old tart like the rest of us.'

'They're doing a series on political journals,' explained Edward, 'and it was my turn.'

He hadn't smiled once. I found myself hoping that he was a man who never smiled, but who would break the habit of a lifetime for me.

'Harriet does *Time for Talk* with David Doubtfire,' said Dominic.

'I know. I've heard her.'

Dominic put his arm round my waist. 'How was it for you? Did Digger Dave lay his chairpersonly hand on all the right zones?'

'It was pretty dire. For me, anyway.'

'The plaint of women the world over,' sighed

Dominic. 'Look, mind if I go and gee up these drinks?'

Edward Lethbridge and I were left standing surrounded by cases like two people who'd packed for a weekend away and then thought better of it. He seemed quite content to stand there in silence but I was in the mood to make an effort. 'How do you know Fergal and Dominic?' I asked.

'Fergal wrote a piece for me a few years ago. About teenage girls and the pill. We printed it, but I disagreed vehemently with every view it expressed.'

Knowing Fergal's opinions I was able, by a process of elimination, to identify Edward's. Best to tread carefully then.

'But you've kept up with him.'

'Idealogical polarity can make a very sound basis for a relationship.'

'I must remember that.'

At last, the others emerged from the pub and distributed the drinks. Edward's was a large, neat whisky. Philip, who always felt upstaged by the Oddfellows, gulped his and began to make 'can't hang about' noises. No-one tried to detain him and a couple of minutes later he had leapt into a cab at the traffic lights.

The conversation had veered, as it so often did in the company of the Oddfellows, to sexually transmitted disease.

'The only reason they've all got it in Africa,' bellowed Fergal, 'is that the poor buggers have about as much idea of genital hygiene as you or I do of tracking white rhino. The privates parts of the Malimbo tribe, to give a classic example, are just one ruddy great nest of infection. They've got everything up their wedding tackle but sewer rats. In some of their villages, I kid you not, I've seen cocks that would...'

'Let me just get this straight,' began David.

'Okay, okay,' went on Fergal. 'I'm saying that our dusky brethren are much like women drivers—don't much care what goes on under the bonnet so long as it gets them there. And when it finally forces itself on their attention, it's generally too late...'

Dominic weighed in with some nightmarish experiences he'd had in Thailand in the seventies, and I glanced up at Edward. His hawkish profile was as impassive as a totem pole.

Quite suddenly he turned and fixed me with his pale, penetrating gaze. I felt as though I'd been caught with my finger in my knickers.

'Would you like dinner?' he asked.

I was stunned into a cloddish silence.

Edward tilted his head slightly. 'Mm?'

'Dinner?'

'Yes. Food and drink, generally taken in the evening.'

'Of course, I'm sorry. I don't know—I think I'm all right.'

His eyes were not so much frosty now as chips of ice, and his voice took on a touch of cold steel.

'I wasn't suggesting you were undernourished. It was mutual society I was interested in.'

'What a lovely idea...' As I blithered I

126

experienced a familiar, half-forgotten sensation—that of being greatly inflated by a bicycle pump with its tube inserted between my legs. It meant I wanted to have dinner with Edward Lethbridge. I really, really did. But good old Blue Funk, the housewife's friend, was programmed to rescue me even now when I didn't, in theory, need rescuing.

'I'd have loved to, Edward, but I have to get back.'

'Then back you must go.' Was that it? He drained his scotch and swooshed down from his great height to place his glass on the pavement.

'Who's going?' cried Fergal. 'Edward? Not staying for another snort?'

'No thank you.' He picked up his case. It was as though having sounded out the possibilities and found them lacking he was washing his hands of the whole pack of us. I watched, paralysed with frustration, as he shook hands with David and had his shoulder slapped by the Singing Gyni's. He then took my hand with neither more nor less warmth than anyone else's. 'It was nice meeting you again, Harriet,' he said. 'Shall I give your regards to Persephone when I see her?'

'Yes, do.'

'Good night.'

Away he strode, tall and erect, his long, patrician nose cutting the night air like the prow of an ice-breaker. God but I was a wally.

Fergal put his arm across my shoulders, releasing a warm waft of body odour from

127

the gaping front of his sheepskin coat.

'You look melancholy, darling. 'Nother g and t?'

'No, no thank you.'

'What's the matter with everyone tonight?' Fergal put his lips to my ear. 'What did you make of Edward the Avenger, then?'

'Why Avenger?'

'Sees it as his mission to clean up the country,' said Dominic. 'And I don't mean litter.'

'Seemed like a nice enough chap to me,' said David. 'Wasn't clutching the Good Book to his bosom or anything like that.'

'Oh, he's not a holy Joe,' said Fergal. Takes a more Old Testament line. Less cheek-turning, more eye for an eye. Hit 'em where it hurts?'

'Is he married?' I asked unguardedly.

Fergal grinned. 'No. And isn't interested either. Keeps his prick to himself and gets his rocks off on Law and Order.'

'I see.'

'So there you are, Harriet,' said David. 'Wasting your time with that one.'

CHAPTER 7

'Who's teacher's pet then?' taunted Bernice after rehearsal the following Tuesday night.

'I don't know what you mean.'

'You know the whole thing. Creep.'

'Somebody has to.'

'Crawler!'

'...if only to encourage the others.'

'*Me* you mean. You mean *me!*'

I didn't bother to argue with her, we were only sparring anyway. Instead I topped up our glasses. Bernice had come back to our house for a drink while she waited for a lift home from Arundel, who had been lecturing a mass meeting of the eastern counties Soroptimists. Bernice's own huge, rusty coffin of a car had failed its MOT for the umpteenth time and had not been granted a stay of execution.

'It's going to drive me wild, this,' she said comfortably, curling her feet up beside her, 'this being dependent on lifts. The only thing is that it will enrage his nibs even more so he may be impelled to buy me the little red Datsun of my dreams. Mind you,' she added, 'it's nostalgic. Like waiting to be collected from teenage parties. Not so much fun, of course, saving your presence...Oh, how I mourn the passing of heavy petting...'

'I can't say I think about it much.'

'Golly, I do,' said Bernice.

I could believe her. Tonight she resembled several kilos of peaches stuffed into a small string bag. Through every chink, gap and buttonhole exuberant flesh peeped and bulged, seeking egress. Even the holes in her tights revealed moons of plump, thrusting leg on the look-out for prey, and her frizzy black tresses waved and rustled about her head like the tentacles of some predatory sea-creature.

129

'By the way,' she asked, 'where are they?'

I did not query the short mental routine by which she had travelled from heavy petting to my children. Was not Clara at this moment at the house with Colin Waller?'

'Clara's with a friend,' I said, 'and Gareth...' I heard the back door slam...'has just got back from training.'

'Someone call me?' Gareth came in and stood over us in his shorts and stockinged feet. His enormous hairy knees, like some product of Ridley Scott's imagination, were near my right cheek.

'No,' I said. 'Not called. Just mentioned in passing.'

'Hallo, big boy,' said Bernice. 'Well done on hitting the big time.'

'Yo,' replied Gareth in his cool-dude, hard-man mode. It drove me up the wall but Bernice, a shining example of the child-free state, had not OD'd on all this stuff.

'YO?' she shrieked. 'What's that?'

I translated flatly. 'It means hallo.'

'Get away, Ma, don't short-change the lady,' protested Gareth, flopping down in a chair. His attitude was one I'd seen described in a body language book as sexually available: legs splayed, crotch and pelvis thrust forward, hands laced behind the head. 'It means how do, looking good, what's going on, how's it hanging?

'*How's it hanging?*' This sent Beatrice into fresh fits of mirth. 'Honestly, Harriet, these kids of yours, they're totally shameless. How's yours hanging, Gareth?'

Gareth gave her his 'no sweat' gesture. Just the same I should have been happier if I'd been certain that his *was* hanging. He was at that stage of a young man's development when the whole of life is one long tussle with rampant priapism, and Bernice wasn't doing anything to help. He swung his legs over the arm of the chair.

'The only conceivable drawback about not being a parent,' Bernice was saying, 'is you don't stay abreast of current trends.' She shifted her position, displaying an even more provocative configuration of peaches. 'What sort of dance are you all doing these days? The only groovy dances I know are the Hitch-hiker and the Funky Chicken. In the unlikely event of Arundel ever taking me to a dancing party I shall be a public disgrace.'

When, I wondered, had she ever been anything else?

'Come on, Gareth,' she insisted. 'Tell me.'

'Dunno. Whatever gets you going.'

'Hooray! That's what I like to hear!' Bernice raised her arms in the air and wriggled her shoulders, making her breasts quiver. Gareth crossed his legs. 'I know what I meant to ask you, Harriet,' she said. 'Will there be a party after the play?'

'There usually is, but Percy hasn't mentioned anything.'

'Should he have? What's he got to do with it?'

'The producer usually hosts the party.'

Bernice's face was a study. 'God in heaven.

Harriet, can't *you* do it?'

'No!'

'Why not?'

'Why the hell should I?'

'Go on, Ma,' interjected Gareth. 'This I've got to see.'

'Exactly,' I snapped. 'I'm not inviting people back here so you and your friends can snigger at them.'

Gareth looked aggrieved. 'Who said anything about sniggering? We could, you know, mix and mingle, top up the drinks. Get the dancing moving along.'

'Do you know, he's absolutely right,' said Bernice unhelpfully. 'I'm all in favour of mixing the age groups. We could have a blast.'

'This is all entirely academic, because it's none of my business,' I protested. 'The party's up to the producer.'

'But Percy's such a wanker,' moaned Bernice. 'I can just imagine it, all fondue and fumbling. Is there a Mrs Percy?'

'Yes.'

'Well, I suppose that might inhibit him a little. What's she like?'

I hesitated. 'She's very nice.'

Bernice and Gareth groaned aloud, and Bernice nodded and rolled her eyes. 'Oh yes, here we go. Harriet cannot be persuaded to say a bad word about her fellow woman. Come off it! When you describe someone as very nice it's a racing cert she's some tight-arsed, blow-waved pillar of the community who makes *Kinde, Kirche, Küche* read like a revolutionary slogan. Now tells us what she's really like.'

'She's fine. A perfectly unexceptionable woman.'

'What are you talking about?' asked Gareth.

'No-one you know,' I answered automatically.

'Mrs—er—Norton, is it?' said Bernice. 'The wife of Percy, our poor man's Blinkie Beaumont.'

'That chap who runs the deli in Parva?'

'Yes.'

'With the really gross hair.'

'You know him?'

'Sure.'

'But do you know her?' persisted Bernice.

'Not really. But,' Gareth beckoned Bernice forward, 'she was wearing beige flares the other day.

'Beige flares? Is that bad?'

'Blimey,' said Gareth, 'you are out of touch.'

'Mea culpa, mea culpa...' Bernice beat her breast.

'Flares are the pits.'

'There you are then,' said Bernice to me. 'It's got to be here if we're to avoid the humiliation of fondue, fumbling *and* flares.' The doorbell rang. 'That'll be Arundel. Gareth, be a love and let my husband in.'

Gareth didn't usually respond well to requests for errands—a professional domestic inertia was the hallmark of his current style—but on this occasion he answered the call like a lamb. Perhaps he was relieved to be offered an opportunity to achieve detumescence in the twilight of the hall. We listened to Arundel bid Gareth good evening and Gareth said yo and that we were in there. We heard Gareth's footsteps going up the stairs as Arundel entered.

'Hallo,' said Bernice, 'how did it go?'

'Quite well, I fancy,' replied Arundel in his bloodless way. 'Good evening, Harriet.'

I wondered if he knew that I knew. 'Glass of wine, Arundel?'

'No thank you. But coffee would be welcome.'

'When I returned with his coffee it was quite plain that Bernice had long since put an end to uncertainty.

'I shall withdraw all conjugal rights,' she was saying, 'unless you get Harriet on to the shortlist at the very least!'

I handed Arundel his cup and he glanced up at my burning face from beneath his pale chameleon lids. His mouth might have been drawn with a mapping pin.

'What a small world it is,' he said. 'But you do both realise that properly I shouldn't be here at all.'

Bernice snorted.

'Sugar?' I asked,

'Thank you, no. So perhaps we could leave the subject quite alone. For both our sakes.'

'Absolutely,' I said. I felt the cold, dead hand of Arundel's dislike upon me. In vain did I remind myself that this was a man like any other and one who had carnal knowledge of my dearest friend several times a week, if she was to be believed. No-one would ever know how impossible it was for Arundel to be swayed in my favour.

'Next thing you know,' remarked Bernice, who had been last in the queue when discretion was handed out, 'she'll be a set book for GCSE!'

I quaffed my wine. I needed it.

'Do you see anything at all of George?' asked Arundel.

'Quite a bit, yes. We're on very friendly terms.'

'Just the same, this must be a difficult time for you. It must be hard, for instance, to get in the right frame of mind for writing.'

'Not really.'

'You must have admirable powers of concentration.'

'I don't believe in inspiration if that's what you mean,' I said, playing my hardboiled professional's card. 'I'm a believer in getting down to it.'

'Ah,' said Arundel.

The bastard. He was reminding me of my failure as a wife, my difficult and inhibiting circumstances, the many grave responsibilities which surrounded me...it wasn't so, but he'd very nearly persuaded me it was. The sickening irony of the situation hit me with full force. Here were Bernice and Arundel who treated each other in a way that might charitably have been called cavalier and, more realistically, hostile. They led almost entirely separate lives, had no children and, now that Arundel's ghastly old father, Bartie, had gone to the great flophouse in the skies, no other dependent relatives. They made no effort, for each other or anyone else.

135

And yet their marriage was intact. Here was Arundel dropping by to pick up his wife like any normal, uxorious provincial hubby. While George and I, who at least liked one another, who had been mutually admiring companions and sympathetic bedfellows, were separated. It wasn't fair, it wasn't right.

Fluffy stalked into the room and sprang on to Bernice's lap, where he at once sank down, purring.

Bernice stroked his back with firm, even movements. 'Nice pussy...good, good pussy...' Arundel's eyes, resting on his wife, glittered.

'Oy.' Gareth appeared in the doorway. 'Phone's ringing.'

'Then why don't you answer it?'

'Don't want to talk to anyone tonight. If it's for me say I'm out.'

'Do your own dirty work!' I hissed as I picked up the receiver. 'Hallo?'

'Yeah—hallo,' said a voice, young, male and proletarian, probably the offspring of some merchant banker. 'Is Clara there?'

'No, she isn't actually. I'm waiting to hear from her myself.'

'Okay. Never mind.'

'Who is that?'

'Colin

'Colin Waller?'

'That's right.

'I thought she was with you. I mean, I dropped her off outside your house.'

'Yeah, well, she's not here now.'

'So where is she?'

'Dunno. Thought she might be with you.'

'Colin—' I spoke extra firmly to stifle the first stirrings of panic. 'Colin, has Clara been with you at all?

'Oh yeah.' Silly me for asking.

'So why did she go, and when?'

'Dunno. She just felt like splitting.'

I entertained an horrific mental picture of my daughter bursting open like the robot in *Alien*, spewing white bread, Mars bars and hair gel in all directions.

'When was that?'

' 'Bout...an hour ago.'

'An hour ago?' I shrieked. I was aware of Bernice and Arundel hovering nearby, intimating that they were about to leave, but I was by now far too agitated to pay them any attention. 'Where to?'

'Dunn...'

'But she must have said something!'

Bernice stuck a hand in front of my face and waved it. I batted it aside like a gnat.

'No,' said Colin, 'she didn't.' The Potters left.

'Look,' I said threateningly. 'It's pitch dark, it's ten-thirty at night, she told me she was going to ring for a lift if your father couldn't run her back...'

'Yeah, which he can't if she's not here, can he?' argued Colin reasonably.

'In my day,' I thundered, indicating at a stroke just how long ago that was, 'if a girl went out with a boy he made it his business to look after her and make sure she got home

137

safely afterwards! And here you are telling me that you don't know where Clara is!'

There was a hissing sound in my ear and someone tapped my shoulder. Once again I batted the hand away.

'Ow,' said Bernice aggrievedly.

'I thought you'd gone!'

'We came round the back.' Clara appeared from the kitchen, looking daggers at both of us. 'She's back,' added Bernice unnecessarily.

'Clara!' I snarled welcomingly. 'What have you been doing?'

'Walking home.'

'Walking? From Regis?' Spot, thinking it was an offer, emerged from his basket and wagged hopefully.

'Don't shout,' said Clara. 'What's all the fuss about?'

'I'll leave you to it, then,' whispered Bernice. As she opened the front door I caught Arundel's look of gloating satisfaction.

Spot returned to his basket. A distant and distorted voice reminded me of Colin Waller, stuck on the other end of the line. I lifted the receiver, my eyes still on Clara's face.

'As it happens,' I said, 'she's just got back. And she seems to be all right, no thanks to you, Colin, I might add. Do you realise she's walked home all the way from Regis?'

'Blimey,' said Colin, 'I'm impressed.'

'Who's that,' asked Clara.

'Colin Waller.'

'Mind if I speak to him?'

'I think you'd better!'

138

Clara took the receiver. I stood next to her with my arms folded, needing only curlers and rolling pin to complete the picture.

'Colin? Hi...yeah...that's right... No, I can't as a matter of fact, not right now...' She glanced at me, but I stood my ground. 'Yeah, a bit...nothing I can't handle...yeah, yeah, okay. Me too. Seeya. Bye, Col.' She hung up.

'Are you going to tell me what all that was about?' I asked.

'Nothing. We had a bit of a bust up, that's all. But it's okay now.' And in truth, now that she had spoken to Colin, she seemed perfectly benign.

'What on earth was he playing at, letting you walk back from Basset Regis at this time of night? And what were you playing at, even to think of it?'

'You're right,' said Clara. 'He needs wheels.'

'But you said his father...'

'His dad was out.'

'You should have rung.'

'I told you we had a row. I walked out on him.'

'That was a very stupid thing to do.'

'No it wasn't. It sorted him out. I won't have to do it again.'

'You should never have done it in the first place. And listen,' I added, as she began to move towards the stairs and the sanctuary of her lair, 'don't ever, ever, do that again.'

'Okay.' She went up a few steps. 'Anyway, I only walked part of the way if you must know.'

'What about the rest?'

'I hitched,' she said. 'Night.'

I returned to the sitting room and sank my teeth into a cushion.

A couple of days later I received a letter, forwarded by Era Books, from Persephone Marriott. In it, she reiterated how delightful it had been to meet me, and enquired whether I might consider attending a little lunch she was holding for prospective guests of *Considered Opinion* at the end of the following week. Had I, she wondered, ever seen myself doing a show such as hers, because she and her colleagues thought I might very well be a *Considered Opinion* kind of person. The lunch, she promised, would be quite pleasant and informal and would give us all a chance to make our minds up. She did so look forward to hearing from me, and hoped my answer would be yes.

I'd barely finished reading it when Vanessa was on the line.

'Harriet!'

'Hallo, Vanessa.'

'I simply had to ring—I saw the BBC stamp—what did she say?'

'She's asked me to lunch next week.'

'Harriet! Brilliant!'

'You think I should go?'

'Do I think you—Harriet, do you realise what an achievement this is? You, Harriet, Blair, have succeeded where captains of industry and Members of Parliament without number have failed! It's a triumph! You can let a day or

140

so elapse,' (Vanessa had not lost sight of the gamesmanship angle) 'and then accept.'

'I'm not entirely sure it's me.'

'Look, Harriet,' said Vanessa patiently, 'if Marriott thinks it's you, then, it's you. Producer knows best, yes?'

'I suppose so.'

'I promise you.'

'And after all, it's only lunch, only a preliminary...'

'Oh, no.' I wasn't to be let off that easily. 'It's not "only" anything. The *CO* lunch is tantamount to being asked on the programme. You'll have to eat your soup with a fork or something not to get on now.'

'I just can't help wondering whether I'm up to...'

'Besides, think of all the high-powered people you'll meet, the sort of people who buy literary novels in hardback, and ask yourself, can I really afford to pass up this opportunity?'

Put like that, it began to look like a sacred duty. She must have sensed my coming round, for she continued, pressing home her advantage: 'I mean, take for instance that chap she was with at the Gadfly, that E Lethbridge. He's been on quite a few times. And the *Bystander* does reviews. You'd be mad not to go!'

'Yes,' I said thoughtfully. 'Yes, Vanessa, I think you're right.'

The *Considered Opinion* lunch was held in a private room at the Ormrod Institute, a grim red-brick building just off the Edgware

Road. I thought it shrewd of Persephone to choose such a forbidding venue for her auditions (for whatever she'd written, I cherished no illusions about this being a social occasion). A Portrait of the eponymous Ormrod, a Victorian philanthropist, in the hall of the Institute, served to remind us how trivial were our concerns and ambitions compared with the Greater Good of Mankind. Such eyebrows! Such whiskers! Such magisterial jowls!

I left my coat with a trembling old man, pocketed my ticket, and went to the Ladies, which had red tiles on the floor and white ones on the wall, and vast chipped basin on which lay tiny shards of pale green soap, scored with deep, black cracks. A woman in a gingham-patterned nylon overall sat playing patience. There was only one other patron, a tiny, well-groomed creature in a grey suit and high-necked white blouse. We went about our respective rites with complete self-absorption, ignored by the attendant, silent but for the occasional trickle of water, the whisper of hands brushing fabric, the slap of the playing cards.

The grey-suited woman left first, but when I reached the Acton Room on the second floor I almost bumped into her just inside the door.

'Oh! Hallo again!'

'Hallo—what a coincidence.'

'Have you two already met?' Persephone came steaming across to us.

'Only just. In the Ladies,' I said.

The grey suit was introduced to me as Tish Wetherall, Tory candidate in a forthcoming

West Sussex bye-election.

'I'll leave you to talk for a minute or two,' said Persephone. 'Drinks are on their way. It's so *lovely* to see you both.'

Tish Wetherall and I, left bobbing in Persephone's wake, smiled anxiously at each other. A tray came round with white wine, orange juice and mineral water. I stared at it. Was this part of the audition, a test of character? My hand hovered over the glasses... I wasn't driving, had nothing to lose, and was shit-scared. I took the wine.

'Is that Perrier?' Tish Wetherall asked.

'Yes, madam,' replied the waitress with a 'what else?' inflection.

'Oh dear,' said Tish, 'what a pity,' and took the orange juice, adding, while the waitress was still within earshot: 'I make of a point of only drinking Malvern of Buxton.'

She had scored points on a couple of fronts here, but I considered that I'd clawed back a few by not entering the competition at all.

'This is all quite impressive, isn't it,' Tish said. We looked at the white-robed table laid for lunch, the sideboard bristling with fine wines, and at our fellow guests.

I nodded. 'Do you know all these people?'

'Yes—yes, I think so. Those I don't know I recognise.'

'I only know Persephone,' I said. 'And you of course.'

'Perhaps I can help.' I realised I was in the presence of someone who took herself very seriously.

'Thank you.'

'The dark girl is Anne Dwyer, Persephone's chief researcher,' she said, 'she'll be the one who found out about you.'

I couldn't let this pass. 'No,' I said, 'I met Persephone socially.'

'That's the style,' said Tish frostily. 'Never waste a good connection.' And never expect humility from a politician, I thought grimly. Tish continued: 'The man talking to her is Doug Archer, head of the Allied Fuels Union. The one in spectacles is Jonathan Royce, Labour spokesman on Welfare. And the other one is Hugh Lorimer, of course.'

'Good Lord, so it is. Has he lost weight or something?'

'People put on nine pounds in front of the camera, you know,' explained Tish patiently. She was beginning to get up my nose.

Anne Dwyer came over, bringing with her the union leader.

'Now I'm going to split you two up if you don't mind,' she announced. 'Harriet, this is Doug Archer of the AFU. Doug—Harriet Blair, bestselling author. Tish, why don't you come and say hallo to Jonathan. Lunch soon,' she added, 'we're one short, but we shan't wait.'

Doug Archer and I surveyed each other. Now, of course, I recognised the bootbrush hair, awning eyebrows and ill-fitting suit of innumerable TUC podia. He was shorter than I'd imagined—in his case the nine pounds seemed to have been lopped off at the end—and had a pleasing no-frills directness. 'I read one of your books on my flight to Poland last September,' he said. 'I could not have been more surprised if he'd admitted to being the man in Shirley Maclaine's memoirs.

'Which one was that?'

The Remembrance Tree.' Ah yes, vintage Blair, written while under the influence of extra-marital passion—no bosom left inert, no manhood unstirred...

'What did you make of it?' I wanted to know.

'Great stuff. Just the sort of story I like.'

I found myself glancing at his drink, but it was hardly touched. 'I must say you surprise me. I always thought most of my readers were women.'

'Aye, well, women buy 'em and the men sneak a read as soon as they're able,' he said. 'Got any more coming out?'

'I have as a matter of fact, quite soon. But it's a different sort of novel.'

'What sort would that be?'

'Rather more—contemporary.'

'Pity.' I felt crestfallen. He peered in my glass. 'You drinking that?'

'Yes... Why?'

'Nothing. Only I know a bit about wine, and this lot ought to be ashamed of themselves.'

I warmed to him. 'Have you done this before?'

'Wouldn't be here if I had.'

Ask a stupid question, Harriet, and you get a blunt answer. 'It's pretty nerve-wracking, isn't it?'

He set down his glass, folded his arms and ranged himself alongside me to survey the room. 'You've got nothing to worry about, Mrs. Blair. You're in, take my word for it.'

'Do you really think so? I've been wondering what on earth I'm doing here. It's been a real effort reading the papers every day, and it's taken me all week to work out what my opinions are.'

'Doesn't matter,' said Doug, 'you're in. Good-looking woman, no political masters to answer to, fresh perspective... Her Ladyship's already decided you're just what she needs.'

I didn't know whether to feel flattered or terrified. 'I'm not even sure I want to be on.'

'That,' said Doug, 'is your greatest asset.'

Persephone summoned us to the table. 'Harriet, Doug, we've decided to go ahead. Our last guest is an old hand anyway.'

I looked questioningly at Doug and he inclined his head to mine, muttering: 'Another one to help with the vetting process.'

On the table, prettily displayed quenelles of trout were already laid at our places, framed by phalanxes of silver and several glasses per head. Persephone directed the seating plan. Hugh Lorimer and Jonathan Royce sat at either end of the table. I was on Lorimer's right, with Anne Dwyer opposite, and the empty seat on my other side. Doug sat opposite, between Anne Dwyer and Tish Wetherall, and Persephone was beyond the empty chair.

Hugh Lorimar introduced himself and shook my hand. He had tufts of hair in his ears and nostrils and a cross, squinting expression like a baboon. 'Tuck in,' he suggested. 'You might as well.'

We sat. The napkins were like stiffly laundered sails of white linen. Bottles of the despised Perrier stood on the table, and two kinds of wine were being offered. I made some quick calculations.

'I'd love some white,' I said to the motherly waitress who had the sympathetic air of a warder serving prisoners on death row, 'but I'll have some water too, if I may.'

'Certainly, love.'

'A statesmanlike decision,' said Hugh Lorimer, tucking his napkin into his collar. He must have been the only person there with a genuine healthy appetite, unspoilt by terror or the need to concentrate on others. Just the same, he poked at his quenelles with his fork, like a biology master preparing to dissect a rate. 'How I hate this pretend food,' he remarked testily. 'What happened to good thick soup?'

'Stop grumbling, Hugh,' said Anne Dwyer with an amiable firmness, like the lady of the house reprimanding an irascible old uncle on Christmas day. 'You're hopelessly out of touch. The kind of food you like would send our guests to sleep. Which we certainly don't want,' she added, smiling at me with a steely brightnesss.

Hugh started shovelling down his quenelles and I glanced down the table. Tish, Persephone and Jonathan Royce were already debating some fiscal matter. Doug was assessing the latest wine with a scowl and ignoring both food and conversation. Unfortunately I was overwhelmed by the need to pay due attention to both, while my mind was blank and my throat closed like a self-sealing valve.

Hugh Lorimer had finished his quenelles and was well into his bread roll. Anne Dwyer leaned forward, one hand holding a dainty forkful, the other resting on her glass of water. 'So what do you hope for from the budget?' she asked.

'Are you going to eat that bun?' murmured High Lorimer.

'No, do.' I pushed the roll in his direction. 'I—er—I—suppose everyone wants to be richer, don't they? But I'd certainly be prepared to pay higher taxes if I felt the money was going where it's needed.'

'And where is that?' her brow furrowed quizzically as she introduced the forkful into her mouth.

'Well, into education for a start.'

'Excuse me.' Hugh Lorimer stretched across me for more butter.

Doug asked: 'Where are your children at school, Harriet?'

He could not have fed me a better cue. 'They're both going through the local state system,' I said, 'and doing very well out of it as far as I can tell. But that's because the teachers and pupils, and the parents, work extremely hard to overcome deficiencies in the basic provision.' There was one of those fleeting lulls, in which I realised I had an audience of six. I faltered and halted. Then Persephone struck up again at her end and Anne Dwyer turned to Doug.

'You have children, Mr Archer...?'

Hastily I ate some of the quenelles and spread the rest about the plate among the carrot matchsticks and ringlets of endive and radicchio.

'Tell me,' said Hugh Lorimer, 'my wife wants to know. When are you going to write another of your ripping yarns? She's a fan, claims to have read every one so far.'

I took a deep breath. It looked ominously as though this was one starlet who was never going to play Portia. Still, nothing ventured.

'I have another coming out soon, actually,' I said. I was beginning to feel like a tape of myself. 'A contemporary novel. It addresses itself to one or two themes that have been interesting me for a while.'

Hugh cocked his head, frowning. 'Is humping one of them?' he enquired.

Halfway through the main course—rack of lamb with new potatoes, broccoli and peas—the eighth man arrived. Persephone rose from her place with a welcoming smile, but it wasn't till he'd sat down on my right that I realised it was Edward Lethbridge.

'I shan't eat, thank you,' he said to the waitress, 'unless there's a sensible pudding. But I will have a glass of the red if it's the '78.' Even sitting down he towered over me. His face was very pale, with bruise-coloured shadows under the eyes. As he explained his lateness to Persephone I observed a minute shaving-nick on the point of his jaw. His bicycle pump was in perfect working order.

Hugh Lorimer was mopping up gravy and mint sauce with his third bread roll and I saw a homing-in look in Anne Dwyer's eye. I decided to take the initiative. 'Hallo again,' I said. 'I didn't expect to see you here.'

'Hallo! Nor I you. You're a postulant, I take it?'

I nodded. 'But you're not.'

'No. Persephone likes to have an experienced panellist at these lunches to get a second opinion.' He lowered his voice. 'Something of a chore.'

Doug Archer leaned across the table. 'I say...'

Edward raised his eyebrows, which had a tendency to fly away at the corners, like Jack Nicholson's 'Yes? Mr Archer, isn't it?'

'It is. If I may say so, Mr Lethbridge, that magazine of yours has a lot to answer for.'

'I certainly hope so.'

'I'd like to hear your justification for that piece you ran about the gasworkers.'

'Certainly. How long do you have?'

'As long as it takes.'

'Then if you're sitting comfortably, I'll begin...'

I'd have been quite happy to listen, but Anne Dwyer leaned across and tapped my wrist.

'Harriet,' she said, 'a moment or two ago Doug and I were discussing the attitude Great Britain should take to this coup in Hai Kwai.

What's your view on that?'

Hugh Lorimer leaned back, arms braced on the edge of the table, fingers drumming gently. He belched. Where, for pity's sake, was Hai Kwai? And had there been a coup? And did I, in all honesty, care?

'That's a difficult one,' I began. Anne nodded encouragingly. 'We need to make our position clear while not interfering at this stage...'

Somehow I busked it. Some long-buried instinct for survival guided me through the minefield of potential gaffes and inaccuracies and I emerged on the other side flushed and sweating but not entirely disgraced. My reward was a nod and a 'that'll-do-nicely' smile from Anne Dwyer.

Hugh Lorimer swung his head about like an old charger snuffing the breeze. 'What are they giving us for afters?' he asked.

The answer was caramelised oranges, or cheese. We all had the oranges except for Hugh and Edward. Persephone changed places with Anne and Hugh changed places with Jonathan Royce. We discussed the freedom of the press and connected matters, and Doug became extremely heated. Jonathan, it became apparent, was even more nervous than me and Edward remained completely silent. Under these circumstances it was relatively easy for me to play my plain woman's card to good effect. I was able to sound both radical and moderate at the same time which was quite a feat by anyone's standards. I even made Persephone laugh at one point, but I didn't look at Edward for his reaction, he seemed a man wholly committed to his Stilton and Bath Olivers. Down at the other end Tish seemed scarcely to have drawn breath throughout lunch, her face was flushed and her eyes bright. She had the air of a woman who knows she has done well.

Over the coffee Edward turned to me and said: 'This may sound a little odd, but I have some shopping to do in Marks and Spencer when I leave here. I gather they have some rather good lambswool pullovers at reduced prices at the moment, but my taste in these matters is notoriously suspect. Could I prevail upon you to come along and give me a hand?'

It was such a blameless invitation, and combined dignity and boyish ineptitude so charmingly, that what else could I do?

'Of course,' I said. 'It'd be a pleasure.'

Downstairs in the Ladies Tish was eager to know what I'd thought of her. 'Do tell me, how do you think it's gone,' she asked breathlessly, dabbing her nose with powder like a hamster washing its whiskers.

'It didn't seem too bad,' I said, 'but then I've got nothing to compare it with. I don't suppose I'll go any further, anyway.'

'Ah, but you're a wild card! You have no political masters to answer to. Was I all right on pensioners' day-care?'

I wondered why she imagined I'd been listening to her all through lunch when I'd had my own performance to consider.

152

'You were wonderful,' I said irresponsibly. 'Lucid, forceful and sympathetic. You won't have done yourself any harm at all here today, Tish. The PM would have been proud of you.'

'Oh, God!' Tish clasped her hands and prayed to the neon light. 'I do hope you're right!'

A few minutes later I was walking up the Edgware Road with Edward. 'What an extraordinarily annoying little woman that is,' he remarked.

I tried to extend my stride to synchronise with his, so as not to appear too little myself.

'Who?'

'That Wetherall woman. Tish—I ask you. I've never been able to understand an adult who goes around calling themselves by a nickname.'

I filed this away. 'She was all right really.'

'Don't disappoint me, Harriet. She was awfully silly. And when she began talking that twaddle about benefits...words fail me.'

It's awfully easy to be treacherous when you're off to Marks and Sparks with a tall, dark, handsome hardliner.

'Yes,' I said. 'Me too.'

CHAPTER 8

In the hierarchy of seduction, choosing pullies in M & S must, on the face of it, come pretty near the bottom. Which all goes to show you can't be too careful.

153

I took a fateful step that afternoon when I agreed to spend half an hour in Menswear with Edward Lethbridge. There was, I discovered, something peculiarly intimate about helping a man choose clothes. George had brooked no interference in the matter, and had only in the direst emergencies despatched me, with detailed written instructions, to purchase socks or shirts on his behalf. And yet here was this cold-eyed, hawk-nosed, raven-haired hounder of video pirates deferring to me as though I were the source of all wisdom on matters sartorial. He displayed a touchingly abysmal ignorance of sizing, style, colour and general appropriateness, and as we sifted through the Sale merchandise together it was not unpleasing to be taken for his wife by the motherly assistant.

It didn't end with pullovers. When we, or more accurately I, had chosen a couple, one navy and one red, both with crew necks, it transpired that Edward was getting a little short of socks, and could do with some underwear as well. To this day it's my proudest boast that I am the woman who got Edward Lethbridge into boxer shorts. We bought several pairs in Madras checks and candy stripes, and then selected some dashing Argyll socks.

'I'm enormously grateful,' he said as we stood in the queue for the till. 'I'm a complete duffer about clothes.'

'You don't look it.' I eyed his dark grey double-breasted suit which had a massive quality, as though hewn from some substance other than cloth. 'That suit wasn't bought here.'

'No, I'm a little tall. I go to a chap in Jermyn Street who just does the same suit over and over again for me, with minor variations in weight and colour. I dare say he despairs of me, but he's too well-bred to mention it. We understand one another.'

I hoped the Madras shorts and Argyll socks wouldn't cause the Jermyn Street chap to despair further.

Edward paid for his purchases in cash, taken from a large and battered brown leather wallet. As we made our way to the door, Edward clutching a fistful of shiny green carrier bags, I ventured the question that had been at the back of my mind for the past half hour or so.

'How do you normally manage your shopping?'

'Normally?'

'I mean, if you dislike it so much, and find it so taxing—who do you get to help you?'

'Oh, I see. Fortunately I have several kind friends whose taste and good sense I can trust. One of them can generally be pressed into service when the need arises. Persephone, for instance, can always be relied upon.'

I thought of Persephone...the legs, the shorthand-kiss at the Gadfly.

'You two are old friends?'

'Yes. Old and true friends.'

We emerged into what had become rather a nice afternoon, with pale sunshine and high, floating clouds and early daffodils glinting in Hyde Park.

'Would you like some tea?' he asked.

'That sounds lovely. But are you sure I'm

not keeping you from your editing?'

He gave me a wonderfully stern and chilling look. 'The thing about being an editor is that your timekeeper is your publication, not some other fellow. We come out on a Thursday, so Friday is a quiet day. Shall we?'

We went to tea-rooms in Park Lane. What with one thing and another I felt quite Anna Neagle-ish. It wouldn't have taken much for me to swing gaily round a lamp-post and burst into song. We were shown to a window table and Edward ordered Earl Grey and Eccles cakes.

'I understand you're a writer,' he said.

'Yes.'

'What kind of thing do you write?'

'Oh...novels.'

'Should I have read any?'

'Heavens, no.'

'Why ever not?'

Reader, I lied to him. 'Because they're very small, introspective, rather dull books.'

He seemed quite content with this and didn't bother to argue. 'I see. But very well-written, I'm sure.'

'Other people must be the judge of that.'

'Indeed.'

A policeman strolled past the window, making it even more like one of those 1940's musicals, and to change the subject I said: 'Isn't it nice to see a bobby on the beat like that? It makes one feel so safe.'

'Safe?' Down went the Eccles cake and up when the eyebrows. *'Safe?'*

'In a manner of speaking.'

'Let me tell you something, Harriet.' He looked briefly but intensely out of the window as if gaining control of himself, and then turned back. 'In this country today, safety—physical, spiritual and moral—is an illusion. We are all of us under threat.'

His voice was cold and even and sharp, like a sword. It occurred to me in a vague, distant sort of way that he might be a little mad, and that I did not agree with a single word he was saying, but neither of these thoughts prevented me, as he began banging on about urban policing, from picturing him in the boxer shorts.

'...letting the fabric of our society rot and disintegrate through television-induced inertia...'

I nodded, and poured more tea. Sylvia Plath had written about women loving a fascist, but I'd always imagined my own preferences to run counter to her theory. It wasn't Edward's opinions I found arousing so much as the cold fire that fed them. If that same fire could be channelled elsewhere, what a conflagration there would be... That such a diversion was unlikely, to say the least, simply added to its attraction. Here was a man outstandingly equipped for sexual passion, but wedded to his bizarre ideology. I could see that I stood about as much chance of getting past the lambswool-pullie stage as Edward did of editing the *New Statesman*. And that made me feel—well—pumped up.

'...on a Home Office committee investigating hooliganism,' he was telling me now, 'so I shall be travelling around a good deal over the next few weeks.'

'How interesting,' I said. 'What exactly will that involve?'

'I shall try and see things for myself. Be present at the places where trouble occurs and form a firsthand impression of how it started and by whose agency. The police and the public can give one their views, but I intend to form my own as well.'

'Couldn't that be dangerous?'

'I shall simply be observing. I shan't, on this occasion anyway, be taking issue with anyone.'

'Who else is doing this?'

'On the Beamish Committee?' He did, now, give a wonderfully sardonic, disparaging smile. 'Assorted trick-cyclists, breast-beaters and apologists of the bleeding-heart Left. All looking for ways in which society is to blame, whatever that may mean. In this country,' he said, leaning forward with eyes like glacier mints, 'we have lost the ability to identify our enemies.'

'Have we?'

'We no longer like to apportion blame in case it tarnishes our view of ourselves as kindly, tolerant people.'

'But you would—apportion blame?'

'Certainly. Fairly, of course, but blame, like credit, must be given where it's due, and swiftly punished.'

It was a long time since I'd spent so much time with someone with whom I so fundamentally and wholeheartedly differed. Unpoliticised as I was, I had carried with me into early middle age the baggage of Sixties attitudes picked up at university. Love, Peace and Hair was our creed, as we wandered about like Ferdinand the Bull, smelling the flowers. Speaking of which, Edward's own hair, I noticed, grew in a widow's peak...

'...the absolute necessity of saying, "this is wrong, and must not go unpunished," ' he said. 'As a parent, surely you must agree with that?'

This put me on the spot. As a parent I went in for wild inconsistency with flashes of inspired improvisation.

'Oh yes,' I said, 'of course I do.'

Edward nodded approvingly. 'Before I go on my travels,' he said, 'how about a spot of lunch?'

The ability to lie convincingly, I reflected, was the author's greatest gift.

An extra rehearsal was called for that evening, but did I care? No, sir! For the first time I actually felt like Yvonne, the woman of the world—warm, wise and witty, a person others would confide in at the drop of a hat. Why, on this one day I had hobnobbed with a trade union leader, a Tory MP and a nationally famous media mandarin, and bought boxer shorts for the Right wing's answer to Charles Dance. I was in a mood to out-Yvonne Yvonne.

In fact, the play seemed better all round. We did Acts Two and Three, of which we were not yet heartily sick, and Bernice managed a close approximation of her lines unaided.

When we'd finished, Percy asked us all to gather round, an avuncular smile on his face.

'A *great* improvement, everybody,' he said. 'It

really is beginning to come together at last. In fact if the upward curve continues our problem will be how not to peak too early!'

We chuckled obligingly. Percy held up his hand to indicate the end of the Good News.

'However. We are still rather short of technical back-up. I did put a notice in the news-sheet, but there's been very little response. In fact it would be fair to say there's been no response at all.'

We assumed appropriate expressions of self-righteous dismay, and whispered to one another how absolutely typical it was. None of this was anything new, of course, but it was the cast's prerogative to see themselves as crack troops, keeping the flag of the Performing Arts flying over the massed TV aerials of Magna. Brian and Delia Arnold, who had been seen to confer briefly, now craned their necks and lifted their respective index fingers.

'Any suggestions?' asked Percy. 'Yes, Brian and Delia?'

Brian it was who spoke up. 'Look, Percy—in our experience it's all hands to the pumps at times like these. Delia and I have quite a bit of experience of set construction and painting, and we'd be perfectly willing to organise regular workshops in our double garage to do whatever needs doing.'

We were aghast. Blacklegs! The Play may have been the thing, but the cast would have rather performed on upturned milk crates and in semi-darkness than do any of the work themselves. And we could always, of course (it had been done before) cancel the production if the necessary manpower did not materialise. That this was the cause of blessed relief to many of the Arcadians was not publicly acknowledged.

Here at least Percy was in tune with the rest of us. He shook his head and spoke firmly. 'That is good of you both, but no. This is a thriving organisation with fifty members, on paper at least, and it simply isn't right that two-thirds of them aren't pulling their weight. I won't have my actors wearing themselves out building scenery till all hours. It's not on, and it shouldn't be necessary!' We rhubarbed self-righteously like a crowd of extras in *Julius Caesar*. 'On the other hand,' went on Percy, 'we could put out a pro-forma letter explaining just how serious the situation is. Telling the membership that the production is in jeopardy because of people's unwillingness to do this vital backstage work.'

Bernice put her hand up. My heart sank.

'Percy—?'

'Yes, Bernice.'

'May I ask what actually needs doing? I mean, the play's set in rehearsal rooms in a provincial town, and it's more or less contemporary, so surely we can just get up on the stage and do it, Bob's your uncle.'

Percy gave an amused, kindly smile. 'Bernice, I hope you won't mind my saying so, but what you have just said proclaims you as a newcomer.' He looked at the rest of us for endorsement, and we gazed sympathetically at poor, benighted Bernice. 'A play is a team effort,

161

what appears on stage is simply the tip of an iceberg. Even a production like this one, which is light on scenery and costumes, generates a hundred and one vital practical tasks which must be done by someone.'

Bernice, obviously unconvinced, shrugged. 'Okay. I'll take your word for it.'

Just then a shadowy figure appeared near the door, a glint of eye-whites, the frayed silhouette of ruffled hair.

'Jimmy!' cried Percy. 'Just the man! Can you come over here and tell us exactly what backstage jobs remain to be filled?'

Jimmy marched forward. His hands were in his pockets but you could see they were bunched into fists. His shoulders were hunched and tight, as if pulled up with a drawstring. Whatever the Ministry of Defence establishment got up to, I did hope Jimmy wasn't near any switches.

Percy grabbed him by the arm and pulled him centre stage. 'Shoot,' he said, and I found myself flinching in case Jimmy should take this instruction literally.

His staring eyes swept over us and found us, as usual, lacking.

'I need a stage manager, someone on props, a gofer, and someone on tabs,' he said. 'Proper ones, not idiots.'

Percy nodded. 'That's about what I thought. We need at least four quick-witted, able-bodied people for these important jobs.'

Bernice nudged me. 'What are tabs?' she whispered.

'Curtains to you and me.'

She raised her voice to address the company at large. 'What's so technical about pulling curtains?' she wanted to know. 'I mean anyone can do that, can't they? Hell, I'll do it, I'm not on stage at the beginning or end of anything.'

Jimmy's marble-eyes came to rest on Bernice. She at once gave him her most expansive, beddable grin. But she had on this occasion wasted it on the one mature male on earth who was a hundred per cent proof against her charm.

'I want someone competent on the job,' said Jimmy. 'Not some member of the cast faffing about.'

'Sorry I spoke!' said Bernice with a laugh, looking round for her moral support which the rest of us were far too chicken to give. 'I just can't believe pulling curtains open and shut is difficult.'

Jimmy pushed his fingers upwards through his hair, finishing with a slight tug. 'Whoever's on tabs,' he said through gritted teeth, with his eyes shut, 'has to be in constant contact with me on the cans. This play has a bastard of a lighting plot—' this we recognised as a compliment—'and it's no good me getting my end right if some joker doesn't pull the fucking tabs on time.'

'Quite right,' said Percy. 'It's crucial. Let's leave that aside for the present. What about these other things?'

'I must have a gofer,' said Jimmy. 'When I'm up on that lighting tower I can't see to every damn thing myself. There's got to be someone

163

on the ground to take messages and prevent cock-ups offstage right, where there's no-one on cans.'

We nodded. How well we knew! At the previous year's pantomime Jimmy had actually imposed a total blackout on a squadron of weeping fairies and woodland creatures because the Ugly Sisters enjoying a can of best in the wings with their wigs off, had omitted to douse their panatellas. If there was one thing worse than a perfectionist, it was a perfectionist with tunnel vision, like Jimmy. No revenge was too dastardly or counter-productive for him to exact if crossed.

'I wonder,' said Percy, 'whether that job and that of stage manager, or props, could be combined?'

Jimmy glared at him. 'If you want this play to be a success you won't fuck about making bloody silly economies,' he snarled.

Percy was finally stung. 'It's not a question of economies,' he retaliated, 'it's not as if it's going to cost us anything anyway.'

'But it bloody well will if the gantry gets fused by some prat rushing about like a gnat in a paper bag trying to do three jobs at once,' said Jimmy. 'You asked me what was needed, and I'm telling you. Now if you'll excuse me I've got some work to do on that dimmer switch.'

He jumped off the stage and we parted to let him through, watching him apprehensively as he picked up his huge metal toolbox. The dimmer switch in the village hall was a Jardine innovation which had been a bone of contention with the

Finance and General Purposes Committee both before and since its introduction.

As if reflecting our nervous mood the overhead lights suddenly faded to a faint, crepuscular glow. But none of us liked to complain.

Bernice had got her red Datsun out of Arundel, an operation akin to getting blood from a stone, and which clearly demonstrated her hold over him. So enraged was she by Jimmy's ultimata that she invited herself back for a drink and drove me the three hundred yards to my door in the style of a New York cabbie with an ulcer.

'I never heard such bollocks!' she fumed, pulling up with two wheels on the pavement. 'Who the hell does he think he is, dictating terms to the rest of us like that?'

'The man who can consign us all to outer darkness, that's who.'

'Fiddle-de-dee, any fool can point a few lights at a stage!'

'That's where you're wrong,' I said. 'It's a very skilled job and Jimmy's very good at it.'

'He'd need to be!' I winced as Bernice slammed the door. 'If he can't switch on a few blasted lamps then I'm sorry for him. He's got sod all else going for him.'

'He's a professional,' I said patiently. My mood was still sunny. I unlocked the front door and sniffed for smoke as was my habit.

'So was Crippen,' said Bernice.

'Have a drink and forget it.'

'Good idea. Where are the kiddies, are they in?'

165

'Yes, I think so.' I heard the quack and jangle of the TV. 'Go and take a look.'

I poured two glasses and went along to the sitting room. It was in semi-darkness, and the beady red eye of the video recorder indicated that a film was showing.

Bernice was sitting on a beanbag, whose seams I could actually see gaping. One or two tiny white polystyrene balls had already escaped and lay on the carpet nearby. On the sofa were Clara and a youth with hair 'en Bros' whom I took to be Colin Waller. Gareth sprawled in his sexually available position in the comfy armchair. There was a strong smell of stale cooking oil and the unlit grate was clogged with greasy white paper. Fluffy and Spot, flanks distended and whiskers glistening, lay comatose on the hearthrug. Of course, this was the night the Prime Enterprises stalked the streets of Magna in a specially converted van which served fast food at one end and videos for hire at the other. I had been known to take solace at the Muck Wagon myself. Only the knowledge that every other house in the village contained a similar scene tarnished the wicked pleasure of feeding junk to both body and mind simultaneously.

'Evening—'

'Ssh! This is great, this bit.'

Colin Waller cast me a nervous glance and Bernice stretched up her hand for her glass. On the screen there appeared a youth who had apparently swallowed a large octopus. For a couple of minutes his subcutaneous tissues did a St Vitus dance, then he sank to all fours and began to sprout facial hair and fangs. When his contortions seemed to be at an end, I tried again.

'Evening, all. Hallo, Colin—it is Colin, I take it?'

He nodded.

'May I?' I asked, and squeezed on to the end of the sofa next to Clara. It was only a small sofa, but she contrived to clench her muscles in such a way that no part of her body touched me. I thought she was damn lucky Bernice hadn't tried to sit there—but then Bernice did not suffer from the plague of consanguinity.

The werewolf, tail waving like Spot on the make, pottered out of his bedsit in search of prey.

Bernice covered her eyes. 'Oh God, this is going to be ghastly!'

'Yup, juicy bit coming up,' agreed Gareth.

The werewolf made short work of a courting couple on Hampstead Heath and then set off in search of afters. Its face had a puzzled, glowering expression which reminded me of Hugh Lorimer.

I wondered what Edward was doing. Listening to opera, perhaps...or dining alone at his club, the Blood and Thunder, to which he had invited me to lunch next week...maybe he was in his austere bachelor flat, munching cheese on toast as he worked...or speaking eloquently on my behalf to Persephone Marriott—no, that thought was rather less pleasing, and I deleted it. I dwelt instead on our precious moments together...the boxer shorts...the Eccles cakes...urban policing...

'AAAAAH!'

My eyes snapped open. The werewolf, refreshed by supper, was enjoying a spot of mindless evisceration in Golders Hill Park. More interesting by far was the effect this had on his audience. Colin had used it as a pretext for putting one arm round Clara and the other hand on her thigh; Bernice had wrapped her arms around Gareth's leg—tonight mercifully clad in jeans—and had buried her face in his knee, her shoulders shaking with mirth. Only Gareth remained motionless, though there may have been less obvious bits that moved, and his face, directed at the screen, wore a dim, slightly sheepish smile. Though it was impossible to tell in the dim light, he had the air of someone blushing.

The scene on the screen altered, and we were with the puzzled denizens of New Scotland Yard. Colin took his hand from Clara's thigh and Bernice said in a muffled voice: 'Someone tell me, is it over?'

'Yes,' I said, 'you can come out now.'

She flung herself backwards on to the beanbag, arms splayed, shrieking with laughter.

'What a perfectly appalling thing that is!' she hooted. 'Horrid, horrid...!'

'Just you wait,' said Gareth, still wearing the little smile and not looking at her. 'In the end he finds he can't change back and he starts eating himself.'

'Oh no!' Bernice put her hands over her face,

then parted them like shutters to look at Gareth. 'Where does he start?'

'At the tail, of course,' said Gareth, and Bernice covered her eyes again, giggling. She was like a great, amiable, abandoned dog, inviting everyone to tickle her tummy—or at least her enviable torso, displayed to advantage this evening in an angora pullover. The pullover was patterned with lambs, frisking in rows, getting bigger where they were stretched over her bust, trotting away into relative obscurity towards the waistband of her black ski pants. I would have entrusted Bernice with my life—but not with anything else. Her loyalty and affection were beyond dispute, but her libido romped free and untamed like some gigantic sea creature frolicking in the ocean beyond the control of man.

Under cover of the CID's deliberations, I checked out Colin and Clara. Colin, clearly unsettled by both my presence and Bernice's behaviour, was using a technique borrowed from the animal kingdom, that of remaining absolutely motionless in the hope of going unobserved.

'Colin,' I said, just for the fun of seeing the sweat burst out on his upper lip, 'how about a cup of tea?'

'No—er thanks.'

'Darling?'

Clara shook her head and yawned.

'Bernice—Gareth—tea?'

They neither of them appeared to hear. Clara turned to Colin. 'D'you want to come up?' He nodded, and they rose as one and made for the door. Clara, entirely composed, Colin scanning the carpet for rattlesnakes. I experienced a pang of nostalgia for those dear, dead days when one had to find a pretext, however threadbare, to get a boy up to one's room.

'How will you be getting home, Colin?' I enquired with my most forbidding solicitude.

'My dad's coming.'

'I see. He'll be able to make it, this time, will he?'

'Oh yeah.'

'Mu—*um!*' said Clara.

'I was just checking. We don't want anyone else walking three miles in the middle of the night.'

'Take no notice,' said Clara to Colin. 'Come on.'

The film was ending, in a flurry of gratuitous and highly coloured slaughter. The words 'The End' seemed to me like a comment on the preceding hour and a half. Gareth switched off the television and began stretching and scratching, a cue for Fluffy and Spot to do the same.

'Pretty amazing, eh?' he said.

'Astonishing,' agreed Bernice.

'British technicians, of course.'

'Really? Thank God we lead the world in something, even if it's only celluloid carnage...' She heaved and struggled, trying to get up. 'Hell's bells, I'm going to need a block and tackle to get me out of this thing...Gareth, be a love.'

Gareth took both her hands and hauled her up. 'There you go.'

'Thank you.' She dusted herself off, making everything quiver. 'Harriet, did you say something about tea a moment ago?'

'I did, yes. Do you want one?'

'Perhaps it would be a good idea. I don't want to get nicked, and me in my brand-new motor.'

She sank down again, this time on the sofa, and I went out to the kitchen. Fluffy, who had run out ahead of me, was crouched on the draining board licking a bowl that had contained cornflakes. Spot sloped in and stood glumly by the back door, staring straight ahead through the frosted glass. I let him out and chucked Fluffy out after him. I wondered, if Edward could see me now, what his condition would be. My mood had dimmed slightly under the influence of the domestic scene with its grim reminders of responsibility, and sexual activity not my own.

I sighed deeply and Spot returned and gazed at me, sighing back. I took Bernice's tea into the sitting room. But she and Gareth were exactly where I'd left them. As I walked in Gareth said: 'How's the play going then?'

My jaw dropped at this unprecedented display of interest in something outside himself.

I handed Bernice her tea and sat down. 'How do you mean?'

'The play. How's it going?' he repeated, rearranging the words slightly to assist me.

Bernice answered. 'Our leader says it's improving, but I'm just the new kid on the block so I've nothing to compare it with.'

'It is a lot better,' I said.

'But then some lunatic started haranguing us about backstage problems, grossly exaggerated as far as I could make out, and the next thing we know it's all doom and disaster and the whole thing's going to be cancelled.'

'Well, not *quite*,' I put in. 'Only if we can't find the people.'

'Yeah?' said Gareth. 'Tell me about it.'

I did wish I could stop feeling suspicious about this conversational advance.

'...three perfectly simple tasks that any fool could do,' Bernice was explaining *con spirito*, 'but you'd have thought he was talking about prefrontal lobotomy!'

'I don't mind doing something,' said Gareth.

Furtively I put my fingers to my pulse to check that I wasn't in some extreme and abnormal physiological state.

'Great!' cried Bernice. 'Would you really?'

'Yeah. Sure. Why not?'

In the next fifteen seconds alone I could think of half-a-dozen reasons why not. I found my voice.

'Gareth, love, you're not a member.'

'So?'

'You'll have to join.'

'Why? I thought they were desperate.'

'You're not insured otherwise.'

'Okay. How much?'

'A fiver.'

'I got it.'

'But *why?*' I squeaked, all pretence at rationality cast to the winds.

'Why not?' I did wish he'd stop saying that. 'Something to do.'

'You'll have to attend rehearsals.'

'Yeah. So?'

'I mean it's no good just turning up when you feel like it.'

'Fine.'

Bernice flapped her hand at me. 'For heaven's sake, Harriet, stop knocking the idea, it's absolutely marvellous, we shall have darling Gareth around to brighten our dull old lives! Let him do it, woman, for God's sake.'

'But we need three,' I said, 'and he's only one.'

'Oh I dunno, he's worth at least one and a half,' said Bernice, a remark, which I chose to ignore.

Gareth got up, and Bernice followed suit, with a movement that made the lambs jerk as though an electric current had passed through them.

'I'll stroll along next time,' said Gareth. 'Night, all.'

'Night, sweetie,' said Bernice, adding, when he'd left the room. 'What a poppet, and so mature.'

I was not about to enter a discussion on the maturity of my offspring, something I spent much of my time trying to ignore.

I accompanied Bernice to the door. In the road outside, its front bumper almost nudging the rear of Bernice's Datsun, was a white Sierra. A man sat in the driving-seat, tapping his hand on the steering-wheel in time to inaudible music.

'Oh I say,' said Bernice. 'A gentleman caller, just waiting till the coast is clear...?'

I gave her a withering look and leaned slightly in the direction of the stairs.

'COLIN!' I bellowed. 'Colin, your dad's here!'

Bernice looked impressed. 'How can you tell?'

'Experience.'

'You know, Harriet,' she said, kissing me, 'I'm worried about you. You seem very tense to me. You really must give yourself permission to have a little *fun.*'

I watched as she bounced out, exchanged a few cheery words with Mr Waller through the window, and after a couple of false starts which grazed the Sierra's bumper (and for which she didn't even receive a dirty look), drove away. Colin slithered past me into the night and got in. The open car door emitted a short burble of Jim Reeves. Poor Colin, street cred shot to pieces at a stroke. Half-an-hour later, as I rubbed baby lotion into my neck, I reflected that as regards fun, it wasn't the permission I lacked, but the conditions.

CHAPTER 9

March, and the children's half-term, came in to an accompaniment of high winds, heavy rain and record low temperatures for the time of year. Stu stood up to her hocks in mud in the paddock, the incipient daffodils were bent double before the blast, and the cat roosted in the airing cupboard. On my front fence, Damon's poster had to be swaddled in several layers of cling film to protect it from the elements.

I had, as promised, let him know the dates of Gareth's trip to Barford United, and his response had been swift and sure.

'LOCAL BOY PICKED FOR BARFORD!' shrieked blue writing on an orange Day Glo background. 'BOOK YOUR SEATS AND TRANSPORT WITH PRIME ENTERPRISES *NOW* TO AVOID DISAPPOINTMENT!' There was the date and time of the game, and the name of the opposition. No mention was made of the First Division match which followed, and for which this was only the warm-up.

'My word, Damon,' I'd said when he brought it round, 'you have been busy.'

'That's right,' he agreed. 'Got a nice little coach booked, and a choice block of seats right over the tunnel.'

'But do you think that many people will want to come?'

'You're joking!' said Damon. 'What? First Division club, everything laid on, spot of local interest—it's a great day out.'

'I suppose so. Where are you making your profit, though?'

He looked pained. 'There is such thing as community spirit.'

'Yes, there is, but you're a businessman.'

'I got some T-shirts printed for next to

175

nothing, and Terry's bringing the van along with a few refreshments.'

'I see.'

'So how many you want then?'

I had been taken aback by this. Damon's charabanc did not accord with my image of myself as the mother of the Boy Wonder. Still, I didn't want to hurt his feelings.

'I think,' I said carefully, 'that we'll be independent.'

'Your husband's not going, by the way,' said Damon.

'Sorry?'

'I called on him. He'll be in Denmark.'

Oh, he would, would he? I assumed a that's-right-I-remember-now expression. 'Of course, I'd forgotten. Still, its doesn't make any difference. I think I'll go separately if it's all the same to you, Damon.'

'Suit yourself.' For all Damon's savvy he had not acquired the knack of behaving graciously in the face of refusal.

'But if I feel hungry,' I added, 'I'll know where to come.'

'Gotcher.'

Clara had also, not surprisingly, declared herself unavailable for the fixture. Gareth seemed unperturbed by the news that only I would be going, but I thought it a poor show, and said as much to George when he came round on the evening of the preceding Saturday.

'I mean you *knew* when it was going to be.'

'Yes, but I didn't check my diary immediately,

176

did I? And the Copenhagen trip has been fixed for months. I'm as sorry as you are, but it can't be helped.'

'You ought to be there.'

'Why? You'd be going anyway, and you're not particularly interested in my company, so I don't see what difference it makes,' said George, with an uncharacteristic touch of petulance, and I had no ready answer.

The fact was that since Barford's elevation into the First Division its fans had felt it incumbent upon them to assume the mantle of soccer hooliganism, and had acquired quite a reputation in those circles where such things are discussed. I'd even heard Gareth use the phrase 'the beasts of Barford', and their exploits had made the papers on more than one occasion. I wasn't at all sure that I fancied going to the ground on my own, but neither would I admit as much to George. I almost wished I'd taken up the offer of Prime Enterprises. Almost.

Fortunately perhaps, there were other events standing between me and the Barford game which enabled me to set aside my anxieties for the time being. Chief among these was lunch with Edward at his club on Thursday, which stood out like a beacon in what looked like being a long week of literary inertia and domestic wrangling.

On the Tuesday Gareth attended his first rehearsal of *Trick of Hearts* and was accepted, *faute de mieux,* in the role of Jimmy's gofer. Dilly Chittenden said that since she was going to be sitting there anyway she might as well pull the curtains, and Glynis Makepeace volunteered her husband, the hapless Robbo, as A.S.M, which we all took with a pinch of salt. Jimmy said he supposed this would have to do. No wonder he was always maddened with rage— he persisted in the fantasy that the Basset Arcadians would suddenly bring forth technicians and stage hands of West End standard, completely out of the blue and in defiance of every known precedent.

Despite my anxieties, Gareth surprised me by performing his allotted tasks quite adequately and with something almost approaching diligence. Having marked down Jimmy from the first as a middle-aged head-banger he assumed a demeanour of lordly impassivity towards his criticism, not bothering either to explain or complain. Gradually, I became less tense, and even permitted myself a glow of maternal pride when, at the end of rehearsal, Percy thanked Gareth profusely for stepping into the breach.

'My pleasure,' said Gareth.

'He's much sought after, you know,' said Bernice, and went on to tell everyone about Barford United. If I had done this I should have been all but turned to stone by the venom of his stare, but this evening he seemed quite content to accept the plaudits of the Arcadians.

'Yeah,' he said, 'sorry I shan't he here for the next one.'

Jimmy Jardine jerked his head and hissed in his breath, but his protest was swamped by the general assertion that of course that didn't matter at *all*, and everyone *quite* understood. It was all very gratifying, but I still couldn't rid myself of the small wriggling worm of doubt, and the nagging question: why?

'What did you think of it?' I asked afterwards as Bernice ran us home in the Datsun.

'It's all right,' he replied, using the marginally more enthusiastic of his two laconic inflections. 'Not as bad as I thought.'

'Praise indeed!' said Bernice.

'What about—you know—the actual performances?' I pressed.

'Steady on, Harriet,' said Bernice, 'there's no need to invite trouble.'

'I'd just be interested to know.'

Gareth shrugged. 'They're okay. I mean you're not going to be giving Kim Whotserface any sleepless nights, but you know...'

'Kim who?'

'Thingy. Basinger.'

'Kim *Basinger?* What's she got to do with it?'

'She's an actress, isn't she? A pretty good actress, I reckon.'

I was sure Gareth was not supposed to have seen her in action. Bernice cackled with laughter and ground the gears with a flourish. 'Harriet, it's acting lessons for us—*straight* round to the plastic surgeon in the morning.'

'She's not an actress,' I protested. 'She's a film star.'

'So?'

'There's no comparison,' I said huffily.

'Yeah,' agreed Gareth, 'that's true.'

Bernice shrieked with laughter again and

stalled the car on the pavement outside our house. 'Hooray for Gareth!' she cried. 'I knew it would be a giggle having him on board!'

I declined an invitation to do *Time for Talk* on Wednesday afternoon so that I could see Gareth off on the train to Barford. Reg Legge had rung me to say that the new lads, of whom there were several from all parts of the country, would be met personally, by him, at the station, and escorted to the hostel where they would be staying.

'I'll look out for him,' Reg assured me. 'We know each other.'

For a moment my imagination ran amok with visions of green carnations and bunches of keys, but Gareth's reaction was stupendously scornful.

'What does he think I am?' he complained. 'A little kid? I suppose he's going to line us all up in a crocodile and make us look both ways before we cross!'

'Don't be silly,' I said, 'he's just taking a responsible attitude, and quite right, too. There'll be plenty of boys who've never been away from home before, you know.'

'It's *unbelievable.*'

'Well, it's a relief to me, anyway.'

'You're as bad as he is. I just hope Legge's not going to cluck over us like an old mother hen the whole time, because that's going to get *right* up my nose.'

'I'm sure he won't,' I said. I was racked by so many conflicting instincts that my brain felt plaited.

In the driving rain on Regis station I ambushed Gareth with a kiss.

'Hey, what are you doing?'

'Ring me when you get there, won't you?' I said. 'There's sure to be a pay phone, and you can reverse the charges.'

'I'll ring, I'll ring!'

'Have a wonderful time...'

'I'm *training*, Ma.'

'...and I'll be there to watch on Saturday. Damon's bringing a whole coachload of supporters.'

'Great. I'm bound to have a mare.'

'Of course you won't. We'll all be rooting for you.'

'That's what I mean.'

In the end I was quite glad when the train pulled out bearing Gareth and his graceless gloom with it, and I could dash back through the puddles to the car.

The house felt quiet and cosy. Fluffy remained in the airing cupboard, purring gently like a furry electric meter. Spot twitched convulsively in his deep sleep on the hearth-rug, pursuing neighbours' bitches through a dream landscape. There was no rehearsal, and there was lunch with Edward to look forward to.

Clara and I watched our favourite TV programme, a series set in the social services department of a north London borough.

'This is rather nice,' I said, 'all girls together.'

For once Clara did not disagree. 'It's a bit better watching this without his snide interruptions, I must say.'

'I wonder how he's getting on...'

'Like a pig in shit, I should think.'

'Clara, please.'

She wagged a finger at the screen. 'I reckon this woman, the tough egg, is the one who's going to have an affair.'

'Do you? But she doesn't like men.'

'She pretends not to. I can see it coming.'

The phone rang, and we neither of us moved. It continued ringing.

'Go on then,' I said, 'it's bound to be for you.'

Clara hauled herself up and moved crabwise in the general direction of the door, her eyes still on the screen.

'She's in with a chance with that black youth leader, I reckon...' she left the room and answered the phone. In a minute she was back, and in her chair.

'For you.'

'Really? Who?'

'Didn't say his name, but it sounded amazingly like your little stray lamb.'

'Gareth?'

Clara nodded. I went out to the phone. 'Hallo? Gareth?'

'Yo.' I could hear voices, and a sound like caps firing, in the background.

'How's it going. What are you doing?'

'Phoning you.'

'Yes, but where from?'

'Lucky Break Snooker Club.'

'Where's that?'

'Downtown Barford.'

'Good Lord. Can you afford that, I mean shouldn't Reg Legge...'

'Settle down, Reg brought us. It's all on United.'

I didn't find this very reassuring. Still, if this was Barford's way of blooding their young guns, I supposed I should have to go along with it.

'You're not drinking, are you?'

'Now let's see...' I sensed heavy humour about to break the horizon. 'I do seem to have a glass in my hand, and every so often it rises to my lips...'

'Don't be childish.'

'Lemonade and blackcurrant.' So he would be sober, with rotten teeth. 'Hang on, need another coin.' He put another in.

'I told you to reverse the charges.'

'No problem, this one'll see us out.'

'Have you met any of the players?'

'Rick Poole's taking us for training tomorrow. By the way, I'm going to get some new boots while I'm here. They've got every make there is, and there's discount for our lot.'

'Well...what will you do about paying?'

'I'll bring you the bill.'

'Of course,' I said humbly. I was certainly being had for a mug, since the Italian boots Gareth favoured cost at least twice what I'd have bought for him at Regis Sports, so any discount would mean nothing in real terms. These were the moments when I needed George, who was even at this moment availing himself of lavish expense-account hospitality in Copenhagen.

'What did they give you for supper?' I asked.

'We had a choice. Just about anything with chips.'

'And what did you have?'

'Just about everything. With chips.'

I bit back the comment about high-fibre, low-fat food which rose spontaneously to my lips. Barford United FC had secured a place in the First Division on a diet of refined carbohydrate and saturated fat, and who was I to criticise?

'Look, I've got to go,' said Gareth. 'See you after the game on Saturday, right?'

'Right.'

I went back to the sitting room. 'He seems to be enjoying himself' I said.

'What did you expect?' said Clara. 'Here, she is going to get off with that youth worker, what did I tell you?'

The Blood and Thunder Club in St James's was a tall, once fine eighteenth century building which gave the impression of being supported by the buildings on either side. Its grand entrance, with a flight of steps flanked by pillars, had a slightly knock-kneed, sway-backed look, and once inside you could tell you were in a male fastness whose deep, twilit peace had remained undisturbed for a couple of centuries. Custard-coloured walls and ceilings stained sepia with nicotine, fine and elaborate mouldings blurred with cobwebs, chandeliers too far away and table lamps too heavily shaded in parchment to shed much light, furnishings with an air of permanence as if they had put down roots through a carpet the shade of stewed prunes. I went into something designated the Downstairs Drawing-Room, and found Edward sitting just inside the door reading one of the more upmarket tabloids. This he shut with a swish when he saw me, and jumped to his feet.

'Harriet, how nice. Shall we find a more salubrious corner? I only parked there in order to greet you.'

We moved to the clammy chintz embrace of two chairs near the window overlooking the street. Swathes of net curtain which would have made even Noleen tremble gave the view of road and pavement a foggy Holmesian air. A strapping elderly man with a barrel chest and strutting walk of an army PE instructor came and took our order for drinks. The room was twice the size of Basset Magna village hall and there were perhaps a dozen people in it, of whom I was the only woman.

'The Downstairs Drawing-Room is mixed,' explained Edward. 'Everything above this floor is a strictly masculine preserve.'

'I see. Tell me about the club. How did it start?'

Edward obligingly embarked on some long rigmarole about the Napoleonic wars, while I nodded intelligently. and drank him in. He was wearing the usual great, dark suit, but I caught a flash of Argyll sock when he crossed his legs, and the thought of the striped boxer shorts next to his skin made me shiver.

Our drinks arrived, with the menu, and Edward said: 'Thank you, Jeavons.' My menu had no prices marked, and Edward urged me to have whatever I liked. 'It's not elaborate, but it's well-cooked and filling,' he explained. 'An enhanced version of what the members used to eat at boarding-school. A good rule of thumb when choosing is, the plainer the dish the better it is.' Accordingly I went for the shepherd's pie, and he for the Lancashire hotpot. I became conscious of a not-unpleasant whiff of institutional cooking in the air. I thought of all those men, on the upper floors, the massed ranks of shared experience, tucking into their meat and potatoes, talking about sport and politics and work and sex... I looked at Edward, who was choosing wine, and saw him, suddenly, as an emissary from another world. I could not believe that the Downstairs Drawing-Room and the Ladies Dining-Room were his preferred social settings, and it did nothing to dim his lustre that he had made this sacrifice for me. I felt a surge of tenderness towards him, as one might for a dangerous animal seen pacing a cage.

Jeavons escorted us through to the gravy-brown dining-room and we took our places at a table big enough for six.

Edward leaned forward. 'Enough elbow room to drink your gravy off the plate.'

'It's a very fine room.'

He glanced up and around. 'It's not bad. But you should see upstairs.'

'I'd like to,' I said pointedly.

'You'll have to take a job as a window cleaner. This is the most traditional club in London.'

'Why do you belong to it?'

There was a hiatus while he tasted the wine and pronounced it admirable. 'Your very good health, Harriet.'

'Cheers.'

'Why do I belong? Because it's also the best club. One of the oldest, the most comfortable, the most confident...'

'Confident?'

'Yes. It doesn't try to be "trendy",' he pronounced the word as if it were the name of some disgusting affliction, 'it's quiet, and dignified and immutable. It provides a safe haven.'

'You feel the need of that?'

I wondered why I was being so abrasive, and decided that I had written about too many feisty heroines in my time; this spiky behaviour had become second nature.

'I like the illusion of it,' he replied. 'It's my particular form of escapism.' I thought about this as lunch arrived, and vegetables were served. There was far too much of it, great steaming pillows of old-fashioned food, hot, undemanding and comforting. We began to eat.

I pressed on. 'You don't think it's retrograde— decadent, even?'

'Certainly not. I think that frightful place, the Gadfly, that Persephone frequents is decadent. Effete. A ghastly, arch mockery of what a club ought to be.'

Actually, I agreed with him, except for one crucial detail.

187

'At least Persephone and I can go there freely.'

'You're here today.' He was unruffled. 'Ladies are perfectly welcome here as guests, but this has been a Gentleman's Club for two hundred years. Besides there are precious few gentlemen—or ladies, saving your presence—at the Gadfly.' He softened this with a cold, courtly smile. I was ambushed by a shocking lurch of lust. I suddenly realised that I was actually inviting him to be rude, to speak to me harshly, because it was a massive turn-on.

I despaired of myself. Yet again I could not ignore the similarity to all those novels of mine in which the chap who gave the girl a hard time was the one rewarded by her undying love and the speediest possible termination of her virginity. God knows, I never believed all that even when I wrote it, and yet here I was endorsing the scenario over shepherd's pie and buttered carrots. I wanted to bow the knee before Edward...I wanted to iron his hankies, roll his Argyll socks, mop his brow and be inflated by his bicycle pump...

'I don't,' he said, taking more mashed swede, 'set any store by the current mania for trying to please everybody all the time. One should identify one's likes and dislikes and behave accordingly. With all due civility, of course.' Again the smile.

'And the devil take the hindmost?' I suggested.

'In my experience, it's not the hindmost whom the devil takes, but those unfortunate souls who wander up blind alleys in the search of Nirvana.'

I couldn't win, and I loved it.

We cleared our plates—I was sure he approved of a healthy appetite—and the conversation became more general. Or at least it became more specific—polite enquiries about where I lived, my domestic and professional arrangements and so on—but it felt more general because we were not flaunting our colours as we had been. He asked me 'with all due civility' what George did, and I made a point of saying how amicable was our separation, which I instantly realised he found baffling.

'The term "confirmed bachelor" has become debased,' he said, 'or I should use it of myself. I find the mores of modern marriage entirely incomprehensible.'

'Just because two people find they can no longer live together happily doesn't mean they have to be sworn enemies, surely?' My unwillingness to mention aberrations on both sides made my argument sound a trifle limp.

Edward raised his eyebrows. 'Why should you expect to be happy all the time? The search for happiness, or constant gratification, is one of the greatest causes of misery in our society.'

'You know what I mean.'

'No. I take the marriage vows extremely seriously. They are chief among the reasons I have never married.'

I bridled. 'I take them seriously, too.'

I was allowed the last word on that subject by the return of the menus. On Edward's recommendation we both decided on the treacle tart and custard and this led, as night follows day, on to a discussion of dietary fads in which Edward attacked and worked over *cuisine minceur,* leaving it for dead. Every so often, as he trampled over my most cherished convictions, he would look into my face and favour me with a quick, blinding smile, like a motorist flashing his headlights, which ensured that I remained dazzled and acquiescent. He was a fascinating and alluring blend of chivalry and ruthlessness. As we left the dining-room at the end of lunch I realised that while I was well on the way to being infatuated, I still had absolutely no idea what sort of impression I had made on him. It was unnerving, like observing someone through a one-way mirror. I could see him, but it appeared he only saw himself.

In this I was soon to be proved wrong. As we collected our things from the porter Edward, having helped me on with my coat, opened his briefcase and took out something in a paper bag.

'Harriet, before you go...'

'Yes?'

'I have one of your books here. I wonder if you'd be so kind as to sign it?'

My heart stopped for a second or two. Then it began to go like the APT, sending all the blood from my stomach, where it had been comfortably attending to lunch, to my face. I was a flaming torch of embarrassment. I watched him draw the book from its paper sheath like someone in a morgue pulling the sheet from the face of a cadaver.

My worst fears were confirmed. It was a paperback, some six hundred pages in length, with the words *The Rapture and the Rose* embossed in shiny red lettering on the cover. Also on the cover were: a Dolly Parton lookalike in mediaeval dress and considerable disarray; a villainously moustachioed man in a cape; a blond youth in tights, flourishing a sword; a black horse with flaring nostrils; a spray of roses with blood dripping from their thorns; and a cast of dimly etched-in extras with expressions ranging from annoyance to dismay. If my book had been a skater it would have scored nought for both Technical Merit and Artistic Impression.

Edward opened it at the title page and passed it to me, along with a black Parker pen. 'Just a signature would be fine.'

He didn't say anything else. He didn't need to. What had I said? '...very small, introspective, rather dull books...' and how had he replied? 'But very well-written, I'm sure...'

I scribbled beneath the awful, awful title. What had possessed me to say such a thing? Had I supposed he would be so uncurious as not to look out for one of my books? And now he not only had one in all its overblown, overheated technicolour glory, but he knew me for a liar as well.

'Thank you.' He returned the book to the bag, the bag to the briefcase. We emerged on to the steps and the commissionaire hailed a taxi.

'You take this one,' said Edward. 'I shall walk to the office.'

'Thank you.' I directed my remarks to the air over his right shoulder. 'And thank you for lunch.'

'My pleasure entirely. I shall be out of town for a while as I explained, but perhaps when I return we could repeat the engagement?'

Cruel, oh cruel. 'That would be nice.'

'I'll be in touch.'

I sank into the back of the taxi like a woman on the run, sweating and gasping.

I had completely, and irrevocably, blown it.

CHAPTER 10

On the Saturday morning I received a note on the engraved heavy vellum of the Blood and Thunder Club, addressed unequivocally to Mrs Harriet Blair. 'My dear Harriet,' Edward had written in a thick, upright hand like iron railings, 'I so enjoyed our lunch together at the Club yesterday, and trust I did not bore you with my opinions. You are altogether too good and forbearing a listener. I was even able to forgive your little joke at my expense concerning your novels. And taking a tease, as my mother was wont to say, has never been my strong suit. I may even, in time, get round to reading the book you so kindly signed for me; I know you are a great favourite with Persephone whose taste I generally endorse.' At this point I found that my face was wreathed in a great, witless grin. 'By the way,' he added, 'I saw Persephone that evening, and I understand you can expect to hear from her. And from me, of course, when the hurly-burly's done, all the best, yours, Edward.'

I read the note through several more times until the grin had reached other parts of my body, and I was absolutely convinced that the danger had passed. So there was a God! Edward must have taken my paralysing inertia panic for playful coolness (he'd obviously missed the colour of my face) and decided that he would apologise for his seeming inability to 'take a tease', the poor lamb. I didn't deserve this small victory, but by God I was going to make the most of it! And what was this—I could expect to hear from Persephone, could I? It was all too much—weeks in the wilderness and now an embarrassment of riches. I was even able to contemplate the trip to Barford with equanimity. What were a few lager louts to a woman who was about to be invited on to *Considered Opinion?* And what cared I for the lack of an escort when Edward awaited me after the hurly-burly?

Full of optimistic energy I went jogging, and saw Damon marshalling his forces in the village hall car-park. Marking time for a minute or two I was able to distinguish Robbo Makepeace, Trevor Tunnel and quite a crowd of the Tomahawks, both players and management. There were one or two mothers in padded jackets, toting cool-boxes, and a group of teenage girls conspicuously under-dressed for the weather and carrying banners. Damon wore an ice-blue rosette the size of a dinner plate, and white open-knuckle gloves. Music—it sounded like *The Birdy Song*—wafted from inside the coach as the party climbed aboard. Nearby stood the Muck Wagon, with Terry at the wheel, blue ribbons dangling from its wing-mirrors, like a plain bridesmaid.

Any doubts I had harboured about going on my own were finally dispelled.

'Are you quite sure you don't want to come along, darling?' I asked Clara, who was in the kitchen eating the first of several breakfasts when I returned.

'No thanks, honestly. I've got things to do.'

'You'll be all right?'

She sighed.

'Will you be on your own all day?'

'Dunno. Colin may come over.'

'Well, be good, won't you?'

This didn't even merit a sigh. My maternal duty done I turned my attention to what to wear for the match.

As mother of the Boy Wonder I certainly wished to appear smarter than the jeans and puffa jacket brigade travelling in Damon's bus, but not conspicuously over-dressed. In the end I opted for a black pleated skirt and shirt with a white sweater, flat-heeled boots and a black and white houndstooth tweed jacket. I did have a light blue Jaeger throw, but decided against wearing Barford colours in any shape or form. Sensible, understated, non-partisan elegance would be my watchword, time enough for turning heads when I attend the Cup Final ten years hence.

It was a little warmer today, but the sky was still churning with bad-tempered clouds so at the last moment I equipped myself with a golf umbrella and George's ancient pewter hip flask with a tot or two of supermarket brandy.

Barford United was on the outskirts of the city on the apex of an area known as The Wedge. Driving to the ground I passed the Lucky Break Snooker Club, and could readily appreciate why Reg Legge had taken his tender charges there: it was easily the most salubrious establishment in the neighbourhood. Barford was a university town with a proud history, but as one penetrated deeper into The Wedge one had a sense of Gown having been clobbered senseless by the DM's of Town.

I had no problem finding the ground. The stands, flagpole and massed floodlights of Barford United FC loomed over the surrounding streets like the ramparts of some feudal pile, exacting fealty through a mixture of threat, promise and paternalism.

Today, threat seemed in the ascendancy. Once within sight of the ground the Metro and I became part of a turgid tide of people and traffic all heading in the same direction. It struck me that a car was the worst place to be. If you couldn't be a pedestrian, marching six abreast with your peers and chanting partisan anthems, then you were better off on a motor-bike, or even push-bike, snaking between the bumpers, or in a coach, safely insulated and raised high above the mêlée. In the car I felt uneasily like a slow-moving, ground-level target. I turned on the radio, but the introduction of *Any Questions* from a school hall in Northumbria seemed an invitation to unwelcome attention, and I hastily switched it off again and tried to look like the sort of person who regularly attended soccer matches.

I was congratulating myself on not giving in to the temptation to wear Barford blue, and glad that everything about me proclaimed my disinterested status, when my eye was caught by a banner slung across the rear window of a coach just ahead of me.

'CONNINGHAM COLTS RULE!' it proclaimed. On either side of it were banks of grinning youths in hats and scarves. A couple of them raised their thumbs. I was wearing the opposition colours.

As soon as I was able I turned off the main road, away from the unwelcome spotlight of the Conningham bus, and my attention was taken up by the more immediate and pressing question of where to park. I figured that if I was about half a mile from the ground and the traffic was this bad at a quarter past one, it was going to get a lot worse before it got better. I was going to have to find a berth for the car as soon as possible.

I was in a maze of identical small streets, all vying with one another for the arbitrariness of their one-way systems and the paucity of available parking. To ensure that the footie-fans reached the ground in the highest possible dudgeon, the streets had also been intensively coned, and dug up here and there by the Water and Electricity Boards. After fifteen minutes spent investigating every possible lateral and longitudinal route across the block I found a space outside a Greek supermarket, obviously cleared by the enterprising proprietors in the interests of passing trade.

I parked the Metro and, feeling I should express a proper appreciation of the facilities, went into the shop and bought two bars of Cadbury's fruit and nut.

'How you must hate home matches,' I remarked to the woman at the checkout.

'Not at all,' she said, 'it's all good business.'

'You don't get any trouble, then?'

She smiled affably and shook her head. 'Not usually. Barford has a reputation, after all.'

This was encouraging. 'For good behaviour, you mean?'

'No, no, no!' she laughed as she handed me my change, and altered her tone to one of theatrical villainy. 'For being the meanest!'

At the ticket booth for the Ruddles Memorial Stand I struck a hitch.

'Sorry, love. No seats on the day.'

'No-one told me that!'

'Perhaps you didn't ask, love.'

'But—' I stood aside to let a group of ticket-holders surge past—'but are you saying you've sold out?'

'That's right. Big game today, we're fighting to hang on to our place.'

'But for heaven's sake— Look, I only want to see the warm-up game.'

He looked at me pityingly. 'Sorry.'

I lowered my voice and looked him directly in the eye. 'I'll pay the full price, and then give up the seat to whoever's booked it for the match. That way you'll get paid twice for one seat.'

'Nope.' He shook his head. 'Sorry, darling. No can do.'

Another string of ticket-holders, God rot them, separated us. I began to feel frantic. Could this really be happening? It was one passage of arms I had not anticipated.

I closed in again. 'Please, can't you make an exception just this once? My son's having his first game for the Youth Team.'

'They're all somebody's little darling,' said my friend on the turnstile, 'though it's hard to credit it sometimes.'

I was coming rapidly to the boil. 'This is quite ridiculous! There's a whole coachload of people from my village come along to support my son, and they'll all be in there waving and cheering, and I'm his mother and I'll be stuck out here!'

'Perhaps they booked in advance.'

'They did. I'm just pointing out the ludicrous, petty-minded stupidity of his situation—'

'Calm down,' said the man, ensuring that my blood pressure rose by several degrees. 'I never said you couldn't get in.'

'Yes, you did, more than once!'

'Correction.' He closed his eyes for a moment as if praying for patience. 'Correction. I said you couldn't buy a seat.'

'What's the difference?'

'The difference is, lady,' he waggled his head at me, 'you could go on the terraces.'

'All right,' I said, 'I will!'

Even had there not been signs it would have been impossible to miss the terraces. I was borne along in a swift current of pedestrians that at first spread the width of the street, was then compressed, jostling and clamouring, into a narrow alley skirting the back of the stands, then burst forth and spread out again at the far end of the ground where a Colditz-like fence, two huge iron gates and a row of clanking turnstiles acted as a sieve. A handful of policemen patrolled the edges of the crowd, and the fence, with an air of studied easy-goingness, to show they were just bobbies on the beat engaged in a little run-of-the-mill community work. They didn't fool me. I felt as though even if I hadn't already committed some offence I was likely to in the next few minutes.

Determinedly I elbowed my way through the crush, ignoring the imaginative suggestions which came my way. This time I had no problem buying a ticket. I crossed to the nearest turnstile and pushed the ticket into the slot. I then stepped forward, expecting the metal bar to yield obligingly, as it should have done. Instead it remained rigidly in place, fetching me a nasty crack across the pelvis.

I turned the ticket round and tried again. Nothing. The bar was intractable. A ragged chorus of advice and comment, more or less good-humoured, broke out behind me.

'Bloody hell, what now...'

'Give it a good shove, darlin!'

'Someone give her a leg up!'

'What's the flaming hold up?

I turned round. 'I'm sorry,' I snapped, 'it doesn't seem to be working.'

There was a kind of fatalistic communal groan-cum-grumble and those nearer the back moved off in the direction of the neighbouring queue. A youth with neatly serrated cheeks like a cheese grater leaned round me, took my ticket and inserted it himself. It was a relief to see that it didn't work for him either. His place was taken by a short, dapper man in a three-quarter mac who also met with no success.

'Dud ticket, love,' he said, handing it back to me. The noise behind me was beginning to swell like a storm getting up over a cornfield. It was irritating to be confirmed in what I already knew.

'Please,' I called, 'could someone tell the chap in the kiosk that I've got a faulty ticket!'

Shortie-mac tried to squeeze past me, but I was loath to lose my place. A policeman with a walkie-talkie came through the crowd towards us. He had the alert, cheerful air of a babysitter who suddenly finds his presence justified when the baby wakes up.

'No need for you all to hang about here,

lads,' he said sensibly. 'Plenty of other places you can go through.'

'If she'll get out of the way we can get in here!' objected grater-cheeks. Shortie-mac nodded in agreement. 'It's this lady's ticket that's the problem, not the gate!'

'They're right,' I said. 'I simply need another ticket. I have asked.'

'Never mind,' said the policeman kindly. 'Let's see.'

He held out his hand for the ticket. This was too much. 'It's *not working*,' I said. The hand remained out. I gave him the ticket. Behind me the crowd grew denser. I remained wedged firmly in the iron arms of the turnstile. The policeman, satisfied that my summary of the situation was correct, placed a solicitous hand beneath my elbow. 'Okay, madam. You come with me. On your way, lads.'

The queue began to pour through. I was escorted along the fence to the first of the massive gates. 'Stay there,' said the policeman. He must have been a dog-handler. I stayed. He went to the side window of the nearest ticket kiosk, knocked, asked for something, and returned with a gigantic key straight out of the brothers Grimm. 'Here we go here we go,' said my saviour with unconscious irony.

I was admitted with a positively Transylvanian clanking and rasping, and the gate was slammed shut behind me before hordes of aggrieved fans could follow. I headed for the entrance with cries of 'All right for some!' and 'What did you have to do, darlin'?' ringing in my ears.

I don't know what I'd expected the terraces to look like, but what I *hadn't* expected them to look like was—well—terraces. I came up the steps to emerge on to the lower slopes of a concrete paddy-field, broken here and there by railings and all over which clumps of fans sprouted like rice plants. There was still quite a bit of room, more in fact, I noted with satisfaction, than there was in the stands. I began to feel a little calmer and considerably more optimistic. I went down the narrow steps to a place quite near the front, behind and slightly to the right of the goal. A grandstand view to be precise. I scanned the seats over the tunnel and at once spotted Damon's party, a spinney of waving light-blue banners. I waved energetically with both arms in the air, but there was no response. They were all doubtless tucking into Prime Enterprises' fast food. I actually felt rather sorry for them in the sheltered conditions of their choice block of seats. I was where it was at. They didn't know what they were missing.

Two boys of about twelve came and stood next to me. They were eating chips with an accompaniment of greenish curry sauce in a polystyrene tub. They didn't seem in the least put out to be standing next to a middle-aged woman with a golf umbrella, wearing the opposition colours. I felt a glow of well-being. This was radical, grass-roots stuff, the camaraderie of the terraces, apparent differences were sunk in a shared enthusiasm for the great game of football. The smell of the sauce tickled my nostrils. I turned and beamed brightly at the lad next to me.

'Those do smell nice,' I said. 'I wonder if I could have just one chip?'

He beamed back. 'Buy your own sodding chips,' he said.

United won, but Gareth could not be said to have had a hand in their victory. It was strange how the hero of the Basset Tomahawks, the famed and feared gorilla of the back row, whose long shadow struck terror into opposition strikers, faded into relative obscurity among the fit and practised young braves of United. In spite of being continually on the move, and apparently uncowed by the occasion, he scarcely got a touch until well into the second half, when he heeled a ball back to the keeper and was nearly responsible for an own goal. This incident seemed so to unnerve him that he managed to avoid contact with the ball for the remainder of the match. The scenario of *Abide With Me* faded rather, and my feet began to feel cold. I'd finished the fruit and nut. I decided to go and do some shopping during the main match, and return for Gareth afterwards.

'Who's that big kid at the back?' enquired one of the lads next to me of his neighbour, as the two youth teams trooped from the field. If I could have blocked my ears, I would have done.

'Dunno,' replied his friend. 'He shoulda stayed in bed.'

I flamed with maternal indignation and might have taken the fatal step of bandying words with him, had not a big man just behind us tapped the boy on the shoulder and said: 'Goes to show how little you know, son. That Number 11's marked his man like paint all afternoon, and always been in the right position, stopped his man doing anything with the ball. He may not be showy but he's a good player. Plays with his head.' The man tapped his temple with his forefinger to show what he mean. 'Know what I mean?'

I nodded vigorously. The glow returned. *Abide With Me* sprang once more into focus.

Encouraged, I turned to leave. But a lot had happened since the start of the youth game. I was confronted by a solid wall of muttering, shuffling, rumbling humanity. United's bid to avoid relegation had pulled them in from far and near in their thousands, and with the preliminaries over they were psyching themselves up for the real thing.

I took a deep breath and got my head down. It took me ten minutes to fight my way to the exit, zig-zagging back and forth across the terraces, squeezing between unforgiving anoraks and kagouls, my feet skidding on a treacherous layer of cigarette butts, sweet wrappers and greasy paper. To add to my discomfort it was pointed out to me all along the way that the pitch, in case I didn't know, was in the opposite direction.

When I reached the top of the steps I leaned on the wall for a minute to catch my breath and suddenly remembered George's hip flask. I had unscrewed the top and was about to take a reviving swig when I felt a tap on my arm. An elderly man in a John Lennon cap was jerking his head and wagging his forefinger at me like a metronome.

'What? Sorry?'

He repeated the gesture with a bigger jerk of the head. Following the direction of the jerk I saw two policemen standing by the wall on the far side of the steps, and understood the message.

'Thanks!' Hastily I returned the hip flask to my shoulder-bag just as the policemen, like twin searchlights, turned my way.

'Just going,' I told them, and scuttled down the steps against the tide of those still arriving.

I reached the turnstiles bruised and breathless with my heart racing. The turnstiles, of course, were locked. Neither was there anybody in the ticket kiosks.

I railed against my misfortune to those nearest me, but it was a waste of time.

'I just want to get out!' I wailed. 'How do I get out?'

A few looked over their shoulders at me and at once pressed forward more urgently, not wishing to contract the disease. One kindly soul, a woman, spoke to me loudly and clearly: 'You do know there's another game, dear?'

'Yes, I do, but I don't want to see it!'

'Don't blame you,' put in a youth on my right. 'Conningham's going to get stuffed.'

The black and white ensemble was catching

up with me. 'I couldn't care less!' I barked.

'Got used to it, eh?' retaliated the youth.

George had always advised me against joining in arguments in which I had no place. But in this instance I felt it had been forced on me. 'Far from it,' I said. 'I don't even have much interest in football if you must know.'

'Just like your team,' came back my sparring partner, quick as a flash. We were becoming the focus of some interest, and a Barford supporter at my right shoulder guffawed at this sally.

'I just want to get *out!*' I shouted, bringing the point of the golf umbrella down sharply for emphasis, and striking the instep of the man next to me, who let out a howl of pain and fury.

It's an atavistic female fantasy, that of being fought over by men, and one I'd often exploited in my novels. But on this occasion I seemed to have overdone it. Within seconds of my inadvertent assault on the Barford man, my profuse and flustered apologies were drowned in a great communal cheer the sort that must have greeted the end of rationing, and I was swept aside against the turnstile, my backside receiving bruises to match those at the front.

I may have started it, but it had definitely been in the wings awaiting its cue. The speed with which the brawl gained strength and impetus testified to that. Suddenly it was there, fully formed and in its prime, a great heaving, flailing, parti-coloured monster.

The woman who'd spoken to me earlier came and stood next to me. 'Oh Gawd,' she said, folding her arms, 'here we go again.'

'The Beasts of Barford?' I quavered.

'Like to think they are,' she replied drily.

It didn't last long. First the policemen homed in, wading into the mêlée and bidding the participants to settle down and leave it out, grabbing a collar here and a scarf there, losing their dignity and their helmets in the process but not looking specially put out about it.

Then there was a roar from the terraces, signalling the arrival on the pitch of the Barford and Conningham teams, and the whole crowd, still fussing and feuding, moved off in the direction of the steps.

'Bye, dear,' said my friend. 'Hope you make it.'

The policemen reclaimed their helmets and adjusted their dress. I was just about to approach one of them and ask yet again for his good offices with the giant key, when I spotted Edward.

He was standing, notebook in hand, just inside one of the gates. He wore a muffler, a British Warm Overcoat and an air of scientific enquiry. It was obvious he had not yet seen me, and I froze as he walked to the centre of the concourse and addressed one of the officers.

'Constable,' he said, 'do you have any idea how this affray started?'

Who knows what comfortable, non-committal, unhelpful words the policeman might have spoken, given half a chance? But instead one of the stragglers—it was he who had taken me for a Conningham fan—yelled gleefully: 'Over

207

there, squire! That's her—attacked my mate with an offensive weapon!'

Edward's gaze followed his pointing finger. Our eyes met. As I stood there like a wax effigy my shoulder bag slid slowly to the ground, and George's hip flask emerged with a clink and disgorged its contents on to the concrete.

CHAPTER 11

I awoke on Sunday morning beneath a blanket of gloom so dense and heavy that I was unable at first to recollect its cause. I just lay there, half stifled by it, hoping it was a dream or, if not, that I could lose consciousness again as soon as possible.

When memory did return it brought no relief, but sent me plunging even deeper into the abyss of gloom.

It was not that Edward hadn't accepted my explanation with perfect politeness. And the police, taking their cue from him, had let me off with a caution and let us both out. I felt like an offender being escorted by my probation officer.

'None of that's true,' I burbled. 'I assure you—'

'Please, Harriet,' he said. 'Don't apologise.'

'But what must you think of me!'

At this he'd given me a curious, veiled look. 'Let's not discuss it any further.' We had walked back along the alley at the side of the ground and come upon the Muck Wagon parked near the main entrance.

'Do you serve tea?' Edward asked Terry.

'Do dogs like lampposts?' Terry replied. 'Afternoon, Mrs Blair.'

Edward looked from one to the other of us. 'You two know each other?'

'Terry used to be my—he used to be a blacksmith.'

'I see,' said Edward, to whom it was obviously as clear as mud. We took our tea and I withdrew to one side to avoid further conversation with Terry.

'I assume you came here looking for trouble?' I asked. 'Or at least, let me re-phrase that—'

'No need. I did indeed come looking for trouble, and I found it. Barford United has a reputation.'

'You heard.'

'I made it my business to find out. Excuse me.' He took a large white handkerchief from his trouser pocket and began dabbing the front of my jacket. It was the first time, other than shaking hands, that he'd touched me, and I was too wretched to enjoy it. 'What is this?' he asked.

I looked down at the khaki-coloured stain. 'Curry sauce, I bet.' The little bastards had been too tight to spare a chip, but they'd managed to spill sauce on me.

'I'm fond of curry myself,' said Edward. 'Perhaps we might have one together some time.'

The likelihood of this seemed so remote that a hollow laugh escaped me.

Edward put away the handkerchief. 'Have I said something amusing?'

'No.'

'Are you going to watch the match?'

'No.'

'What are your plans for the remainder of the afternoon?'

'I'll probably do some shopping and then come back to collect my son.'

'He's watching?'

'No, he was playing. For the youth team.'

'I see.'

It was obvious he didn't. The whole scenario was opaque to him. With every word I uttered I was making any advance in our relationship more hopelessly improbable.

'Unfortunately,' said Edward, 'I have to attend a student rally in Manchester.' He even had a cast-iron excuse for escaping me. He added: 'I shall be travelling part of the way on the Conningham soccer special, which I think will prove interesting.'

'I'm sure.'

'Your son isn't travelling in the team coach?'

'No, no.' I waved a dismissive hand over my curry-stained black and white. 'No, he's Barford.'

'Ah. I see.'

We returned our cups. 'Very nice, thank you,' said Edward to Terry. 'A far cry from shoeing horses, surely.' He eyed a pile of Terry's uncooked burgers speculatively.

'More demand for this, though,' said Terry. 'I'm in business with a partner, we identify a need, a gap in the market, and move in to fill it.' I could hear him quoting the thoughts of Chairman Damon.

'Very laudable,' said Edward. 'What other needs have you identified?'

A horrid surmise gripped me, but too late. Terry had unbolted the louvred panel at the side of the serving hatch, and released it with a flourish. It rattled up with a sound like machine gun fire, revealing row upon row of videos for which the word nasty was laughably inadequate.

'Ah,' said Edward. 'I see.'

I writhed at the memory and buried my head beneath the pillow with a moan. I was so alone! In his room the Boy Wonder slept the sweet sleep of success dreaming, no doubt, of sliding tackles, diving headers and balls finding the back of the net like homing pigeons. In hers, Clara would be curled beneath a tangled heap of bedding, like a hamster, serene in the knowledge of Colin's affections. Bernice had Arundel. Even Declan had the tacitly acquiescent Noleen. And bloody George was with the Danes.

About an hour later I staggered up, made a cup of tea, let Spot out and Fluffy in, and retreated back to bed with the papers. The bells of St Cuthbert's tolled, summoning the Magna faithful to one of Eric's stern, fibrous Lenten sermons. There was an evil pleasure to be had in pulling the duvet up to one's chin,

211

sipping heavily sugared tea and preparing to ingest whatever scandal the Sundays had seen fit to serve up. Attempts to be good had got me nowhere, I might as well be as bad as circumstances would allow.

The very first thing I found was a piece about the Beamish Committee, its members and aims. There was a photograph of Edward looking his most Rochester-ish and even this imperfectly reproduced image, I discovered, went some way to activating the bicycle pump. I remembered the Conningham soccer special and wondered if, as I lay here in my comfortable bed, he was stretched out bruised and bleeding on some remote station platform, victim of his own hubris...

I stormed through paper after paper, seeking comfort and finding only stories that mocked my affliction. Bimbettes told all, pensioners fell in love, smug couples analysed the success of their marriages, sexually active teenagers described their action-packed weekends—it was all too much.

But it all counted as nought when I turned to the centre pages of the *Sunday News Review*. There, staring back at me, was a woman, who should surely have known better, masquerading as Madonna. The effect was bizarre and repellent, a curious display of inept vampishness. In the foreground was a young man dressed like Rupert of Henzau, brandishing a whip. A cheetah gaped. Cherubs bridled. The woman sulked beneath an unlikely pagoda of hair. It was awful. Awful. And it was me.

By the time the children had crawled from their beds and begun incinerating toast in the kitchen I had pulled several miles of ivy from the hedge, split enough logs to see us through the whole of the following winter, and tidied the shed. With the flesh still insufficiently mortified I began sharpening the edges of the largest herbacious border. I was scarlet-faced, aching in every part and filled with such a violent misanthropy that it was a pity I wasn't on the terraces at that moment—I could have given the entire Tartan Army a run for their money.

Glancing up I saw Gareth's form hunched over the table. On this, his first morning home, I might normally have been disposed to make him a cooked breakfast, but today I was prepared for only that human contact which touched on life and death. Even my craving for a cup of coffee would not get me indoors while there was someone there who might speak to me.

Just then I heard Gareth give his special, unmistakeable, disparaging laugh—a sort of cavernous bark such as I've heard ascribed to lions hunting in the African bush. This was followed by Clara's name shouted at full blast, and another, more uninhibited laugh. I kept my eyes on my work, the blades of the shears snapping like piranha fish. When, after a minute or two, I did permit myself a covert look in the direction of the house it was to be greeted by the unwelcome sight of the two of them staring back at me, grinning like gargoyles. Quickly I returned to my edging, but not before I'd seen that they held between them the shameful *Sunday News Review.*

Of course it was only a matter of seconds before Gareth, ever one to pursue his advantage, was at my side, hunkering down chummily and waving the horrid picture under my nose.

'Stands back in amazement!' he said. 'What's all this then?'

'Shut up,' I said. 'Shut. Up.'

'Nice one,' he continued, as though I hadn't spoken. 'Today, Sunday centrefold, tomorrow Page Three.'

'Very funny, Gareth.'

'No, honestly, this is a wicked photograph, Ma.' He waddled along sideways, still crouching like a chimpanzee, to keep pace with me. 'They really did the business on you.'

'The business?'

'They worked you over. You look pretty cool. What did they do?'

I may have been incensed by the photograph, but I was even more incensed by Gareth's suggestion that I had been a mere pawn in Hal Worship's game. I didn't bother to answer, but clacked the shears half an inch from the toes of his trainers.

'Who's the geezer?' he asked, pointing to Callum.

'Nobody,' I muttered.

'Nobody? Steady on. If ever I saw a bloke who looked like somebody, it's this poser.'

'Callum.'

'Callum?' Gareth snorted. 'Bli-mey!'

'It's a perfectly ordinary Scottish name.'

'So's Rory, but you don't get many of those to the pound either. Callum!' Gareth chuckled happily to himself. I toyed with the idea of snipping off his precious extra-wide plaid laces. 'What is he?' he asked. 'A model?'

'I don't know.'

'Nice work if you can get it. Hey, who did your hair?'

'Paul.'

'Paul, Callum—Ooh!' said Gareth.

Joints cracking, I got to my feet. 'Gareth.'

'Yeah?' He got up too, zooming past me like someone in a lift and gazing benignly down on me from his great height.

'Buzz off.'

'What's eating you?'

'I'm trying to get on, that's all.'

'Sorry.'

'So if you don't mind.'

'Okay.'

He folded the *News Review*, then looked at me, struggling with a snigger. He lost, and the snigger scuttled out and settled on his face.

'What's the joke?'

'No. Nothing.' The snigger stuttered, revved and became a snort of laughter: 'You!'

He strolled off, swinging the magazine in one hand. A couple of minutes later I distinctly heard the 'ting' of the phone as he alerted his peers that there was a good laugh to be had from the Sunday papers.

There was an extra-curricular rehearsal called for that night. Generally speaking the evening of the Sabbath was kept sacred to sloth, but with only four weeks to go till the performance Percy was anxious to instil a sense of urgency, and to keep us on our toes. We had not booked the hall, but were to gather at the Rectory, which had the most space. 'A chance to concentrate on lines,' the note had said, 'and to iron out any last problems on characterisation/interpretation.'

Eric was watching television when I arrived, and rose from the sofa as Dilly showed me in, with the air of a man who had been told to behave.

'No evensong?' I asked, to rub salt in the wound.

'Not today,' he said. 'Group Eucharist this morning, if you remember.'

'An evening off,' I said, 'how nice.'

'Yes. A chance to see how the other half live,' I supposed that had to be fifteen all. The whole world got up my nose this evening.

'Come along, Ricky,' said Dilly, plumping cushions like a thing possessed, 'go and fetch the biscuits from the side in the kitchen would you, and then why not go and have a bash at next week's sermon or something, there's nothing for you to do in here.'

Eric looked wistfully at the television as Dilly switched it off and closed the doors over the screen. As soon as he'd gone for the biscuits Dilly confided in me that her husband was like a lost soul without a service on Sunday evening, meaning that he was under her feet. When he reappeared she snatched the biscuits off him and propelled him out of the door. 'I'll

216

give you a shout when we want the kettle on, love!' she called after him. 'Good practice for Front of House!'

I never ceased to be intrigued by Dilly. She seemed not to have divined the difference between being a good company wife for the Sales Manager of Aztec Electronics (as Ricky had been before the Call), and being the helpmeet of a country vicar. No matter how many cake stalls, nearly-new events, playgroup parties and carboot sales she presided over, she still came across as a woman on the make. This evening she was got up for Percy's informal rehearsal in baby-pink stirrup pants and a clinging pink polo-neck top with a white appliqué trim. Her pink pearlised nail varnish matched this ensemble and she was made up with Cindy-doll perfection. We sat down and Dilly lit a cigarette. 'Done anything exciting since I last saw you, Harriet?'

'Um—no, I don't think so.' It would have taken too long to tell her.

'Just writing away, I suppose.'

'That's right.'

'I saw your lass out with the pony yesterday. It's a lovely hobby for a girl, isn't it?'

'Yes...' I grappled with this one. 'You saw Clara? Riding?'

'Yes. Well, I tell a lie. She had her riding things on, but she was taking another kiddie for a ride.' Her choice of words was unfortunate, I thought.

'Yes,' I said, with unnatural calmness. 'She does that sometimes.'

217

'Your pony looked really lovely.'

'She did?'

'A good turn-out, isn't that what you horsey people call it?'

'They do, yes. Are you sure it was Stu?'

'Oh, positive!' The bell rang and Dilly got up to answer it. 'Little white pony, and her hair was all in little pigtails, she looked a picture, excuse me!'

I considered this as the other members of the cast arrived and took their places round Dilly's cheerily blazing gas logs. Trevor Tunnel said he'd been proud of Gareth at Barford, and Glynis endorsed this on Robbo's behalf. Where had I been, Trevor wanted to know, and was suitably impressed when I told him.

'Harriet, that wasn't a good idea, not a good idea at all.'

'It was perfectly all right.'

'We were given to understand there was a bit of trouble just before the big game.'

'Oh?' I said airily. 'I must have missed it.'

'Missed it?' Interposed Barry. 'Knowing our Harriet she probably started it!' And everyone had a good laugh.

Dilly did a quick headcount and yelled at Eric to put the kettle on. Bernice was last to arrive as usual, shouting 'Two more please!' at poor Eric, and bringing Gareth in her wake.

'What are you doing here?' I wanted to know.

'Blimey, act pleased to see me, I would.'

'No, but—'

'I called to offer you a lift, and there he

was,' explained Bernice, squeezing on the sofa between Barry and Glynis. 'So I brought him!'

'But he doesn't need to be here,' I protested.

'I can be here if I want to,' said Gareth stolidly.

Percy intervened. 'Of course, Gareth.' He was wearing his glasses on top of his head. 'It's nice that you're so keen. Personally I think that that sense of involvement can only be commended. I wish there was more of it about.' Wrist slapped, I sank back, but not into obscurity.

'And who,' cried Bernice, dragging *Sunday News Review* from her tote bag, 'has seen *this?*'

I did not invite Bernice back that evening, and neither did I encourage Gareth to conversation. When we got home I went up to Clara's room and knocked on the door.

'Clara!' I shouted, and then louder, to penetrate the massed synthesisers of the Nation's Number One: 'CLARA!'

She did not reply, but the music was turned down, the door unbolted and she peered out at me. 'Keep your hair on. What's up?'

'Did you take some child riding yesterday when I was out?'

'I did as a matter of fact.'

'I have told you I don't approve of this casual hiring.'

'There wasn't any hiring.'

'Then who was it?'

'Lucy Mulholland.'

'Who's she? We don't know anyone called Mulholland.'

219

Clara shrugged. 'That's who she was.'

'Mrs Chittenden said Stu was all plaited up. Looking a picture was how she put it.'

'So?'

'Don't be obstructive, you know what I mean.'

'I sold her, didn't I?'

'Clara, I've told you...' I realised what she'd said. 'You what?'

'I sold Stu.'

'But—who to?'

'Mrs Mulholland for her little Lucy.'

'Clara!'

'What's the problem? You wanted to sell her, didn't you?'

'Yes, *I* wanted to sell her in a proper, above board, orderly way, for a decent price.'

'I got five hundred for her.'

I put my hands to my temples, which were beginning to throb. *'How* much?'

'Watch my lips. Five hundred.'

'But Clara...' Whatever wind there had been in my sails had now been well and truly sucked out. 'Clara...I took the ad out of the paper.'

'Colin and me stuck a few around Regis.'

'But what did you say?'

Clara waved a hand dismissively. 'Usual sort of thing, kid's show pony...'

'Show pony?' I squeaked. 'Anyone with half an eye can see she's not!'

'Some people,' Clara explained patiently, 'have more money than sense. We made her look beautiful, we put talc all over her, and blacked her hooves, and put gel on her plaits.

220

Colin came over and walked her round the field till she was knackered, and then we put her in the stable till Mrs Thing came.'

'But didn't this—this Mrs Mulholland want to know where *I* was? I mean in her place I'd have wanted to speak to an adult.'

'I said you'd been held up judging at a show.'

'Judging at a show?'

'I wish you'd stop repeating me. Yes, I said you were judging best child's riding pony at a show in Norfolk. They're moving to Kent so she'll never find out. She barely knew one end of Stu from the other. She was ever so nice though.'

'How old was the child?'

'Lucy? Dunno. Seven? Eight?'

'Clara, listen to me...'

'Want to see the dosh?' She retreated into her room for a moment and reappeared with a fat handful of notes, which she passed to me. 'There you go.'

It was true. Five hundred pounds in cash. 'Why not a cheque?'

'I offered a discount for cash. Quick sale essential because we're going abroad.'

'Discount...' my head was beginning to pulse like a wobble-board. 'Clara, we have to talk about this. It was very, *very* naughty of you. Totally out of order.'

'But why? Everyone's happy. Mrs Mulholland thought Stu was ace, Lucy thought Stu was ace. Stu's gone to live in the lap of luxury and we've got five hundred smackers.'

I was too tired to argue. 'We'll talk about it tomorrow.'

'Good on you, Mum,' said Clara. 'Can I keep half, as commission?'

The next morning the children had returned to school and I sat down in front of the typewriter like a boxer facing an old and wily adversary. Ten minutes into my perusal of the blank sheet George rang from his office in London.

'Hallo, I'm back.'

'Hallo.'

'Just wondered how our hero got on in his professional debut.'

'Very well, according to those who know.'

'Did you get a chance to speak to Legge?'

'No.'

'I dare say he'll be in touch. Keep me informed. Anyway, I won't take up any more of your valuable time...'

'Actually, George, there is something.'

'What?'

I told him about Clara. 'So you see I think a fatherly hand is required. A bit of advice about money, and ethics and trading standards—the sort of thing you're so good at.'

'What a fun parent I must be,' said George drily.

'You know what I mean.'

'I don't actually. I think Clara's to be commended for her entrepreneurial flair. Pocket the ackers and let well alone.'

I was aghast. 'But George, she *lied*.'

'Not about the actual commodity, though.

222

Not about the horse.'

'By implication she did.'

'I don't see it. The mother saw the horse, the child rode it, they were satisfied, they paid the price. Quite honestly I should be grateful it's off your plate.'

'I see, George. Thank you.' I hung up on him and sat there quaking with annoyance.

He, of course, rang back. 'Oh, and Harriet.'

'Yes.'

'Open an account for her with her share. We can teach her a bit about money-management. This could be just what she needs, don't you think?'

'I...'

'Got to shoot off. See you soon.' This time he hung up on me.

Lew was next on the line, applying the usual balm to my injured pride. 'Harriet, what *were* you worrying about, it's a simply super photo, it's not going to do you any harm at all, believe me. I've already had calls from one or two people who've seen it and they agree with me. Really.'

'I can't think why.'

'I'll tell you. Because you come across as a very thoughtful and serious person in the text, and a very raunchy and glamorous one in the photo. The best of both worlds, in fact.'

'Or best of neither.'

'Now then, Harriet, you're looking at that hole again, and not the doughnut.'

'That's right.'

'Let me cheer you up then. Vanessa forwarded

me all the stuff from Betabise this morning—
have you had it yet?'

'No,' I said grimly, 'but then I'm only the
author.'

'Harriet! Don't *be* like that. I guess the post
just takes longer in your part of the world.
Anyway it might interest you to know that
Reap has gone straight on to the shortlist!'

'I don't believe you,' I said, and meant it.

'You don't have to. You'll be receiving a
letter from them yourself any moment now,
but I can assure you it's true. Rhiannon Parsons
writes—er—that...' Here Lew was scanning a
letter, 'that the total entry was not as large
as expected and the initial weed-out left some
fifteen novels which have now been reduced to
a final six, and these six have been passed on
to the panel of judges...she's delighted to tell
us that Harriet Blair's novel *A Time to Reap* is
on this shortlist, and that she looks forward to
meeting us all at a reception for the shortlisted
authors at the end of this month...and so on and
so on... So you see, Harriet, this could turn out
to be your *annus mirabilis!*'

'It's certainly encouraging,' I said grudgingly.
I was nursing my gloom, but it was impossible
not to be just a little bit chuffed. I only wished
it hadn't happened too late to raise my stock
with Edward.

'It's more than that!' chirruped Lew. 'It's the
start of great things for all of us, I feel it in my
water.'

'Let's hope so.'

'I know so. All my people are on the up and

up. Did I tell you Mo Townley's game's been bought by Xenon, the computer people?'

'No—has it?'

'It sure has. And if they get it on disc in time for the Christmas market our Mo could be earning mega-mega-bucks. I'm talking serious dough here. I said that title of his *Hanging In,* I said it was prophetic. A great idea finds a market in the end, it's one of the laws of Nature.'

I found I was deeply resistant to the warm glow of mutual success with which Lew was trying to envelop Mo and me. Dammit, I didn't want to be corralled with Mo in Lew's highly idiosyncratic hall of fame.

'The way things are going,' went on Lew, 'this time next year I'll have the most covetable list in town.'

When Lew had at last finished, I did a deeply sneaky thing and nipped downstairs to get a coffee without notifying either Declan or Noleen. I was not in the mood this morning for getting caught in that particular pincer movement. I was actually reduced to stooping as I walked about the kitchen in case Declan spotted me. It was undignified, but then I seemed to have declared a moratorium on dignity.

Perhaps, I reflected, Betabise would go some way to restoring it. Determinedly I squared up to *Abide With Me,* scanned what there was of my synopsis and riffled through my notes. In the light of Saturday's events it didn't seem quite such a good idea. Gone was the lady in the fetching hat wearing a tremulous expression of wistful pride. In her place was a kind of female Mad Max, boozing, brawling, and taking on allcomers when not otherwise engaged in posing for salacious photographs. I threw away my synopsis, sketched a horse in my notepad, and drew an elaborate rococo frame round the horse. The phone rang and I sprang on it like a hunter who has been stalking a telephone for hours.

'Is that Harriet Blair?'

'Speaking.'

'Harriet, it's Persephone Marriott here.'

'Oh, hallo, Persephone!'

'It was so nice to have you at our lunch the other day. I do hope you'll forgive us for putting you through all that. We really have to vet the politicians in some way, but I hate doing it to civilised human beings.'

'Not at all, good Lord...I enjoyed it.'

'Did you? Did you really?'

'Yes, of course,' I replied, with rather less assurance.

'Good, I'm glad. You certainly *seemed* very happy and relaxed. A natural, to be honest.'

'Did I?'

'Yes. Anne and I both think we must have you on *Considered Opinion.*' I just had time to realise that Edward had been right before terror put up the storm warnings. 'Persephone I don't think I can do it.'

'We can arrange a date to suit you.'

'No, I mean I don't think I can *do* it.'

'You must let me be the judge of that,' said

Persephone with amiable firmness. You could tell how she'd got where she was today, and no mistake.

I realised it was Yes or No. Dithering would count as No. 'Okay,' I said, 'I'll do it.'

'Wonderful. I have in mind the second week in April.'

'Fine.'

'But of course I'll write and confirm everything. And Harriet—'

'Yes?'

'I can't tell you how delighted I am that you've agreed to take part.'

After I put the phone down I just sat there, grappling with the idea I was going to be on *Considered Opinion*. I, schlock novelist and political illiterate, would be sitting there in my best frock (which one...the blue? the black? A visit to Boutique Meridiana?') And answering questions of pith and moment on national television. Was I completely mad? My hand flew to the receiver; my brain, programmed for panic, threw up a pressing engagement in Auchtermuchty which I had somehow overlooked. But simultaneously some other part of my brain reminded me of Lew's ecstatic response, of how my superiority to Mo Townley would be placed once and for all beyond dispute, of how grateful and admiring Tristan and Vanessa would be...of how Edward was bound to hear of it...I did not dial.

On *Time for Talk* on Wednesday we discussed Rubbish—Is It the Window of your Soul? and

227

the word 'Casual'—Did It Now Mean Anything
But? Rather to my own surprise I found that
I was already getting into gear for *Considered
Opinion.* The swinging yet frivolous line which
I had made my own was gone, sloughed off.
I addressed myself to topics like a secretary
of state in the run-up to a General Election.
Subjectivity, spontaneity and silliness no longer
had any place in my discourse.

'Is there anything the matter, Harriet?' asked
David as soon as we'd finished.

'No, far from it.'

'Only you don't seem yourself. A bit down,
I thought.'

'Not at all.'

'You certainly came down on me like a ton
of bricks,' complained Philip, 'when I told that
story about Lord Beaverbrook and the revolving
bow-tie.'

'It'll be cut anyway,' said Lowther. 'You've
told it before.'

Philip looked aggrieved. 'So what's new?
We've all been grinding on since dinosaurs
ruled the earth anyway. We're practically into
our second generation of listeners so what
the hell?'

Nick came through and caught this last bit.
'It will have to go, actually,' he said. 'It's less
than a year since you told it.'

'Oh, Nick, I never realised you kept a file
on us,' said Nemone, swathing herself in an
aubergine cycling cape.

'Anyway, there was no call to shoot me down
in flames the way you did this evening,' went

on Philip. I could already see the way this exchange would be dusted off, embellished and recycled at a thousand evenings at the Gadfly. ('No consistent thesis...hate to say it, but that's still a female failing...it's like being on air with a bloody bird scarer...')

'Night all,' said Nick, waving us out of the door. 'Have one for me.'

In the lift Lowther said: 'You were different, Harriet. Your voice was lower, has someone said something to you?'

I decided it was time to sock them with the truth. 'I've got a lot on my mind, as a matter of fact. I've been invited to go on *Considered Opinion.*'

This floored them, as I'd hoped it would. Of all those present I was definitely the least likely to be selected for a current affairs programme.

Nemone was the first to congratulate me, clasping her hands and gazing on me with an expression of wonderment. 'Aren't you clever...! But aren't you terrified?'

'Scared shitless,' I told her, knowing full well that a display of rugged unwillingness would infuriate Philip and David still further.

Lowther chuckled. 'You'll be a sensation! You're just what that God-awful programme needs. For goodness sake be yourself, my dear.'

'I wish you luck,' said David. 'Though I can think of almost nothing I'd less rather do, myself.'

'Absolutely,' agreed Philip. 'They say old Lorimer's a bit of a toothless lion these days. Past it.'

They began to discuss just how past it Hugh Lorimer was, and I allowed them to have their fun. I could afford to be magnanimous.

After a drink at the pub I went with the Oddfellows for a curry at the Prince of Jaipur off the Tottenham Court Road, and Fergal was soon enlarging on his favourite topic.

'It's all such balls,' he declared loudly. 'You'd have to be engaged in fellatio day and night for about six months to stand the slightest chance of catching this one. Or else putting spunk on your cornflakes,' he added cheerfully, spooning raita on to his rhogan josh.

'So you don't subscribe to the divine retribution theory?' I asked. I felt sure we'd get this on *Considered Opinion*.

'I do not! There's more tosh spoken to the square foot about this than just about anything else at the moment. I don't mind telling you it makes me bloody furious!'

He introduced an enormous wad of paratha into his mouth and while he was thus effectively gagged Dominic took up the baton.

'I don't entirely agree. Communications between the Almighty and myself may have broken down a while back, but I do feel that this latest wave of plagues and pestilence is the natural result of a prolonged period of general promiscuity in the so-called civilised countries. Leaving questions of morality aside for a moment, if you play dirty games for long enough you pick up bugs.'

'Dirty's the word!' exclaimed Fergal, fighting

free of the paratha and waggling his fork before our faces. 'We all need to pay more attention to those maxims learned at our dear old nanny's knee. If we kept ourselves generally clean, including and most importantly those areas where the sun never shines, there'd be a lot less chance of catching whatever's currently doing the rounds!'

I became aware of an elderly couple at the next table casting white and anxious looks in our direction.

'I can't possibly say any of that on TV,' I began.

'Why not, for Christ's sake?' Fergal wanted to know. 'It's precisely because everyone's too chicken-shit to speak out that we're wading knee-deep in a pit of ignorance now!'

'Perhaps,' I said quietly, trying to lower the volume.

'Beg your pardon?' bellowed Fergal.

I almost whispered. 'I said you could well be right.'

'Of course I'm bloody right, lovey!'

Suddenly Dominic rescued me by asking: 'How's Edward?'

'Edward?'

'Edward Lethbridge, our mutual friend. Wondered if you'd seen anything of him since last we met.'

'No, I haven't.'

'Very wise,' said Fergal, scraping the remains of a vegetable biriani from the service dish on to his plate. 'The man's a maniac.'

'He's out of town, I believe.'

'Is he? Where is the bastard?'

'Doing some research for some committee he's on.'

'That's right,' said Dominic. 'He told us. Off looking for troublemakers.'

'Can't think why,' said Fergal, 'when he can converse with any number of them just by staying at home.'

'You know his speciality, don't you?' said Dominic, leaning towards me with a leer.

'Speciality?'

'His special antipathy. The one that gets him going.'

'No.'

'Soccer fans. Doesn't much matter whether they're hooligans or not, Edward would like to subject the whole tribe to Death by a Thousand Cuts.'

Fergal peered at me. 'Harriet, old girl, you should never have had the dansak. You've gone a shocking colour.'

CHAPTER 12

'I can see I've almost worked myself out of a job,' said Percy winsomely as we all stood on the stage, 'which is just as it should be. The ball's in your court now, folks. If you have worries, prepare to voice them now. Speak now or forever hold your peace.'

Stunned by his free-ranging use of metaphor

and quotation we remained silent. Our circulation had dropped to such an extent that animation was out of the question anyway.

'So!' Percy went on. 'How's it feeling up there at D-Day minus two weeks?' I heard a kind of honking sound, part sneeze, part sneer, and looked at Bernice from whom I was sure it had issued. She stood wrapped in her crombie overcoat, the collar turned up and concealing the lower part of her face: her eyelids drooped.

The Arnolds embarked on some convoluted query about the positioning of the tea things in Act Three. I tried to remember the statistics on single parent families in the inner cities, and whether or not the pre-school provision in same could be considered adequate by someone of vaguely liberal persuasion such as myself. It was odd, I thought, watching first Brian's and then Percy's lips move, how at social gatherings there was no opinion so wild and unfounded that one would not cling to it like a maddened Jack Russell, and yet as soon as one was formally invited to voice one's views in public they deserted you en bloc.

'...one of our best yet,' Percy was proclaiming complacently. He, of course, was now entering that happy phase during which any producer, cheered by the prospect of mawkish last-night speeches and a bottle of gift-wrapped Glentrivet, changes from dictator to den-mother. From being an insubordinate, insensitive rabble we had become his few, his happy few, his band of brothers, the custodians of the Temple of

Thespis in the howling cultural wilderness of Basset Magna. From here on in, leaving aside the occasional nervous taking, Percy would be all heart. I wondered if we would get a question on the development of rural areas.

'...the right moment to mention our post-production party.' Percy was moving forward by leaps and bounds now. 'Ladies bring a dish. Gents bring a lady—or even the wife if you must. And a bottle per couple would be much appreciated.' I looked again at Bernice. Gareth was standing just behind her—had he been there before? His face wore its customary expression of slumbrous detachment. I studied him thoughtfully. His work on *Trick of Hearts* had given no possible cause for complaint, in fact he had proved an exemplary gofer. He was completely immune to Jimmy's rantings—perhaps he was used to that kind of thing at home—and several people had made a point of congratulating me on his contribution. I dropped my gaze the five or six inches to Bernice's face. She had lifted her chin above the level of the crombie's collar, and was smiling. For a woman who was still improvising a good deal of her part she looked disgustingly complacent.

Suddenly she turned her head and looked directly at me. I grinned affably. Some kind of cheer went up, recalling me to the here and now. I realised it wasn't just Bernice who was looking at me, but everyone. Instinctively I glanced down at myself to check that I was fully dressed—it was a waking nightmare that afflicted me quite frequently these days.

'How very kind of you, Harriet,' Percy said. 'But I don't see why you should.'

I wondered what on earth I had said, and if, like the rantings of the delirious, it had been shocking, and whether it had invoked Edward.

'Sorry?'

'The party,' prompted Percy.

'Yes—ladies bring a dish, men bring a—'

'Young Gareth says you're preparing to have it at your house.'

'Does he?' Everyone laughed indulgently while I looked daggers at Gareth.

'Do I detect a crossed line?' said Percy, to more laughter.

'No,' said Gareth. 'We discussed it, remember?' He favoured me with one of those blank yet pregnant stares which family members use to pressure one another in public. Bernice was just perceptibly nodding.

'That's right,' I said, 'so we did.'

'Are you quite sure you haven't been framed?' asked Percy. If the arsehole wanted to make sure I'd have the party at my place he'd gone the right way about it.

'Quite sure, thank you,' I responded crisply. 'It's a lot closer to the hall and I've got plenty of room. You're welcome.'

'Very well, I vote we accept Harriet's offer with a good grace,' said Percy.

I caught Gareth's eye and he twitched his head with a blink as if to say 'Attagirl'. The patronising little devil. Of course I'd been framed.

The Betabise reception for its shortlisted authors was held on the roof garden of the organisation's head office in South Kensington. Rhiannon Parsons, in her fulsomely worded invitation, had spoken of 'an opportunity to celebrate excellence with wine, food and song, in beautiful surroundings' which should have warned me at once what we were in for.

The roof garden was like an overblown version of the garden-on-a-dinner-plate which the children of Basset Magna entered for the Summer Show. Lush potted greenery surrounded mini-lawns dotted with statuary. Crazy paving paths meandered here and there, all eventually leading to a central gazebo with an ornamental, domed roof. There was even a pond with water lilies, and Muscovy ducks sculling around.

The fifty or so people present milled about either in the garden or the adjoining Brontë Suite (I was sure it had been re-named for the occasion) like game in the African bush assembling near a waterhole. Of food and drink there was plenty, of song so far none, although something in the Richard Klederman mould rippled in the background.

Lew and Vanessa were escorting me. They had obviously made a solemn pact never to leave me on my own, though whether for fear of what I might do or what others might do to me, I couldn't begin to surmise. At any rate, I wasn't up to a great deal of mixing and mingling as my feet were killing me. I'd spent the afternoon scouring the West End for a suitable frock, something which would do for this event and *Considered Opinion*. The result was a false economy, since I'd felt obliged to eschew the two dresses which would have been ideal for each occasion and to go for the compromise candidate which wasn't perfect for either and which I suspected did nothing for me. It was a black, pleated chiffon shirtwaister, which I had then attempted to enliven with some jewellery from Butler and Wilson which looked as though it had hurtled straight from the mineshaft to my body. Every time I caught sight of my reflection in one of the plate-glass sliding doors that separated the Brontë Suite from the roof garden I felt that I had not achieved the integral, top-to-toe look which is the hallmark of the stylish woman.

Mind you, my eclectic appearance was not out of place. Sartorially speaking the party presented a smattering of conspicuous consumption, a good deal of commendable and sometimes successfully put-together high street chic, and a fair amount of out-and-out eccentricity. The gathering hummed with that most distinctive of sounds, the Incipient Hype.

Vanessa and I took up a position between a couple of date palms, and immediately over an under-floor heating duct, which ensured that while our hands and feet were numb our crotches were cosy. Acquaintances, would-be acquaintances and the merely curious or desperate moved towards us through the vegetation and she would then present me with an artful flourish, part pride, part modesty, all lethal charm. I would offer myself up for inspection doing my 'you'd-never-know-me-from-my-publicity' bit, with varying degrees of success. Lew took upon himself the role of hunter-gatherer, making frequent short sallies to the bar, the buffet and the book display, to fetch refreshments and check that copies of *Reap* had not been obscured or deleteriously moved. I tried to work out which of the other guests were my fellows on the shortlist, but we had not been given any form of identification and I gave up. It was all very discreet, in fact painfully so. Conscious of the possibility of seeming crass arrivistes, the Betabise people had opted for taste and restraint. The poor things had not realised that the average literary gathering had about as much taste and restraint as a gypsy horse fair. Most of our hosts were only recognisable by a minute black and gold lapel in the shape of a 'B', and the waitresses wore dresses identical to mine. Rhiannon Parsons turned out to be an immensely tall, immensely thin bespectacled beauty like a giraffe.

'Isn't this wonderful?' she kept murmuring. 'Isn't this wonderful?' And when we agreed that it was, she would gaze myopically at me as if seeing me for the first time and ask: 'Harriet...are you enjoying yourself?' I wondered exactly how many concepts per week she analysed, and to what effect. She introduced me to the Betabise Marketing Manager, Andy Fairclough. He had a well-tended black moustache and an onyx signet ring.

'We decided from the first that we wanted a hands-on approach to this competition,' he confided in Vanessa and me. 'The last thing we wanted to be was some sort of corporate Dutch uncle, commercial sponsors just handing over the lolly and taking no other interest. That's why we're having this delightful gathering tonight, before the actual prize is awarded, to demonstrate just how much we value all our entrants, not simply the winner.'

I expressed my appreciation as an entrant. The warm air coursed up my legs and made me think, for some reason, of Edward. Andy swapped his empty glass for a full one off a passing tray.

'Of course this is an entirely new venture for Betabise,' he explained, in case that aspect of the affair had escaped my attention, 'though we have been exploring avenues of this kind for some little while.' I pictured Andy and Rhiannon in solar topees, creeping stealthily among the baobab and eucalyptus of the roof garden in search of a suitable concept for treatment. 'And with the marketing and managing of books generally being such a growth area these days we thought this had to be it.'

Vanessa, wearing a little frown of fascination, said: 'What I think is especially attractive about this initiative is its free-ranging brief. "Book of the Year". I like that, awfully. It's robust.'

'Robust! Exactly.' Sensing a kindred spirit Andy directed his moustache at Vanessa. It was then that I realised what I had till then only suspected, that we authors were mere

239

window-dressing in this display of corporate pride. Lew bustled to my side with a plate loaded with finger food, and handed it to me. All the food was taller than it was wide. Cautiously, I picked up a segment of celery on which was piled a whirl of mayonnaise freckled with cayenne, an olive, an anchovy and a blob of caviar. Gingerly I moved it in the direction of my mouth, aware that no matter how wide I parted my lips they would not accommodate the package at the vertical. At the last moment, greatly daring, I tilted the whole lot towards my tonsils and threw it, javelin-like, down my throat.

'There's going to be an entertainment,' said Lew.

I gargled.

'And I've been checking out the others,' he went on, 'they're nothing to write home about.'

I swallowed violently and got down half of what was in my mouth.

'Are you all right, Harriet?'

I nodded, eyes watering, as the rogue canapé swirled about my uvula.

Suddenly Lew clasped my hand and gazed at me with emotion. 'If the judges could be influenced by beauty and elegance, Harriet, you'd win, hands down.'

I made a sound like bathwater running away.

'Harriet?'

I hrumphed and, finally spoke. 'They're not here, are they? The judges?'

'Oh my gosh, no. They're tucked up at home with a good book.'

240

Here Andy Fairclough, with that gift for peripheral hearing that is such an invaluable asset to marketing men, turned back to me. 'The judges have other fish to fry! Besides which, prejudicial conduct...by no means everyone knows how to behave—unlikely, I know, but it could happen. We want this award to be squeaky clean... Aha!' We all three jumped. 'The floor show!'

It was the Oddfellows, resplendent in boaters and maroon and white striped blazers. I experienced that odd sense of disorientation which goes with seeing someone you know wearing their public persona. I saw what everyone else saw—two blameless, jolly, off-duty doctors, trailing clouds of NHS glory and singing in the breezy, well-enunciated manner that had endeared them to thousands. Only I knew how far a cry it was from the bar-room bellowing about private parts which characterised their offstage behaviour. Fergal in particular presented a positive rainbow of contradictions. Here he was, his face pink, glistening and wholesome as a freshly cooked ham, plunking away on his banjo...could this genial songster be the same man who emptied restaurants with his tirades on genital hygiene?

Lew slipped away.

'Clever, aren't they?' Vanessa whispered. 'You know them of course.'

'A little...they do *Time for Talk.*'

Vanessa put her head close to mine. 'Is it just me, or is there something sexy about doctors?'

'I never really thought about it,' I replied,

241

half expecting the cold roast chicken drumsticks on the buffet table to rear up and crow triumphantly. To silence Vanessa I adopted an expression of rapt, smiling attentiveness: the song seemed to be something mildly satirical about literary prizes, drawing an analogy with horse racing. Little rustles of appreciative mirth came from the audience. Wasn't it all civilised, their faces seemed to say, what a pleasant, sophisticated, adult occasion.

The Oddfellows finished their first number, to brisk applause, and launched into an instrumental, announced by Dominic as *The Wordsmith's Rag*. Lew grabbed my sleeve and pulled me a couple of paces backwards into the shrubbery, where we put up a vociferous moorhen. It shot across the terrace, neck outstretched, feet paddling furiously, and entered the water with a loud splash. Several people glanced pettishly over their shoulders, but the Oddfellows plunked and jangled away like the troupers they were.

'What is it?' I asked. I could see Vanessa shooting looks in our direction, but not wanting to let Andy Fairclough out of her sight.

Lew's hornrims gleamed in the semi-darkness, like the great eyes of a slow loris. 'Would you like me to point out the others to you?'

'The shortlist?'

Lew nodded, finger to lips. 'I've been checking them out.'

'Go on then.'

He pointed. 'The short, overweight lady in

the red paisley is Coral Delgado, who wrote *Ming*.'

'As in dynasty?'

'And as in porcelain. It's only a novella, really. Very slight. A delicate piece, unlike its author!' We giggled and Vanessa shot us a reproving look. The Oddfellows went into *Your Feet's Too Big* and some of the audience began to clap along. Lew pointed again.

'That's Philippa Llewellyn, in the trousers.'

'Gosh, she looks so young.'

'A rising star,' agreed Lew. 'But her book's pretty specialised.'

'Remind me.'

'*Slow Boat to Samarkand*. A kind of druggie idyll with intellectual sex. She lives with that *Evening Argus* woman in Kentish town.'

All this sounded to me like the ideal credentials. I sighed. 'Any men?'

'Pippa Llewellyn, you mean?'

'No—shortlist.'

'Yup, now where are they...' Lew tapped his teeth with the rim of his glass. 'Over there!' His stage whisper came out with whiplash ferocity, but the Oddfellows were scatting like crazy now and nobody noticed.

'Where?'

'Squat and hairy—simian, one might uncharitably say—corduroy suit, red spectacle frames. Bruno Barnard, pop-shrink extraordinaire.'

'*Dreaming Spires?*'

'Uh-huh. One to be wary of, I fear.'

'I'm sure.'

'Then there's Erin Payne somewhere about...

243

can't see her at the moment, but she was shortlisted for the Booker a couple of years ago with that thing about her childhood in Sumatra. Exquisite, and exquisitely boring, but she must be in with a chance, you know?'

I nodded. 'And the last one?'

'Roland Cuthbertson.' Lew jerked his head and rolled his eyes.

'Are you okay?'

'Behind us—right now!'

I glanced over my shoulder and saw a large, beefy man with very well-groomed hair, like a just-past-it male model. He was talking to a tall blonde in a purple dress.

Lew jerked again. 'That's him.'

'And her?'

'His agent. Debra Field. Pure poison!'

I peeped again, and this time distinctly caught my name on the evening air. Roland and Debra were obviously engaged in the same exercise as us. The Oddfellows, by means of some tortuous *segue* concerning letters, launched into their final number, *A—You're Adorable.*

'What's the book?' I whispered.

'Don't know much about it. It's called, ah, *Coming Back,* or *Going Out,* or *Leaving Home* or something. Australian, so he must stand a chance, all things antipodean being what they are.'

A third peep revealed Roland and Debra densely intertwined while a stray mallard preened placidly at their feet. I looked speculatively at Lew. But even without the streak of mayonnaise on his nose he would not have done. The dark, magnificently forbidding shade of Edward Lethbridge hovered over us, obscuring the competition.

A light rain began to fall and we went into the Brontë Suite, as the Oddfellows retired to cries of 'Bravo!' and 'More!' While Fergal and Dominic set about laying waste to the bar and buffet, Rhiannon Parsons appeared on the stage, blinking at us over a radio mike, and summoned the shortlisted authors to join her.

'I want everyone to meet the six people who are our guests of honour here tonight, and whose exceptional talents we are here to celebrate,' she cooed. 'When we launched the Betabise Award we hoped it would act as a magnet for excellence, and so it has proved. Though we look forward to honouring our eventual winner, we hope and believe that the real winner will be the world of books, with all the pleasure and colour it brings to our lives.'

'Jesus wept,' muttered Vanessa, as I made my way to the stage amid thoughtful clapping and murmurs of agreement.

Rhiannon lined us up like glamorous grannies at a holiday camp and embarked on potted biogs of cringe-making fatuity. Still, it was a useful opportunity to get a look at my fellow authors close to.

I noted that Erin Payne had one of those faces that seem permanently to be on the verge of tears, and that Coral Delgado's looked as though it were made from the same red paisley as her dress. Pippa Llewellyn was boyish and nervily self-possessed, like a young animal.

Bruno Barnard stood with his arms folded and his head sunk on his chest. Roland Cuthbertson put his hands in his pockets and smiled a smile which I was sure he practised in the shaving mirror, which put Paul Hogan creases in his suntanned cheeks.

'...so may I thank you all for coming here and making this evening so special,' concluded Rhiannon, 'and the biggest thank-you of all to our six authors. Ladies and gentlemen, I propose a toast: to the authors!'

At last we were released back to our minders, but any hopes we might have had of further quiet drinking and gossip were quickly dashed. The minders had formed a group, so that when we rejoined them we were a) not at liberty to rubbish the opposition and b) had to talk to one another.

Roland Cuthbertson turned to me, while keeping his eyes firmly fixed on Debra, who was mesmerising Lew like a purple python.

'It's a real pleasure to meet you,' said Roland. 'I haven't yet got acquainted with your work, but I've read so much that's good about it.'

I should probably have told him there and then that he was a mendacious swine, since I'd never received a review, good, bad or indifferent, in my life, but I had such a small proportion of his attention that it would have been wasted.

'Thank you. Now tell me about your book, Roland,' I said, thereby evincing a proper interest while making it clear I hadn't read it.

At last he tore his gaze away from Debra and

fastened it on me. Vanity had won hands-down over lust.

'I can confide in you as a fellow scribe,' he said, 'and tell you that *Going Back* is not my favourite child. I'm totally amazed to find myself on this list, and in such distinguished company...' Yeah, yeah, yeah '...I felt I was being over-ambitious, and of course the higher you aim the harder you fall, isn't that so?

'Quite.'

'The thing is that for some time there have been questions I wanted to investigate, questions about belonging and not belonging, about rootlessness and displacement, about what it is to rediscover one's personal history. Can you understand me?'

'Yes, I—'

'I also recognised that these questions which all of us who come from what one might term the newer countries, the young societies, have to try and answer at some time in our lives, in whatever way we can and through whichever medium.'

'—?'

'I'm interested in the kinds of perceptions such people have about their heritage, geographical, historical, cultural. Emotional, even. So I *had* to write this novel, in a way, no matter how difficult it proved. I knew I was overstretched from page one, but so often one's brief flashes of real achievement come when one is striving for an unattainable goal...'

On and on he went. I smiled weakly and sipped my wine, occasionally glancing over his

247

shoulder to remind him that I was doing him a considerable favour listening to this egocentric drivel. Each time I did this he wove slightly to left or right to relocate himself in the centre of my focus. After about ten minutes, as he briefly pressed his glass to his forehead to recapture some fleeting notion on the theme of displacement, I feinted deftly to the right.

'Excuse me, will you, Roland, there's someone I must talk to.'

I walked quickly across to where Lew was now deep in conversation with Coral of the paisley cheeks. I had an intuition regarding Coral, and it proved correct. Her ego may have been just as inflated as Roland's, but it manifested itself in a furious interrogation of everyone else, presumably as an investment against the fateful day when she would decide to unburden herself and would need to call in a few favours.

'This must be her! This has to be her!' she cried, drawing me close to her side. 'Lew's been putting me in the picture about you, dear.'

'Accurately, I hope,' I said, secure in the knowledge that it would have been nothing of the sort.

'I'm sure he speaks no more than the truth,' said the poor deluded Coral. Her eyes were a bit paisley-ish as well, and I couldn't help noticing an almost empty bottle of Niersteiner on a chair next to her. Her breath was rich with fumes, not just this evening's, but fumes laid down over many years' serious imbibing.

'He's not an impartial witness,' I said.

'Oh, come on, Harriet,' said Lew, blushing.

Coral brushed our demurs aside. 'He's been telling me how versatile you are. It's not often I get to meet a genuine bestseller in captivity. I'm filled with admiration.'

'Thank you.'

'I'd like to know how a lady like you finds the courage to jettison a proven winning formula and write a serious novel of risk.'

'With difficulty,' I said.

'Of course. I want you to tell me *all* about it.'

I began, with Lew nodding like a clockwork Chinaman. A few minutes into my dissertation I noticed Fergal out in the gazebo, capering about and making faces at me.

'You don't feel,' asked Coral, reaching for the empty bottle and shaking it dispiritedly over her glass, 'that you have taken a step you may live to regret?'

'Certainly,' I declared, 'but one can't play safe all the time.'

I could see Lew's eyes brimming with warm tears of approval. Fergal was beckoning with both hands like a man on an airport runway.

'I mean, of course,' added, 'money.'

It was definitely time to move on again. Leaving Lew to field that one I scuttled through the drizzle to the gazebo.

'Hallo, lovey, I thought you'd never see me!' he cried, squashing me against his blazer.

'It wasn't the seeing you that was the problem, it was the getting away.'

'Popular person, eh, on the fucking shortlist!

249

You could have knocked me down with the proverbial when that Parsons female started making her speech!'

'Thank you, Fergal.'

'Not still doing the bonking in tights, then?'

I glanced about apprehensively. 'I dare say I shall be doing some more historical romances, yes.'

'But this one's not smutty then?'

'Certainly not.'

'Bloody shame. No reason why it shouldn't be, you know. A lot of these high-tone books are stuffed with smut, the two things aren't exclusive.'

'I'm aware of that.'

'So what are your chances?'

I rocked a hand. 'No worse than anybody else's.'

'Anything a humble doctor could do to improve them?'

'No!' My voice rose to a shriek. I brought it under control again. 'It's a sweet thought, Fergal, but please stay out of it.'

'Just wondered. I know one or two pox-pesterers who've got dirt on everyone in town as near as makes no difference.' I shook my head. 'Anyway, the offer's on the table.'

We stared out into the rain. The crowd in the Brontë Suite was beginning to thin out.

'Going to join us for a Greek?' enquired Fergal, unwittingly causing me a sharp pang of nostalgia. 'We're meeting Edward.'

My systems went from melancholy to red alert in less than a second. 'He's back?'

250

Fergal shook his head. 'Just passing through, still doing this committee stuff. We just happened to bump into him earlier.'

'Oh, I see.'

'Come on, lovey, you've got the best frock on and the witch doctor's regalia—you could get the bugger's mind off his loathsome ruddy investigations for five minutes. Do us all a favour.'

I was tempted. More than that, I yearned to go. But the memory of my recent humiliation was fresh and raw. No, if Edward wanted to resume relations, Edward must ask.

'I'm sorry, Fergal, I can't. I'm with other people.'

'He's hung like a jackass, you know. I've seen him.'

I blushed, everywhere. 'I'm really not interested.'

'Have it your own way, lovey,' sighed Fergal, and gave me another mouthful of blazer. 'I'll say I saw you. TTFN.'

Back in the Brontë Suite, Lew came up to me. 'We should think about leaving, Harriet, we don't want to be last.'

'That's fine by me.'

'Vanessa's gone to fetch her coat. Shall we meet by the lifts?'

In the cloakroom Vanessa, in her black suede trenchcoat, was ruffling her cropped hair in front of the mirror. Pippa Llewellyn, in a baggy combat jacket, sat on a stool pulling on boots.

'Hallo,' she said. 'We never got a chance to talk.'

'No, hallo,' I said, and we shook hands.

Vanessa headed for the door. 'See you out there, Harriet,' she said, with a meaningful look.

'Christ!' exclaimed Pippa when the door closed behind her. 'Have you ever, ever been to a more terrible do in your entire life?'

'Not many.'

She zipped up the boots and put her shoes in an already bulging Safeway's carrier-bag. I wondered if she realised how stinging an insult this must have seemed to our hosts. I liked her. 'Going straight home?' she asked.

'I don't know. Vanessa will probably suggest something.'

'Fancy a drink? A proper drink?'

It suddenly seemed a wonderful idea. 'Yes.'

'Great!' she beamed. 'Get your rompers on and we'll go somewhere convivial.'

We emerged to find Vanessa and Lew waiting by the lifts.

'Will you join us for dinner?' asked Vanessa, looking pointedly at me alone.

'I won't, thanks,' I said, 'I must head for home.'

'Very well, it has been a long day. Pippa?'

'No, thanks all the same, I snaffled a doggy bag.'

Lew chortled, and Vanessa smiled glassily. 'Good idea.'

Outside, Vanessa and Lew caught a taxi, and Pippa announced loudly that she'd walk with me to the tube.

'That's got shot of them,' she declared. 'Now let's go to the club.'

CHAPTER 13

The Two Y's was an all-girls establishment of which Pippa was clearly a popular habitué. The atmosphere was lively without being threatening, the decor was dim and reddish, the band tuneful, the clientele friendly and the barman a woman. I couldn't remember when I'd last been in a place I liked so much. Pippa and I danced, talked, drank and generally had a blast. A lot of people had read my books and professed to have enjoyed them. Even more had read Pippa's, and she was treated like some kind of mascot.

I rapidly became quite drunk, not on wine alone but on the joys of sisterhood. 'Who's this person you live with?' I asked Pippa.

'Jane Cutting. She's "Circe" of the *London Evening Argus*.'

Greatly daring I said: 'Do you love her?'

'No. Dance?'

Dazed, I let her lead me on to the floor. The band was playing *Let's Fall in Love*. Pippa took me in an orthodox ballroom hold, friendly but not importunate, and we set off. She seemed so carefree, so happy.

'Then why?' I asked.

'Why what?'

'Why do you live with her?'

'Because she's a good friend and a great lay.'

'Is that all?'

She leaned back and smiled at me. 'What more do you want?'

I sighed. 'I don't know. I wondered whether to tell her about Edward, and whether I could begin to explain the undignified nature of my feelings.

'Are you married, Harriet?'

'Er—yes.' I had to think twice about this these days. 'But not very. We're having a trial separation.'

'Poor you, that sounds like the worst of all possible worlds.'

We danced on, but the magic was ebbing away. How could she understand? I felt like some rusty, disused Dinky car that had been left out in a ditch while others, shiny and cared for, were played with in warm carpeted rooms. Lucky Pippa, so guiltless and fulfilled and uncompetitive. My feet began to drag and my stomach to heave.

The band was now playing *Three Steps to Heaven*—three steps I was more and more certain I would never make.

'Harriet, are you all right?'

'Actually no, I don't think I am.'

'Want to sit down?'

'Definitely.'

We found a table in the corner near the bar and Pippa fetched an orange juice for herself and a tonic water with ice for me. She was all honest concern. We might have known each other for years instead of hours.

'I'm sorry, you should have said. What's the matter?'

254

'I should never have come.'

'Course you should, don't talk daft.'

'I'm not fit company for a cat.'

'Don't say that, we've got two cats. Come on, spill the beans.'

'Pippa...I've enjoyed your company...'

'Have you? Good.'

'In fact it's because I've enjoyed it that I feel so—so bloody awful!' I burst explosively into tears, the full works. My nose ran, my mouth filled up, streaming mascara was turning me into an Alice Cooper lookalike. I snorted and snivelled and choked, while Pippa wagged a clean hankie before my face and patted me encouragingly on the shoulder. Her lack of embarrassment was both a comfort and a reproach. She was so sensible that I knew she could never be as sorry for me as I was for myself.

'Here, mop up.'

'Thank you.'

'Feeling better?'

'Well...'

'Want to leave?'

'I think I'd better.'

'Okay.'

Miserably, I allowed Pippa to escort me across the dance floor and up the stairs, making graceful excuses for my state as she went. The trouble was, I reflected wretchedly, I fitted in nowhere. I was neither fish, flesh, fowl nor happily married housewife.

We were half-way up the stairs when two girls—they didn't look more than sixteen or seventeen—came careering down, practically bowling us over as they did so, and yelling like banshees. At the bottom, one girl brought down the other with a flying tackle, and the pair of them skidded some yards across the dance floor leaving a trail of scattered chairs and upset tables in their wake. As soon as they slid to a halt they began fighting in earnest, punching, kicking and gouging, to loud applause.

Momentarily distracted, I asked: 'Who on earth are they?'

'Rachel and Winona, they're always doing it.'

'But why?'

Pippa shrugged. 'Lovers' tiff.'

'Won't they hurt each other?'

'Not seriously. It's all just a bit of fun. They have a very volatile relationship.'

That was putting it mildly. The dance floor of the Two Y's now resembled a wild west saloon seconds after the greenhorn has cheeked the heavy. Furniture crashed, people waded into one another indiscriminately and those not fighting cheered, barracked and whistled. The band struck up with *Consider Yourself*. Everyone seemed to be having the most enormous fun.

Pippa peered into my face. 'Changed your mind about leaving?'

'No...no, certainly not.'

We collected our coats and were just crossing the small, mirrored lobby to the street door when it swung open to admit a grim-faced WPC, a young policeman—and Edward.

'Please stay where you are,' ordered the WPC.

Pippa put her arm round my shoulders.

'We're nothing to do with it, officer, we were leaving anyway.'

'Stay there for a moment please.'

The bobby ran down the stairs. We could hear a great cheerful roar as the brawl got into another gear.

Edward raised eyebrows. His glacial gaze raked me up and down, took in my tear-stained face and Pippa in her combat jacket and flying boots.

'Edward,' I said. 'I didn't expect to see you—'

'No.'

'Weren't you—aren't you—having supper with—?'

'Yes, but there was a disturbance in the street. I followed it up.' And look where it led, his expression seemed to say.

'You know this gentleman?' asked the WPC.

'Yes.'

She looked at Edward for corroboration and he nodded. Downstairs the band began to play *Colonel Bogey*.

'Harriet's never been here before,' said Pippa cheerfully. 'Her very first time and there's trouble!'

'Mmm,' said Edward. A strangled cry for assistance came from the bottom of the stairs and the WPC darted away. 'Excuse me,' said Edward, and followed.

'Quick,' said Pippa, 'let's scram.'

When we were about a hundred yards from the street, panting heavily, she said: 'Who was that anyway?'

257

'Oh...a magazine editor I know.'

'Not exactly a barrel of laughs,' said Pippa.

I got home at half past midnight, physically and emotionally wrecked. I longed for an empty, darkened room in which to lick my wounds, but no—Colin and Clara were sitting side by side on the sofa with an air of studied partition. The two centimetres that separated their denim-covered thighs might have been the Grand Canyon. The air in the sitting room vibrated with recently checked lust. The very cushions were freshly plumped, priapic.

A film of the kind Clara was not allowed to watch in a cinema groaned and writhed on the TV screen. I sat down heavily.

'Clara, I hope this isn't a video.'

'It's not. It's BBC2.'

'Well, you shouldn't be watching it anyway.'

'Mu-*um*. It's not all like this.'

'I should hope not. Come on, switch it off.'

'Mum, don't be so embarrassing. It's really good.'

'It looks ghastly.'

'You know perfectly well if I turn it off you'll turn it on again as soon as we're out of the room. Look, there you are, they've stopped now.'

I was tired. 'What's it about?'

'Right, it's about this woman who can, you know, only sleep with people sort of thing if they're rotten to her—'

'A masochist.'

'Whatever. Yes. Anyhow, this man she's sleeping with, that man she was in bed with just then, he's actually a murderer. I forgot to say there's all these child murders going on, and he did them all—'

'And she knows about this.'

'Yes, of course, that's what turns her on. She's undecided whether to, you know, grass on him. The other thing is there's this lootenant, he's not on at the moment, hang on a tick, that's him in the car, he's quite hunky actually. Anyway this woman does quite like him, she's more or less in love with him only—'

'He's too nice for her.' I was getting engrossed in spite of myself. Colin was doing his impersonation of a sofa cushion, absolutely motionless, his eyes never leaving the screen.

The film began to cut between the clean-cut lootenant in his patrol car and the lady of the piece being brutalised by the child-murderer with every appearance of enjoyment.

I took a grip on myself and the situation. 'No,' I said, 'I'm sorry, it's not on. This is exactly the sort of stuff that does immeasurable harm. You wouldn't be allowed into a cinema to see this, Clara, and I'm certainly not going to allow it at home. Turn it off at once. Colin, how were you thinking of getting home? Clara?'

While I was speaking Clara had risen from the sofa, switched off the television, jerked her head at the tight-trousered Colin and left the room. Fuming, I stormed after them and caught up with them in the kitchen. Clara was filling the kettle while Colin sat at the table looking sheepish. I could find it in my heart to feel sorry for him, I didn't suppose he was a boy to whom all this guarded neutrality came easily.

'Colin,' I said, 'is your father coming?'

'No,' he replied, 'it's okay. I got my bike.'

'You're cycling all that way?'

Clara sighed. 'Not a pushbike, Mother.'

'What then?' I glanced from one to the other. 'You haven't got a motorbike?'

Colin, mistaking my horror for admiration, beamed. 'That's right. It's totally def. Want to see?'

I was far too tired to argue. Like a zombie I followed him to the front door He opened it, and executed a flourish like a magician's assistant. There in the road, spotlit by the yellow glow of the streetlamp, was a motorbike that even I could see was totally, totally def. An Arnold Schwarzenegger among bikes, huge, gleaming, gratuitously powerful, with great jutting handlebars like the horns of a buffalo lowered to charge.

I backed off, and whisked back into the kitchen. 'Clara,' I whispered vehemently, 'you are not to ride that thing. Ever.'

Clara shrugged. 'Col, your tea's here.'

Colin came back in, grinning. 'What do you reckon, then?' he asked me as he stirred his tea, obviously still expecting a torrent of enthusiasm.

'Very grand,' I said. 'And very, very dangerous.'

'Depends how they're ridden.'

'That's true.' I gave him what I hoped was a forbidding look, but he was in the grip of a fantasy which prevented him from interpreting anything to his own disadvantage. I was going to have to spell it out.

'Colin. I would prefer it if Clara didn't ride on that bike.'

Gareth had been right. Colin wouldn't hurt a fly. Now he looked despairingly at Clara for assistance.

She was made of sterner stuff. 'Don't be daft,' she said, 'of course I'm going to ride it.'

'There's no "of course" about it. It's out of the question.'

'No it's not.'

I felt veins I didn't know I had beginning to throb. 'Clara,' I said icily, 'Please don't take that tone with me, it doesn't impress me. Colin, I think you should go home.'

Colin was only too eager to comply. The one thing to be said for him was that he must really have fancied Clara to put up with the cross-fire in which she so regularly placed him. He went into the hall and began zipping himself into a leather jacket. Clara started to go after him but I caught her by the arm and hissed: 'You are not to go on that bike, do you understand? Colin is eighteen, no-one can prevent him dicing with death if he wants to. But you are fourteen and I'd never have an easy moment knowing you were tearing about risking life and limb on that thing of his.'

'It's not his,' said Clara, extricating herself from my grasp with a dainty tweak. 'Not at the moment. It's mine.'

She was in the hall before I realised fully what she'd said, and then I bounded after her.

'I beg your pardon?'

Colin was now fully armoured in leathers,

gauntlets and crash helmet, but his eyes looked warily out at me from behind their covering of shatter-proof glass much as Damon's had done in his scooterist days, before he became Magna's answer to Richard Branson.

'I beg your pardon?' I said again. 'What did you say?'

Clara linked her arm through Colin's though he didn't, in all honesty, look like a man who was going to give her much support.

'I said the motorbike is mine. I made the downpayment on it. To give us, you know, a bit of independence.'

Yes, I did know independence, and I was not so old and sere that I couldn't recall what it brought with it.

'Clara,' I said, in as measured a tone as mounting hysteria would allow, 'what do you mean? A thing like that could cost—I don't know—a fantastic amount.'

'Two grand,' said Colin, proud but muffled.

'*Two thousand* pounds? Clara, where did you get that sort of money?'

'I told you, I only made the downpayment, Col's going to pay the rest off.'

'I'm going to pay the rest off,' confirmed Colin from within.

'Okay, but where did you get the downpayment?'

'That money from Stu, my half.'

It was a nightmare, it had to be. 'You spent all that money on that beastly, dangerous thing out there?'

'No, not all of it, of course not!' Clara was

scornful. 'I drew out half of it and tripled it on a hot tip.'

'You placed a bet?'

'No, Col got the tip and placed the bet. And it paid off. And I've still got a hundred and twenty in the account. So everyone's happy.'

It was the second time she'd said that to me. 'Don't say that, Clara.'

'Okay.'

'Because I am *not* happy. I'm absolutely furious and I shall be talking to your father about it in the morning.'

'Oh—he rang. He's going to Japan for a week.'

'Night,' said Colin, and opened the door just wide enough to edge through it.

'Night, Col. Seeya.'

I suddenly felt like lying down right there and then on the hall carpet and falling asleep. Instead I leaned heavily against the wall.

Clara came up and patted my cheek. 'Cheer up, Mum,' she said. 'You're not such a bad old stick.'

I couldn't be bothered to argue with her. She took her tea from the kitchen and went upstairs. In a few seconds I heard Rick Astley warbling happily. I'm a bad old stick! I wanted to shout. I am, I am! I'm a wicked, mean, tyrannical old stick who puts teenage girls in stainless steel chastity belts and lets down motorbike tyres!

As I thought of tyres so there was a high-pitched squeal of brakes outside and the 'thunk' of an engine stalling at speed.

Wearily I dragged myself to the door and

opened it. Bernice's Datsun had replaced the motorbike, and only just missed the lamp-post by the look of it. Bernice was laughing merrily at the wheel, and Gareth was just getting out. I certainly wasn't surprised, I'd forgotten how to be.

'Hallo, Gareth.'

'Wotcher, Ma.' He strode out of the darkness and past me into the house. 'Got those forms?'

'What forms?'

'From Legge. He liked me. He's put X's where we have to sign.'

'Right.'

There were households, I knew, where parents and children spent literally months discussing the children's future. Where had we gone wrong?

I went out and leaned down at Bernice's window.

'What are you doing?'

'What a silly question! Bringing darling Gareth home.'

'But from where?'

'Oh...' she circled a vague hand in the air, 'I was driving back to Barford and I saw him and a couple of others spilling out of some party, so I thought what's the Christian thing to do? And here we are.'

I stared at her. She was certainly lying, but I couldn't imagine why.

Bernice grinned, wide-eyed. 'Going to invite me in?'

'No.'

'I mean, don't beat about the bush, give it to me straight.'

'No. No, no, no.'

'I can take a hint.' She started up the engine, then remembered something and took her foot abruptly off the accelerator, stalling it again. 'Oh—how was the do?'

'Palsied.'

'What about the competition?'

'A shower, bar one.'

'Give me his name—'

'Her.'

'Her, worse still. Give me her name and I'll poison Arundel's mind against her.'

'Don't bother.'

'I see.' Bernice started the car again. 'Pollyanna not wanted on voyage!' She was in alarmingly high spirits.

'Sorry, Bernice.'

'Think nothing of it. What are friends for but to have sand kicked in their faces? Nightie-night!'

'Good-night.'

I watched her drive away. And then turned to be confronted by the locked front door.

CHAPTER 14

I've heard it said, and read it in books, that people take comfort in the creative process. Anger, depression and even madness find a healing outlet in the written word, in painting, in coaxing a human form from a lump of granite. The more disturbed people are, goes the received wisdom, the more they submerge themselves in their work. Indeed, so runs the theory, the artist's most important oeuvres are often produced under stress.

My own experience to date had shown this to be a load of old horse manure. It was not the creative process that consoled, but the biscuit tin, the fridge and, in extreme circumstances, the shop. The day after the debacle at the Two Y's Club, and the unwelcome news of Colin's motorbike, was a Sunday, so I was able to set about some serious eating undisturbed by thoughts of work. I was up, as usual, some time before the children and managed to consume a cooked breakfast, toast and several cups of milky coffee with sugar before preparing a large roast with all the trimmings and several times the required number of roast potatoes. This was a fiendish piece of pre-planning. After all, the best bits of comfort eating was that which took place clandestinely under the guise of clearing up, and of which cold roast potatoes were the *sine qua non*.

After lunch Gareth went off to strut and preen at an away game with the Basset Tomahawks and Clara, who was wisely maintaining a low profile, shut herself in her room with the colour supplements. Spot and I, our flanks bulging with all the extra-curricular eating, staggered round the village hoping to avoid anyone we knew. When we returned I toasted crumpets and made some flapjacks, neither of which, sadly, interested Clara so I was obliged to consume a fair proportion of them myself. I then lit the fire and flopped down in a digestive torpor, reassured that I was not the sort of person that anyone could have found attractive anyway, so none of it mattered much...

'Ma! Wake up! Phone!' It was Gareth, encrusted in mud and smelling like a polecat.

'What...!'

'Phone! It was ringing when I got in, couldn't you hear it?'

'I've been asleep.'

'I can see that. Go on then, it's for you.'

'I don't want to talk. Tell them I'll call back.'

'He said it was important.'

'Who?'

'Edward Lethbridge.'

I moaned despairingly. 'Tell him I'm out!'

'But you're not. I already said you were in! Come on, Ma, I need a shower.'

This was true. Every time he moved little shards of dried mud fell from him and pattered on to the floor.

'You deal with it,' he said, 'I'm off.'

I went into the hall and slowly picked up the receiver. Be neutral, I thought. Be distant. Why should you care?

'Hallo? Edward?'

'Harriet—I trust I'm not disturbing you. I'm sure Sunday afternoons are a precious oasis of calm in your life.'

Yes, I thought; in between brawling at soccer matches and going to gay clubs...

'That's all right.'

'It's just that I only have today at home. I'm away all this week. And I wanted to speak to you.'

'Did you?'

'Yes. Or at least I wondered if we might arrange to meet on my return. The phone isn't really the right medium for what I have to say.'

I could imagine. 'That sounds ominous.'

'It wasn't mean to. After our recent some-what—er—inauspicious encounters I feel the air needs to be cleared.'

Oh God. 'You're right, of course.'

'I'm so glad you agree. Would dinner one evening the week after next be convenient?'

'Yes—yes, I should think so.'

'Monday?'

'Fine.'

There was a pause. Should I be saying something? All the things I wanted to say were wholly inappropriate, like 'Couldn't we forget about the dinner and the lecture and just—'

'Harriet?'

'...yes?'

'Oh, you're still there. You don't need to—consult your diary or anything?'

'No. Monday week's fine.'

'Would you have any objection to coming to my club again? It is at least comfortable and one can talk in peace.'

'Right.'

'Shall we say eight o'clock?'

'Yes.'

'I'll look forward to it. Good-bye for now.'

'Bye.'

I went back into the sitting-room and sank down on the sofa, shell-shocked. What on earth could Edward want to say for which the phone 'was not the right medium'? A swingeing sermon on anti-social behaviour, lax standards and moral turpitude I had no doubt, culminating in the swift and civil termination of our friendship. For that was all it was, I reflected gloomily. The merest of acquaintanceships, begun over woolly jumpers in M & S and advanced in the most discreet and cautious manner possible over meat and two veg at the club. Only my imagination had supplied the flames and ferment from which I now considered myself banished.

It was pathetic, and I didn't want to be pathetic. I did my best to rally my pride. I was a grown woman, for God's sake, and a successful one, what gave Edward Lethbridge the right to be so all-fired superior? Who was he to set the standard for proper behaviour? Good grief, the man was a dinosaur—an ivory-tower, cycle-clips-and-waistcoat, think-tank type of old-school high Tory, who got more worked up about public order than about women! Hah! I found myself imagining what it would be like to be carpeted by Edward in the Downstairs Drawing-Room of the Blood and Thunder...

I would wear black.

I was prevented from becoming wholly obsessive by the intervention of *Trick of Hearts,* the public performances of which were the following weekend.

'I got tickets for that play!' barked Declan when I took him his tea on Monday morning.

'Declan!' I was genuinely astonished. 'I didn't know you were interested.'

'I am not. But the wife is. Get tickets for that play, she sez.'

I simply could not picture a conversation of that length in the O'Connell household.

'I'm glad you're coming, Declan. I'll make sure Noleen gets an advance booking form another time.'

Noleen was not in the house that morning— something to do with the grommets—so I was unable to quiz her about this new interest. But I still experienced a nice warm feeling that Declan was prepared, occasionally, to indulge the poor woman. It went some small way towards relieving my general misanthropy and paranoia, and as a concession I agreed to Declan's ripping up some Rose of Sharon that had been annoying him for months.

Monday evening was the time appointed, by ancient usage, for the Arcadians' get-in at the village hall, so the afternoon was clouded by nervous apprehension. I had, anyway, decided that *Abide With Me* would not be the lush saga of family pride and passion on the touchline which I had first envisaged, but a searing indictment of soccer commercialism. It was going to need completely re-thinking, but I had at last composed the blurb: 'Takes the lid off our national game. The intrigues, the deals, the violence, the cheating—the scandal. *Abide With Me* gives a new meaning to the phrase 'professional foul'. Harriet Blair exposes the meat market of soccer apprenticeship, and the depths to which top clubs will sink to get their man...'

It was a good blurb. Having read it I wasted no time in putting my signature to Gareth's Barford United forms.

The Obergruppenführer for the get-in was Jimmy Jardine, who had decreed that it should begin at six. This meant that for the first hour at least only women and children, and the halt and the lame who had been off work, were available. Not that it made any odds. We all knew ourselves to be rank inadequates in Jimmy's book, fit only to fetch and carry and take whatever verbal abuse was handed out to us along the way. Only Gareth got by relatively unscathed, not because of any skill in engineering or stagecraft but because he was large, fit and impervious to criticism. In most company Jimmy, being possessed of the strength of the totally mad, had an unfair advantage. Nobody could climb as high, carry as much or last as long—except Gareth. Toughened by years of dirty play with the Tomahawks, and more recently by circuit training at Barford, he was well able to support an entire scaffolding tower while Jimmy swung out at a forty-five degree angle to bang a nail into the wall. What was more, he didn't much care if Jimmy fell off, which was a great source of comfort to the rest of us.

With the performance imminent Percy had mellowed, but Jimmy was getting crazier. This evening he appeared before us in the wet and windswept car park of the village hall wearing the clothes that struck terror into our hearts; out-at-knee cords, split plimsolls and a stained green jumper which had been unravelling slowly for as long as any of us could remember, revealing an ever-increasing expanse of Jimmy's painfully thin, white midriff. His hair was on end and his eyes like marbles in mashed potato.

'I need two people with functioning brains to finish painting the flats,' he announced. 'In fact I'd rather have one person who's half way competent than two shambling idiots.'

We shuffled, undecided between not wanting to appear idiots, and not wanting to paint the flats, which was the shortest of all the notably short straws on offer. Most of us old hands had experience of crouching, stiff with cold and nervous tension, a paintbrush in our hands, smarting beneath the lash of Jimmy's tongue.

But Bernice was no such old hand. 'I will!' she cried, rushing in where no angel would have been seen dead. She stood there, hands in pockets, beaming about her with the look of someone who believes herself to be the first of a happy multitude. A deathly, grateful silence greeted her.

'Sounds fun,' she added.

'Yeah,' said Gareth, 'I'll do a bit of painting. Why not?'

None of us was man enough to tell him why

not. We were just glad of the sacrificial lambs.

Jimmy ordered the two of them into the hall, threatening to be with them shortly. He then summarily deployed the rest of us to heft scaffolding poles, move furniture, clear the changing rooms and collect items of scenery from the farm buildings where they had been stored.

Before leaving on this last mission with Brian and Delia, who had sensibly come in their Volvo estate with trailer in tow, I looked in on Gareth and Bernice. They were painting away happily, kneeling side by side on a groundsheet, with the fan heater playing on them and cups of tea to hand.

'Hi, sucker,' said Bernice, 'have fun out there in the storm-tossed night.'

'These things are relative,' I reminded her smugly. 'You'll have the Prince of Darkness in here with you in a minute.'

'So?' said Gareth. 'We can handle it.'

'Don't be so sure.' I pointed at their handiwork. 'You're not allowed any streaky patches.'

'What streaky patches?' said Bernice.

I was about to walk across and point them out when my shoulder was clamped in a steel vice.

'Come on, Harriet,' said Jimmy, 'for Christ's sake get a move on. I'm coming with you in the brake.'

Rough justice indeed. It was two hours before we got back to the hall. My hands were raw, my shins were black and blue and I was so desperate for a pee I could hardly walk straight. When I emerged from the loo Jimmy was hanging by his heels from the proscenium arch, like a vampire bat, and everyone else was standing looking up at him. Only Bernice and Gareth looked cheerful. They had finished their painting and were standing with yet another cup of tea. Bernice was smoking, and idly flicking her ash on to the lid of a paint tin. 'How did you get on?' she asked.

'Shall I show you the bruises?'

'Tough, Ma,' said Gareth. 'You should have stayed here with us. It was a breeze.'

After the rigours of the get-in, and the unparalleled ghastliness of the technical and dress rehearsal, the performances themselves could only be a relief. The certainty that we could not, now, be interrupted helped us to stumble through, and the sub-text of missed cues, garbled lines and botched exits seemed to go unnoticed by our audience, who were tamely satisfied by what they saw. Even Declan and Noleen joined in the clapping on the last night. A profit was made, a picture appeared in the local paper, Percy waxed emotional and, we assured ourselves over the Betabise gigglewater after the final curtain, we had surprised even ourselves with the verve and pace of our performance. As for the party, I had adopted the time-honoured method of clearing the decks, lighting the blue touch paper and standing well back. Gareth and Clara had put up 'NOBODY BEYOND THIS

POINT' notices in all the usual places and I had hired the Prime Enterprises disco for the evening to avoid getting my nice new Audio Tower clogged up with pâté and cigarette ends. The food and drink arrived with the guests, so I had little to do but survive.

Apart from the cast and production team there were a fair number of gatecrashers of the 'I thought I must just drop in and say well done' variety, and a gaggle of Clara's friends, including Colin, who escorted groups into the road every so often for a guided tour of the horrid machine.

'Didn't you invite anyone?' I asked Gareth.

'No, didn't bother.'

'You should have done, you've worked so hard.'

He shrugged. 'No need to get worked up.'

'I signed those Barford forms, by the way. And I've sent them on to your father.'

'Fair enough.'

'You did want us to sign them, didn't you?'

'I don't know that I'm all that bothered.'

'*What?*'

'Settle down, it's not the end of the world. I'm allowed to change my mind.'

He wandered off and was swallowed up in the crush.

It was no good. I understood nobody, no, not I, and nobody understood me. My house was like the seventh circle of hell, with noise, and strangers, and people who weren't strangers but seemed like it tonight. I hadn't hosted a party of this size for years. Not since before George and I separated. Not since—for one ill-advised moment I thought wistfully of Kostaki the Ever-Ready, Kostaki of the warm hands and questing prick, Kostaki who knew nothing about seduction but all there was to know about conjunction... But it was only a transient, opportunist craving. I tried to imagine Edward at an Arcadians' post-production bash, and it was impossible. Instead, as I twisted, frugged and bopped with Percy, Trevor, Brian and Barry, I kept like a talisman in my mind's eye the picture of myself dining with Edward at his club. Yes, black it would be, stark and unadorned. Dramatic eye make-up, but no lipstick. My heels would be low, my nails unvarnished. I would move in a cloud of some musky and elusive scent. I would not smile, let alone laugh: my expression would be confined to the occasional ambiguous curving of the lips. I would speak but rarely, and low. I would toy with my food. I would intrigue and mystify. I would be a closed book that Edward would suddenly (too late!) long to open. I would—

'Gorgeous party, Harriet!' It was Bernice gleaming and rustling in scarlet taffeta with a huge bow on the hip, like a well-filled Christmas cracker. 'I'm just popping along to the Wagon for some ciggies. If Arundel turns up, be gentle with him, won't you? Byee!'

Of course, Arundel had deposited his wife at the village hall tonight, and was returning to collect her so that, as she euphemistically put it, she could enjoy herself. She had certainly been doing that. Many were the husbands, I reflected, who would surprise their wives this night because of Bernice's ability to communicate her enjoyment.

'Okay, folks!' announced Damon, his face a-flicker with coloured lights, 'it's the King!'

Elvis launched into the declamatory opening bars of *Jailhouse Rock* and Eric and Dilly Chittenden ran shrieking into the room, the acknowledged rock-and-roll experts about to have their hour in the sun. Trevor Tunnel, with whom I had been executing a chaste shuffle, dropped my hand like yesterday's newspaper, his confidence sapped.

'I could do with another drink, Harriet,' he confessed. 'You?'

'Good idea.'

We squeezed and sidled from the room, flinching from Dilly's ballooning skirt and Eric's flailing left arm. I waited in the passage while Trevor went to fill our glasses. Cheers went up. I had once been rather taken—or perhaps taken in—by the rector's 'I'm flesh and blood like anyone else' line, but it had palled with usage.

'He's a great guy,' said Trevor on his return. 'One of us. It'll be a sad day when he goes.'

'Why,' I asked, 'is he thinking of leaving?'

'No, no, no, don't worry! No, no, no,' Trevor reassured me. 'I haven't heard anything. But a man like that isn't going to stay in Magna for long. He'll have caught the judge's eye, take my word for it. He's always dashing off to diocesan meetings now.'

Eric appeared briefly in the doorway, bottom sticking out, arm aloft, knees bent. Hush Puppies stomping up a storm. Was it just me, or had his dancing taken on a new dimension since the TV showing of *The Thorn Birds,* in which a handsome Catholic priest hitched his soutane and did the Black Bottom with an alluring flapper...?

'Hello, you two.'

It was Brenda Tunnel, Trevor's wife, the woman who had actually stirred Cecil Declan O'Connell to a passion other than mindless rage. A big woman. As big as Bernice, but as unlike her as a deal table is unlike a Regency chaise longue.

Trevor stopped leaning on the wall. 'Hi, Bren. Enjoying yourself?'

'It's very brave of you, Harriet,' replied Brenda ambiguously.

I mumbled that I didn't know what she meant, but as though to confound me Dilly hurtled through the doorway on the end of Eric's arm, flashed us a hectic smile and was yanked back in again at shoulder height, legs splayed. We moved to a more circumspect distance.

'Goodness,' said Brenda, 'such energy.'

'Harriet and I have been cutting a bit of rug ourselves,' announced Trevor pluckily, looking to me for endorsement.

'We certainly have,' I agreed.

Brenda raised her eyebrows and drew in her chin, an expression which in her considerable arsenal was the equivalent of the Curse of

Skeletor. I felt for poor Trevor.

'I was a very poor partner for him,' I said.

'Oh Harriet, I'm sure that's not true.' Brenda was mollified. 'Though we did used to turn a few heads back in the old days.' She couldn't have been a day older than me, but she liked to shroud her past in the swirling dry ice of myth and legend.

'Don't know that I ever did, Bren,' said Trevor.

'You did! We both did! What do you mean you're not sure you did?'

'Maybe.'

Brenda put her bolster of an arm across her husband's shoulders. I could actually see him sink beneath the weight of it. 'You're putting yourself down as usual, Mr Tunnel.'

Unable to bear any longer the sight of Trevor submitting to this GBH by flattery, I murmured something about making sure everyone was all right, and headed for the dining-room.

Here the atmosphere was humid and hazy, the conversation a roar, and the ground becoming spongy with well-trodden garlic bread and chilli-reddened rice. In the kitchen the serious drinkers were grouped round the table, and a loose scrum of teenagers, including Clara and Colin, filled the remaining space, flushed with what I hoped was my special low-alcohol cup.

'Evening,' said Colin, as though he hadn't seen me before.

'Hallo, Colin. Enjoying yourself?'

'Yeah, it's okay. Bike's going great,' he added,

as though I had shares in it which, in a sense, I suppose I had.

'Clara,' I said. 'Where's Gareth?'

'Search me.'

I backed out of the kitchen. Quite a crowd had gathered at the sitting-room door, and beyond it I could make out the flying heads of Eric and Dilly, Trevor and Brenda. A hand was laid on my arm.

'Where's that nice son of yours?'

It was Delia Arnold.

'Somewhere about.'

'I haven't said thank you to him for all his hard work.'

'That's not necessary, Delia.'

'I don't agree. When we were in Godalming it was customary for the cast personally to thank all the backstage team, especially anyone who was co-opted. It's one of Brian's little things.'

'A very nice idea.'

'Besides, there aren't many lads of his age who would help out a bunch of old fogeys like us!'

Off she went, sparing me the need to reply. I was not sure I could have been polite. Delia was several years younger than me and at the height of her powers so where, I wondered, did she suppose her 'old fogey' reference left the rest of us?

Suddenly, I needed to escape. I went out of the front door and closed it behind me. The bouncy, infectious pop music became just so much jangling, thumping, noise-nuisance behind the closed windows, the dancers a dense forest of gyrating shadows. There were no lights on in the neighbouring houses. Fluffy sat perched on the gatepost like a tawny owl, glaring disapprovingly at me. I breathed deeply and consulted my watch. It was twelve-thirty. It crossed my mind that it was a little late for Bernice to be buying cigarettes from the pub. In fact, I did a quick calculation, it had been more than a little late even when she left. I entertained a fleeting vision of a crazed rapist stalking the streets of Magna...but another vision of Bernice in her tomato-coloured taffeta superseded it, and I could only feel sorry for the poor fellow. It was nice out here. The sky was a kaleidoscope of stars and the air was fresh. Idly I began to walk along the pavement, and Fluffy jumped down with a 'Prrrrp!' and kept me company. The bleat of Buddy Holly became dwarfed by the silvered darkness. I let my mind weigh anchor and drift on thoughts of Edward. You never knew. Perhaps, just perhaps, when he saw me in my Juliette Greco mode, his stony heart would be stirred...

I reached a point in the road, about a hundred yards from my gate, where the cottages opposite gave way to a collection of crooked old fruit trees, known as The Orchard. A track followed the line of the road just beyond the first trees, and the grassy banks that bordered The Orchard was hollowed out here to make parking spaces for residents' cars. Because of my party all the spaces were full tonight.

The Orchard looked inviting and I crossed the road with Fluffy skittering in front of me, his ears flattened, bottlebrush tail waving. As I entered The Orchard I exchanged the benign, open silence of the road for the secret, collusive one of the ancient trees. They creaked and rustled and seemed to cluster round me like curious but affectionate maiden aunts. Fluffy crouched, and sprang, and crouched again, stalking nothing.

For the first time in ages I was reminded of why I liked living in the country. Where in the city could I have wandered like this, just me and my cat in this safe, nocturnal solitude?

I'd scarcely formulated this pleasant thought when I was bathed in white light as a Jag drew up by the bank. Just as suddenly the lights went out and I heard the car door open and close briskly.

There was a click and the thin beam of a torch played around my ankles and crept upwards to my face, dazzling me.

'Hey—who is that?' I quavered, suddenly wishing I were surrounded by brightly lit cinemas, bingo halls and fast-food emporia.

'Harriet. What the devil are you doing here?'

'Arundel!'

The torch was lowered and when my eyes had settled down I made out the tall, beaky figure of Arundel Potter at the end of the road.

'I could ask the same of you,' I replied, trying to sound haughty as Fluffy sprang on to my shoulder and rocked there, his claws digging in agonisingly.

'Do you know,' said Arundel, 'that is the only time I have ever come across that particular rejoinder outside the pages of popular fiction.'

'Another case of life imitating art, perhaps.' I brushed Fluffy off and he landed on his feet with a yowl and whisked off into the undergrowth. I sidled down the bank and joined Arundel in the road.

'Anyway,' he said, 'to answer your question I am here to collect my wife.'

'Ah.'

'And I was under the impression that you were her hostess for the evening...?'

'I am. I was just getting some fresh air.'

'Shall we walk back together then?'

'Yes...why don't we.'

We began to walk, the long beam of the torch bobbing ahead of us.

Who knows what hidden and mysterious forces shape our ends? What secret voices prompt us to do what we do? Why certain impulses take us by storm and demand to be followed? Who knows why Arundel suddenly, and whimsically, swung his torch back and forth so that it shone straight in at the windows of my own car, which I had thoughtfully moved to this side of the road earlier?

Who knows why, but this is what he did. And the probing beam revealed first, through the rear windscreen, an urgently rooting backside and then, through the side window, the top of Bernice's head with its distinctive mop of black curls caught in red ribbons, and her bare breasts gleaming like a couple of cherry-topped bombe surprises, which Gareth was greedily devouring.

We stopped. The torch beam glared unforgivingly. The silence was deep enough for the muted sighing and grunting in the car to grate on us with the soft insistency of a cracked record demanding to be taken off.

Gareth looked up first, his expression hovering on an uneasy cusp between ecstasy and horror. Then Bernice tipped her head backwards to gaze at us in upside-down dismay.

Arundel switched off the torch with a gesture like Indiana Jones cracking his bullwhip. Bumpings and mutterings indicated the attempts of the lovers to separate and adjust their clothing.

I was disorientated and didn't know where Arundel was until his voice came from behind me, near his own car.

'Send her along here, will you,' he said, his voice like a blunt razorblade. 'When she's ready?'

I nodded, which wasn't much help to him in the dark, but anyway he had climbed in and slammed the door with the offstage ferocity of the pistol shot at the end of *Hedda Gabler*.

The miscreants emerged.

'Gareth,' I said. 'How *could* you?'

'No need to go spare,' said my son.

'Go to your room.' It was the most humiliating thing I could think of.

'Night,' he said.

'Bye, sweetie,' said Bernice. And then, 'Where is he? Old misery guts?'

I jerked a thumb. I never expected an apology from Bernice, but some display of remorse, however fleeting, would have been nice.

'I ask you,' she went on. 'Only Arundel would

go round shining torches into people's cars. But if he's expecting me to eat humble shit he's got another think coming.'

Off she marched. The Jag door slammed. Arundel's headlights, on beam like some tool of Nazi interrogation, slashed over me as I stood in the road. Far away Buddy warbled that every day, it was getting closer...

But the Betabise Award was a mere speck, dwindling, to disappear over the horizon.

CHAPTER 15

While dining with Edward I kept seeing that scene in my mind's eye, as if to remind me of the yawning cultural gulf that divided us. If Edward had had a son, that son would never have had it away with, say, Persephone Marriott. Even less in the back seat of a Metro. And in the unlikely event of any such thing happening, Edward would have called down murrains and thunderbolts on all concerned, there would have been no question of Carrying On as Normal.

I was wearing the black, but it felt like mourning. It was hard to be intriguing and mysterious with a conscience like mine. To make matters worse, Edward had not yet got round to saying whatever it was he was building up to. On the contrary he seemed in vacant and in pensive mood, and kept falling silent and staring at me as though trying to reconcile the woman before him with the one he had recently discovered. Polite conversation faltered along, staggering and stumbling over the hidden agenda.

'What have you been doing since we last met?' asked Edward over the main course.

The results of actually telling him were too horrible to contemplate. 'Oh...just working away.'

'I've always considered the writer's life an enviable one.'

'Why is that?'

'Tranquil, solitary, reflective.'

'That's how it should be, certainly.'

'You feel the world is too much with you?'

That was one way of putting it. 'Yes.'

He seemed to think about this for a moment or two. 'On the other hand one must presumably live, in order to write.'

'I suppose so. But in an ideal world one would be able to choose one's experience. Simply muddling along isn't necessarily helpful.'

Edward frowned. 'You feel that is what you do? Muddle along?'

'Much of the time, yes.'

'You certainly seem to be a woman of many parts,' he offered.

If this was my cue to present a justification for past actions I did not take it. Whatever Edward thought of me, he was probably right.

He cleared his throat. 'Are you ready to cut a dash on *Considered Opinion?*'

'I don't know about a dash. I suppose I'm as ready as I'll ever be.'

'I'm on that night as well. Fortunately.'

Oh hell. 'Oh good.'

'Yes.' He stopped suddenly and gazed at me as though expecting some startling declaration. I pursued and stabbed a sprout, shooting it on to the floor. I was having difficulty eating. I knew that later on I'd wolf down a bowl of Weetabix in the kitchen and dream of this meal.

As the waitress retrieved the sprout and told me not to worry, Edward said: 'You seem tense, Harriet. Are you quite all right?'

'I'm sorry, I'm not very hungry.'

'That's quite permissible. I just wonder why.'

'I've had rather a wearing week.'

'Perhaps you attempt too much. Diversification taxes the energy terribly.'

I suddenly felt the lecture looming up, and I couldn't bear it.

'Pudding?' he asked.

'No thank you. Look, Edward...'

'Yes.'

'Let's not beat about the bush any longer, shall we?'

'I wasn't aware that we were.'

'You told me that you had something to say to me. Something you didn't want to say over the telephone.'

'Did I?'

'Yes. You know very well that you did.'

'In that case I can only apologize for being pompous.' For the first time Edward seemed discomforted.

'Don't, please. I'd just like to save you the trouble of saying it.'

287

'I see.'

'I know how I must seem to you and I'm sorry. I can only say it's not my fault, and I regret it.'

'Harriet...'

'I can't keep up this pretence any longer, Edward.'

'Pretence?'

'You know what I mean—you've seen for yourself how I really am, the kind of life I lead. It's a mess. I'm a mess. My marriage failed because I had an affair with a doctor. My son is a sex maniac and my daughter is a spiv. I lied deliberately about the kind of books I write—'

The waitress appeared with her notepad. 'Coffee?'

We both shook our heads. 'And now that I have written something more serious,' I went on, 'I have managed finally to alienate one of the judges for the Betabise Book Award, so the book will sink without a trace as it richly deserves to do. Furthermore, I do not agree with a single one of your political views, and if I gave another impression then it was mere hypocrisy on my part, because I wanted to start an affair with you. Since I now see that's out of the question, I suggest we go our separate ways as quickly as possible. That's what you were intending to say to me, but now you won't have to.'

My voice had risen and several heads turned. The Juliette Greco impersonation had certainly been chucked out of the window. I was being

288

about as subtle and enigmatic as Freddie Starr at a sporting club hen party. But it was a relief. 'And now if you don't mind I think I'd better go.'

Edward set aside his napkin in the manner of a man who would otherwise have swung a punch. A small muscle worked in his cheek. 'Would you like me to organise you a taxi?'

'Thank you.'

I watched as he walked with his long, Masai-warrior stride out of the restaurant. After my daring performance, reaction set in. My chin went into spasm and I could feel my nose reddening in anticipation of a good blub. I rummaged for the only available hankie, a lipstick-stained tissue from my make-up bag. I knew what a pathetic and foolish figure I must cut, the product, as Edward would have put it, of wandering up a blind alley in search of Nirvana: alone in a gentlemen's club, dressed like Mrs Danvers, snivelling with frustration, busting to get laid by the man I had just sent packing. I had spoken no more than the truth: I was indeed a mess. I thought again of Gareth and Bernice testing the Metro's suspension, and actually envied them their lusty spontaneity. Kostaki and I had been like that. Or at least Kostaki had. It seemed that where sex was concerned I was a bulimic—either bloated or starved, never satisfied.

Edward returned and stood over me. 'It'll be here in a minute. Shall we go?' We went across the hall and down the stone steps into the chilly outer lobby. Edward reclaimed my coat from the porter and helped me on with it. He was painfully suited to the role of silent, dignified courtier, the bastard. My taxi drew up and stood thrumming gently at the kerb. I turned to Edward. 'Thank you for dinner.'

'It was my pleasure. I'm only sorry...'

'Good-bye, Edward.'

For the first time in ages I actually played it right, and disappeared into the night without looking back. This was only for fear of spreading mascara on his lapels, but he wouldn't know that. Too late, I remembered *Considered Opinion.*

When I got back to Magna the children were in bed, mercifully alone. On the pad by the hall phone was a message from Bernice, scribbled in Clara's handwriting: 'Don't sulk. Please ring.'

I tore it up, but as I was stirring my cocoa the phone rang, and it was Bernice herself.

'Okay, okay, okay, but what's the point of recriminations? He's a healthy, red-blooded youth, and I'm married to Arundel.'

This was all I needed after what I'd just been through. 'Bernice.' My voice actually quivered with fury. 'Bernice, he's under age. You were taking advantage of a minor.'

'You're implying that there was nothing in it for *him?*' Bernice's voice rose incredulously. 'I must say, I take exception to that.'

'You've got a nerve! Don't you have any sense of what's right? Any idea of what's appropriate? You're my oldest friend...'

'So you'd prefer he did it with a total stranger?'

'You *know* what I mean. It was a betrayal...'

'Steady on!'

'Besides which, have you no...'

'Shame? I've forgotten what it looks like. And, as I recall, it wasn't so long ago that you were enjoying relations with the Greek Kildare just about everywhere except the bedroom, and loving every minute of it.'

'That was different!'

'Oh yeah?'

'We were consenting adults.'

'It may surprise you to hear that I didn't exactly have to manacle your son. He's so horny he could poke a girl's eye out!'

'Bernice!'

'It's true. They all are at that age. It's good for the little buggers to have somewhere safe to put it.'

'Safe, hah!'

'Of course safe. I'm experienced, kindly, uncritical, on the pill and an all round good lay. Plus I'm frustrated as hell. An adolescent's fantasy woman. I honestly don't know what you're getting so worked up about, Harriet.'

All of a sudden, neither did I. I was tired. I was miserable. I needed a friend. My tone of voice had attracted Fluffy and Spot, who stood watching me, mutely apologising for anything they might have done or be about to do.

'Harriet, are you still there?'

'Yes.'

'Take my advice and put it right out of your

291

mind. It's only Mother Nature. If it hadn't been for the Prof with his beastly little torch you'd never have known a thing about it.'

'What about Arundel, though?'

'What about him? I gave him a roasting.'

'*You* gave *him* a roasting?'

'Of course! He shouldn't be so smutty and suspicious.'

'He was quite justified as it turns out.'

'Not at all. I've always made it perfectly clear. If I'm dissatisfied with what's on offer at home I shall look elsewhere.'

'Did he—did he say anything about Gareth?'

'Oh yes, plenty!' Bernice laughed. 'Only to be expected, product of his upbringing, nobody learns Greek any more, nobody gets caned, nobody speaks the Queen's English. He blames you, of course.'

So Edward had been wrong. There was at least one man who had retained the ability to identify his enemies, and had no trouble apportioning blame.

'But don't let it worry you,' Bernice continued. 'I know how tigerish you are in defence of your young. Far better that you should be cast as the Wicked Queen than that your darling Gareth be branded as the jolly rogerer he undoubtedly is!'

She laughed again, sure she had said all the right things.

'But Bernice,' I whispered. 'What about Betabise?'

'Now Harriet,' she said firmly, 'that is unworthy. Arundel may be a tightfisted killjoy but he is a professional. And he would *never* let a little thing like this affect his judgement.'

The very next morning, ironically, I got my official invitation to the Betabise Book of the Year Award Dinner. I also received a postcard from George in Japan, though he must have been back in this country for some days. Both these missives reminded me that my absentee spouse was long overdue for child-fatigues.

I was in no mood for tact or discretion—I rang him at the office. 'George? You said you wanted to be involved.'

'That's right, I do.'

'Well, now's your chance. Both Clara and Gareth need bringing into line.'

'No change there, then.'

'There's no cause for levity I assure you. I need your support, I need you to bring a firm hand to bear, and that as soon as possible.'

'Of course.' George was at once all concern. 'What do you suggest?'

'I have to attend a book prize dinner in a fortnight's time—I'm on the shortlist as a matter of fact—'

'Harriet, that's brilliant!'

'Thank you. Anyway, I shall have to be away that night, and, quite frankly, with the way things are at the moment, I don't want to leave them on their own here. Perhaps it would be a good opportunity for them to come for the weekend.'

'Certainly. Hang on.'

I heard him consult his diary. Just let him be

in Helsinki that weekend, I thought, and I'll—

'Looks fine. I've written it down. In fact I should enjoy it, it's weeks since I spent any decent amount of time with them.'

'But George—'

'Mm?'

'Please, I want you to put the fear of God into them. Clara's into sharp financial practice and Gareth's into sex.'

'I have to say,' said George, 'that it sounds like a winning combination.'

'Just do it,' I said.

The children didn't think much of my projected appearance on *Considered Opinion;* it was a really, really boring programme; but I made them promise to record it so that I could assess my performance. Trevor Tunnel, on the other hand, gave me to understand that the whole of Basset Magna would be incommunicado that night, clustered round their television sets with an intensity of concentration not matched since the last royal wedding. If he meant this to be encouraging, it didn't work. I was terrified, not just of doing the programme, but of having to confront Edward once again, even if it was for the last time.

George sent me a good luck card. On the front it said: 'Nervous? Don't be.' And inside: 'Just remember MILLIONS of people are watching you.' Underneath he'd written, 'And I'll be one of them. Here's looking at you. G.'

Considered Opinion was recorded a couple of hours before its actual transmission time, presumably so that those panellists who lived in London could nip home and see how they did. When I arrived at the studio at seven I was frisked comprehensively by a security guard, in case I had microfilmed cuttings, books or rolled-up crib sheets sewn into the waistband of the black chiffon shirtwaister. In the green room, where a table was laid up for four courses, I was introduced to my fellow panellists. Tish Wetherall was not among them. Edward had not yet arrived. But there was Doug Archer of the AFU, and the fourth panellist was a young junior minister as smooth, fragrant and slippery as a cake of soap.

Persephone moved among us, taking soundings and trailing bait, making sure we all appreciated just how violently we disagreed with one another. She was wearing a heavily beaded ethnic jacket, a calf-length black skirt and ankle boots. Her spectacles dangled on a black velvet ribbon. Her hair was caught up in a couple of fierce-looking ebony combs. She positively exuded that careless brainy glamour which had so impressed me at our previous meetings. Even someone who did not know her would still have been able to guess at the brilliance of her legs.

Edward had still not arrived when we sat down to dinner. Anne Dwyer's place was empty—she had gone to elicit questions from the audience. Yet another motherly waitress—was there an agency, I wondered, which specialised in them?—came round with an excellent white wine and we attempted to force gull's egg down our constricted throats.

'We're not looking for any googlies,' said Persephone, 'just good, thought-provoking, topical stuff.'

Hugh Lorimer grunted. He'd finished his eggs, and now he swung his chair round in order to watch a recorded news bulletin on state-of-the art TV in the corner.

'I see we're one short,' said the junior minister brightly. 'Will the rest of us get overtime if he doesn't turn up?'

'What makes you so sure it's a he?' said Persephone, nailing with a look.

Doug, who had given his eggs to Hugh Lorimer, waved his glass in my direction. 'We already have our token woman.'

'I resent that,' I said.

'That's the spirit,' said Doug, and winked at me which, if I was going to be consistent, I should have ignored icily, but which, in the circumstances, I thought rather sweet.

Edward arrived halfway through the chicken in parmesan sauce, upstaging us all with his air of gaunt distraction. If anything I found this haggard, rumpled Edward even more alluring. I positively ached to bring him the comfort of a good—well, fairly good...woman.

He said no to food but accepted a glass of wine. 'So what will it be?' he asked of the table in general. A women's issue for Harriet, the privatisation of the Harefield works for Mr Archer, the St Dennis islanders for you, Minister—and what do I get, Persephone?'

'Don't tempt me,' responded our producer with admirable zest. 'And don't make so many assumptions. Harriet, for instance, is not here to be hived off as some kind of representative of her sex.'

'Pity,' said Doug. 'She'd do it nicely.'

Hugh Lorimer turned back to the table to dispose of his dish of *sorbets variés*, and then returned to the television with a chunk of Wensleydale and a stick of celery. Several crumbs of the cheese fell, and lay upon his tie. It was my hope—a forlorn one I suspected—that the make-up girl would overlook these crumbs and leave them in place to be commented upon by several million uncharitable viewers.

Conversation was desultory. Edward seemed preoccupied and, after his first sally, fell silent, ignoring everyone, including me, and referring to a small, dog-eared notebook. The junior minister huddled over the telephone by the door, hastily grabbing a last clutch of statistics. One by one we were called to make-up, and reappeared looking the same but more matte. I could have done with a bit of Paul's determined creativity, but it was not to be. There was no transformation, just Harriet Blair, longing to be anywhere but here.

In the studio I was placed on Hugh Lorimer's right, with the junior minister on my other side. Edward was on Lorimer's left, with Doug Archer beyond him. This meant that if I sat well back in my chair I couldn't see Edward at all. The audience were already in their seats, mumbling suspiciously. They looked as motley and hostile a crew as any my worst nightmares had conjured up. Bearded men

297

in polo necks, impeccably coiffed ladies in earrings and necklaces that matched, smooth black men in three-piece suits, and spike-haired school-children, who looked as if they'd forgotten more than I'd ever know about Major Issues.

I scanned the sea of faces for one friendly, ill-informed-looking one, without success. Oh God. I was here. It was now. This was it. And I was, as Gareth would have said, bricking myself. I couldn't remember when I'd last read a newspaper, or the name of the Prime Minister, or my address—

'We're just going to do a question for level, and to get everyone warmed up,' said Hugh Lorimer, exuding his brand of on-air crusty joviality. The cheese crumbs had gone.

'Where,' he went on, 'is Mr Foley, who is a statistician?'

'Here, Hugh.' Mr Foley put his hand up. He was bald, save for a few hairs brushed smoothly forward from the crown of his head. He wore no jacket. He had on a short-sleeved shirt buttoned to the neck, with no tie. What could it all mean?

'Your question, Mr Foley.'

'Here is my question, Hugh.' Mr Foley cleared his throat. 'If members of the panel were marooned on a desert island and could choose two people to accompany them, one for themselves and one for the good of humanity, which two would they choose?'

A rumble of faintly ominous laughter greeted this. It was like the laugh the pantomime dame gets just before the pudding explodes in her face.

'Harriet Blair?'

'Yes.'

Hugh Lorimer favoured me with his famous quizzical scowl. 'Who would you take, Harriet Blair?'

'Oh—that's easy!' I grinned wildly. 'I'd take Rory Bremner for myself, because he could supply just about anybody, and—er—Prince Charles for the good of humanity.'

A small, polite round of applause. I'd survived. The junior minister opted for his wife and Mother Theresa. Doug went for Billy Connolly and Nelson Mandela. All good, safe stuff.

'Edward Lethbridge?'

'The question is perfectly idiotic,' said Edward. He went on to point out that anyone stranded on an island could do precious little for humanity anyway, so he would take the Bluebell Girls who were beautiful, English and superbly well disciplined, and he would leave it to us to divine the purpose. He got the first really genuine applause, but of course he had an unfair advantage. He had never looked more devastating—dark and aloof, pale and haunted. His little joke—and it had only been a little one—was the more piquant because of the poetic grandeur of his appearance. As I contemplated him, a young man in a sleeveless pullover came to adjust my microphone and the glancing, impersonal contact had a most embarrassing effect on my nipples. I half expected to look down and see them lit up like a couple of miniature miner's lamps. Never mind, I thought. Suffer tonight and then you'll be free, and it'll be back to Basset Magna, *Abide With Me,* the Arcadians and cold turkey...

'...an author, broadcaster and sometime marathon runner.' Me! He was talking about me! 'She describes herself as a committed floating voter, who is especially interested in the issues of education and women's health.' Was that what I had said? It was astonishing what Persephone and Anne Dwyer had managed to distil from the garbled note I had sent them concerning myself. Pray God I wouldn't be found out.

We began. We got the St Dennis islanders, the Harefield works and the new exam structure in schools, so all Edward's assumptions had proved perfectly correct. And till the final question, everything went better than I'd dared hope. I went for a forceful style, blamelessly liberal content and safe targets. I got by.

Typically, it was when Law and Order reared their ugly heads that trouble broke out.

Hugh Lorimer, knowing that we were on the home straight, looked positively genial as he surveyed the audience over his half-specs.

'Our final question is from Beatrice Stewart, who is a student.'

Beatrice Stewart was blonde, plump and peachy with a piping, breathless voice. To see her interacting with Hugh Lorimer was to be reminded of the famous scene in *The Barretts of Wimpole Street* between Mr Barrett and his niece Bella. 'Yes Hugh,' said Bella.

'What I want to know is: How can we curb the rising tide of casual crime and mindless violence, especially that connected with sport, without restricting the freedoms essential in a democratic society?' With a blushing, righteous rustle, she subsided into her seat.

'Thank you, Miss Stewart,' said Hugh Lorimer. 'Harriet Blair?'

I was ready for this one. 'Surely,' I began, 'the greatest freedom we enjoy is that of going about our lawful business or pleasure unmolested and undisturbed, and that is the freedom which must take precedence over all others, especially that of those people who may prove a threat...' It was standard stuff, and it got me through with a scattering of applause.

The junior minister then went into a series of dazzling verbal acrobatics, glittering with statistics, bristling with precedents, scintillating with examples and illustrations. The whole performance was a tribute to the politician's art, a speech designed to dazzle and disorientate the lay listener. A stunned silence followed, into which Doug Archer strode like the heavy in a western who, having watched the Kid twirling his six-guns, picks up the nearest chair and brains him with it. His message was straightforward—yes, we are already in the process of restricting vital freedom all over the place, and if he might just be allowed to cite a mere handful of examples...? He got the biggest clap so far.

'Edward Lethbridge.'

Edward, his elbows on the arms of his chair,

laced his fingers together and then steepled the forefingers and placed their tips on his upper lip. It was impossible to escape the impression that he had taken over the chair of the meeting. He allowed an agonising three or four seconds to elapse before beginning his reply. When he did speak it was in the manner of a man who has only delayed in order to bring his fury under control.

'When I have to sit here,' he said, 'and listen to the kind of arrant, irresponsible, petrified claptrap that my fellow panellists have been mouthing, I find myself seriously wondering whether they, and I, *and* you,' here he pointed, 'are living in the same country or reading the same newspapers. When did we become so timid, so vacillating, so pusillanimous? When did we become *cowards?*' He stared, all fire and ice, at his mesmerised audience. He was utterly splendid.

'Unless, very soon, we begin to identify our enemies, to accuse and to punish the troublemakers, we shall be swept away in a tide of motiveless crime unprecedented in this country's history!'

He was beginning to thunder. It was terrifying, magnificent! My nipples lit up again, even as I realised that if I was not to do a public U-turn I was going to have to disagree with everything he said. It was dangerous stuff. Doug Archer was shaking his head and doing the platform-percher's silent laugh, but no-one was looking. The junior minister gazed in agony at his clasped hands. With my peripheral vision I saw Beatrice Stewart stand up.

'Every one of us,' went on Edward on a rising intonation, 'every one of us who has ever ignored rude and intrusive behaviour on a bus or train, who has failed to upbraid someone for smoking in a no-smoking area, who has tolerated foul language in a public place, who has turned a blind eye to the slipping standards of dress, of morals, of behaviour both public and private—every one of us who has done these things is GUILTY!'

Beatrice Stewart's arm rose, and shot forward. My first reaction was that she was adopting the classic *'J'accuse'* pose prior to some serious heckling. Until I saw a huge tomato cruising through the air, over the heads of the audience, straight at us. I ducked.

It was one of those extravagantly big, opulent, scarlet Italian beef tomatoes and it caught Edward fair and square between the eyes. It splattered generously all over his face and slid squishily down his long nose to fall with a series of plops on the blotter in front of him.

There was an interminable split second of hush. Then uproar broke out. Hugh Lorimer roared at Persephone in the control room to cut, a couple of security guards rushed from the sidelines, a whole phalanx of the audience rose up around Beatrice Stewart like the Hydra's teeth, Doug Archer began to clap and the junior minister said 'excuse me' and disappeared behind the screen. Slowly and deliberately Edward took a large, white, well-laundered handkerchief from his pocket and wiped the tomato off his face. As the action speeded up all round him he rose, very slowly, and pointed once more at the struggling audience. 'There they are!' he boomed. 'There they are, the don't-give-a-damn brigade, the people who make life in this country a misery, the rabble who jeer at the rule of law, who aren't happy unless they're meddling and protesting—'

'Oh, for God's sake, be quiet!' It sounded awfully like my voice. 'Shut up!' It was. 'Can't you see you're only making things worse?' Suddenly I was on my feet and facing Edward. Hugh Lorimer bobbed about between us like a boxing referee. The noise was now deafening, and the audience a heaving, thrashing mass of bodies. Of the poor unfortunate security men there was no sign.

'Yes, Harriet!' hissed Edward, in a venomous undertone that cut through the din like a laser. 'Yes! You would know all about that, wouldn't you? Since trouble seems to follow you wherever you go!'

'How dare you?'

'Please!' spluttered Hugh Lorimer. 'We're here to record a programme!'

'Piss off!' I snarled, and he plumped down in his chair, looking quite green. I was letting the frustration out with a vengeance. 'What gives you the right to judge everyone? You don't live in the real world, Edward, you don't know how people think and feel, you don't feel at all! You're a bloody automaton!'

Sensing I'd probably gone too far Doug tried

to intervene at this point. He leaned forward and snatched at Edward's tie. But Edward, displaying quick reactions and a surprising instinct for dirty tactics, shot his elbow backwards and caught poor Doug in the solar plexus so that he jack-knifed forwards on to the table, scattering blotters, pencils and tumblers and expelling air like a whoopee cushion.

I was exhilarated, and there was a carafe to hand. I grabbed it, scrambled on to the table and poured the contents over Edward's head. Rivers of water cascaded over his head and shoulders, bearing with it the last tomato seeds. Hugh Lorimer let out an inhuman sound. Doug groaned. The audience fought happily.

When Edward, gasping, opened his eyes, they were no longer chips of ice, but pale fire that sent a shiver through me.

A shrill whistle sounded. 'Thank God, thank God!' cried Hugh Lorimer. 'The police!'

Persephone lined us up in the green room like disobedient fourth-formers, and gave us a right royal wigging. She was very, very disappointed in us. She'd had such high hopes, such splendid expectations, and what had happened? We shuffled, smarting under the lash of her tongue, but rather pleased with ourselves nonetheless.

The junior minister, the only panellist not to be impugned, enquired anxiously if the programme would still be going out.

'I couldn't say,' said Persephone sternly. 'A lot of people are going to have to work very

305

hard clearing up the mess you people have made. If we cut in the warm-up question at the end it might just be possible. In all my years as a producer I have *never* had to deal with such an incident. Hugh is one of the BBC's most respected and experienced professionals, but I have never seen him so shaken. It was a disgusting performance.'

'I hope you acknowledge that I was not involved,' said the junior minister.

'I do, minister. But neither did you do a great deal to mitigate the situation,' snapped Persephone. 'Now please go, all of you. There will of course be no fee.'

We slunk off. Outside the studios it was pouring with rain as the four of us emerged. We could not look one another in the eye. Doug Archer set off in the direction of the tube, the junior minister was met by his wife in a chauffeur-driven Rover, and in the split second that Edward and I were left together on the pavement we were ambushed by a keen girl reporter from the *London Evening Argus* diary column, who had followed the police car.

'Can you tell me what's been going on?' she asked eagerly.

'There was a fracas,' Edward told her loftily, as if she had asked a stupid question. 'It has become impossible to state the obvious in this country without suffering actual physical and verbal abuse from all those who are in disagreement.'

The girl looked awestruck. She turned to me. 'May I ask your name?'

'Certainly, I'm Harriet Blair. I was one of the panellists.'

'And what is your view of what took place?'

I decided to give her a scoop. 'Mr Lethbridge is not noted for the moderateness of his views,' I said, 'nor for his moderation in expressing them. There would have been no trouble if he had taken a more temperate line. It was a calculated verbal assault, and I hold him directly responsible for what happened.'

Nervously she turned back to Edward. 'No comment,' he snapped. 'I should go and ask your questions in there if you want the full story.'

'Good idea.'

She bustled off, and Edward grabbed me by the upper arm, abruptly and hard.

'Let go!'

'No.'

He began frogmarching me along the road, sticking out one hand to hail a taxi as he did so.

'Will you leave me alone!'

'Blantyre Mansions, Parsifal Road, please.'

I was bundled ignominiously into the back seat and the door was slammed.

'Edward, what are you doing? How dare you! You have no right to treat me like this...!'

And then, as the song goes, he kissed me.

Kostaki's kiss had been sweeter than wine, but Edward's was pure firewater, a mugging-by-mouth which left me bruised, affronted and gasping for more. When he released me my lips were actually numb, and my whole body felt as though it had been put through a mangle.

'This is intolerable,' I gasped, just like the Lady Genesta Fitzallan in my bestselling *Love at the Gallop*.

'Not for me, Harriet...' He pulled me back against his wet, panting chest and hit me with another kiss. 'It was the self-denial that was intolerable. The wanting you every minute of every day and knowing I must do without.' He kissed me again. 'The fear that you could never feel as I did...as I do...oh, Harriet, Harriet!'

Still clutching me so hard that I could hear his heart pound beneath the clammy shirt he let his head fall back against the seat and closed his eyes, like a man just rescued from drowning. His assurance was awe-inspiring. In this, as in everything else, he took a great deal for granted. In short, he was masterful. And I was in a shameful, pulsating, pre-feminist paradise. In a small voice, I said: 'I meant everything I said, you know.'

Eyes still closed, he smiled. 'I never doubted it.'

'You are holding me here, taking me wherever we're going, against my will.'

'That I do doubt.'

'Your behaviour has been quite scandalous all evening.'

At this he gave a short laugh—the only time I had heard one from him—opened his eyes and looked down at me, eyebrows raised. My small rebellion was put down before it had even properly begun. Another kiss, this time of terrible, thrilling, grinding urgency, descended on me from on high. Like Lady Genesta, I had put up a spirited show but no longer had the strength to resist.

Still holding me with one arm Edward leaned forward and slid back the partition.

'Along here, third on the left.'

'Righto, squire.'

Something about the cabbie's blokey tone stirred a final spark of rebellion. This was the male mafia at work. The cabbie doubtless thought that displays of male machismo such as Edward had just engaged in were the right and proper way to handle a whingeing, stuck-up tart like me. As Edward hauled me out on to the pavement I tried to wrench free, but his grip on my wrist simply tightened like a choke chain, and I was obliged to come to heel as payment was made and change given. My hand hurt and my pride threw in the towel.

'Thank you. Good night.'

'Night, squire.'

Edward pulled me up the steps of a huge mansion block, through outer and inner front doors, across an echoing hall, up a flight of stairs and to his own door, which he opened with three different keys.

The door clunked shut behind us like the portals of Castle Dracula. Edward clapsed me in both arms and crushed me—yes, honestly—against his chest for another kiss. My knees turned to custard, my head swam, the bicycle pump speeded up.

'Come,' said Edward, 'come, Harriet.'

It was like the voice of Jove. I had no option

but to obey, as Edward towed me along a passage and through another door. He had turned no lights on and the darkness was intense, muffling and opaque. I had no sense of direction, of time, or space. I could have been in a ballroom or a broom cupboard. Suddenly my legs were swept from under me and I was swung high into the air and then lowered on to a soft slippery and yielding surface. I didn't dare move, but neither did I want to. All my married life I'd been the kind of woman who did her share of hefting coal, forking bales and lugging rockery stones. It was really something to be treated like a plaything.

And now, Edward was hovering over me, his arms on either side of my head like an eagle mantling its prey. I could just see the glimmer of his eyes in the dark. With almost my last rational thought I told myself to remember this—it was great copy.

'Harriet,' said Edward, on a long, quivering exhalation. 'This has to happen.'

It certainly looked like it. Indeed my disappointment if, at that stage, it hadn't happened, would have bordered on the suicidal. In a final burst of lucidity I whispered: 'But Edward, I don't understand... I thought I'd done everything wrong...'

He began to lower himself on to me.

'You have,' he breathed. 'You have, and you must be punished...'

I once likened sex with Kostaki to being in a

310

tumble-dryer. With Edward it was more like being banged up and down on the stones of a riverbank by some third world matriarch. It was ferocious, persistent and protracted, with any number of false crests and new beginnings. The appropriate musical accompaniment would have been Ravel's 'Bolero' with its dramatic repetitions, terribly spun-out tension and final, abrupt and thunderous climax.

If this was being punished, I could definitely take it.

Afterwards, as I lay there like a discarded rag doll and loving it, Edward got up and lit thick white candles in a many-branched candelabra. He stood for a moment, naked and holding the candelabra, his face eerily lit from below by the flickering flames. Then he set it down on some surface just beyond the foot of the bed and returned to my side.

'Are you all right, Harriet?'

'Yes, thank you.'

'You have no idea how obsessed I have been with you.'

'Poor Edward.' I stroked his cheek.

'I wanted to explain to you the other evening, but you wouldn't allow it.'

'No. Well—'

'Let me help you, Harriet. You must.'

'But I don't need—'

'Hush. Trust me.'

We lay there in his extraordinary room, two figures side by side in the candlelight like effigies on a tomb. Where, I wondered, was the C.P

311

Snow-ish clutter, the fogeydom of the bachelor who didn't know his own size in underpants, the brusque and bristling bedroom of the man who, as Fergal had so cogently put it, got his rocks off on Law and Order? This was a richly textured crypt of velvet and satin, swagged, draped and embellished like a necrophile's fantasy. On one wall hung weapons—a pike, an assegai, two gleaming pistols and, yes, a whip, curled like a rattlesnake about to strike. Huge velvet curtains railed on the floor in extravagant abundance, the bedhead towered over us, boiling over with baroque carving and strange hieroglyphics. On the floor beside the bed was a great black bearskin, its rigid gaping jaws a splash of vivid red amid all the black and purple.

'You will come again,' said Edward. It was a statement.

'Oh, yes.' Again and again and again...

'You may think yourself an ungovernable woman,' said Edward. 'But believe me, I can change you.'

As he loomed over me once more I spread my legs like a welcome mat. He could certainly try.

When I left an hour later I noticed a framed photograph on the wall by the front door. A tall woman with astounding legs, dressed in a minimalist version of a Nazi stormtrooper. Bits of black leather, death's head emblem, cap, revolver, suspenders...obviously someone who needed Edward's attention a great deal more than me.

'Who's this?' I asked.

'A friend,' he replied. But I didn't need him to tell me. I'd suddenly realised who it was.

'Of course,' I said. She must have had the best legs in broadcasting. 'Persephone.'

CHAPTER 16

Yes, Edward and Kostaki were polar opposites. Where Kostaki had been importunate, public, carefree and experimental, Edward was deliberate, secretive, sombre and orthodox. That is not to say that Edward was dull. Far, far from it. It was like being made love to by an avenging angel, carried on mighty wingbeats of reproving lust. His attentions gave a whole new meaning to the phrase 'missionary position'. I hadn't felt so good in years. Three times between *Considered Opinion* and the Betabise Dinner the avenging angel took me beneath his wing. The pattern went something like this.

'Harriet? This is Edward.'

'Oh, hallo, Edward.'

'I wondered if you might be interested in a spot of dinner at the club tomorrow evening.'

'That sounds nice. Let me just check...yes, yes, that's fine. What time?'

'Oh, eightish. I shall look forward to it.'

'And me. See you then.'

'Good-bye, Harriet.'

We were always civil, even prim, at this stage.

Then, over mountains of food at the Blood and Thunder, Edward would begin to draw me out about past misdemeanours, mine and those of my family and friends. I was not concerned with integrity, I exaggerated and embroidered at will. By the time we finally boarded a cab for Blantyre Mansions you could have cut the sexual tension with a knife, and when the many-bolted door finally crashed shut behind us I was ready to take my punishment like a fallen woman.

But though the means of seduction and the surroundings may have been strange, there was nothing untoward about the sex. After more than a decade of marriage, and a hair-raising whirl with the brazen Kostaki, I should have fled in terror at the slightest hint of kinkiness. No, this was standard stuff, writ operatic. I left Basset Magna at six-thirty and was back home in bed with a cup of cocoa by midnight.

Just the same I was glad I'd arranged for the children to go to George on the night of the Betabise Dinner. I rang Edward at his office at the *Bystander* to tell him what I had in mind.

'So I wondered if we could meet afterwards?'

'Of course. A splendid idea. Will you have eaten?'

'Oh yes, the full works.'

'Shall I come and pick you up there?'

'That would be nice—it wouldn't be any trouble?'

'No trouble at all.'

'About eleven o'clock, then.'

'I shall be there.'

314

I didn't tell him that I had the whole night to spend with him—let that come as a lovely surprise. If I won, it would be a Night of Nights. If I didn't, I had the world's best consolation prize to look forward to.

It was just as well I felt buoyant, for I was still riding the turbulent wake of my misdemeanour on *Considered Opinion*. The programme had gone out, in a cobbled-together form, but thanks to the girl from the *Argus* the incident had made quite a few of the papers, with library photos of myself and Edward under headlines such as 'Lady of Letters Makes a Splash' and 'What the Viewers Didn't See'.

Of course it did me no harm at all, in fact over the next few days I found myself having to acknowledge heartfelt congratulations from all sides, and as far as Gareth and Clara were concerned it was the best thing I'd done in years. Even George rang to say he didn't know I had it in me.

'There's a lot you don't know,' I replied.

'Yes, but assaulting people in front of the TV cameras, and on a serious programme like that—frankly I'm staggered.'

'I'm not in the least proud of it,' I lied.

'Let's just hope that Lethbridge fellow doesn't sue,' said George gloomily.

'Yes. Let's hope so.'

Bernice took a different view. She called to offer me a lift into London for the Betabise Dinner. 'I've got to go, you see. Boring, boring, but there it is. Helpmeet time. He's under the impression I owe him one.'

'He's right. At *least* one.'

'Don't start that. What about the lift?'

'No thanks. Anyway, it's hardly proper for a contender to travel in with one of the judges.'

Bernice yelped. 'You really think Arundel could be seduced by anything you had to offer?'

'It's not impossible,' I said huffily.

'Forget it. He's going in by train in the morning so that he can be closeted with the other judges all day, sealing things into envelopes or whatever they do. It beats me how they can take so long reading a few books and working out which one they like best. It'd only take me a few hours.'

'I don't doubt it.'

'So what about this lift? I shall be cruising in in Arundel's horrible great Jag. I'll need someone to giggle with.'

'Thanks, Bernice, but I'll be independent this time.'

'Suit yourself. I've got calls on my time too you know—there's a string of sex-starved schoolboys outside the back door.'

'Bernice. That remark was in the worst possible taste.'

'You can talk. I read the papers, you know. Who is this Edward Lethbridge anyway, and what have you got against him?'

I hesitated. 'Nothing, really.'

'Nothing? I bet he avoids you when you're annoyed.'

'It was just a difference of opinion that got a bit—overheated.'

316

'Harriet.'

'Yes?'

'You wouldn't be having carnal knowledge of this Lethbridge character?'

'Sorry?'

'You *are!* Well, I'll be... And you don't want a lift because you'll be nipping off for a night of nooky with him.'

I thought that whatever else my nights with Edward were, they were not nooky.

'Yes. As it happens.'

'You dirty little devil!' I wondered whether I could engineer a meeting between Bernice and Fergal. 'I smelled a rat when I read about that water-jug caper. That, I thought, is not the all-round good egg who learned her lines before anyone else. That, I said to myself, is a woman aroused!'

'So you were right.'

'Not miffed, are you, at the infallibility of my instinct?'

'No.' I was, rather, but it would do no good to admit it.

'Must go. But quickly—how's darling Gareth?'

'Darling Gareth is staying in at night and doing his homework.'

'What a criminal waste. Still, if he gets a string of "A's" in his exams, you'll have me to thank for it. Indirectly, of course.'

George collected Gareth and Clara on Friday evening. 'I thought we'd go out tomorrow night,' he said. 'Take our minds off the unbearable tension. I booked at this place

Smiths, in Barford, I gather it's the happening eatery among those who know.'

The children's faces took on a look of fixed neutrality. 'Good idea,' I said, 'you can let me know what it's like.'

'As long as they serve one or two dishes which don't silt up the arteries and overheat the blood I shall be quite happy,' said George. 'Okay, kids, let's leave your mother to prepare her acceptance speech.'

He thought he was joking. But inevitably as I got ready the next day I could not help turning over in my mind one or two felicitous phrases—gracious, modest and humorous—that I would be able to use should the need arise. The problem of dress I had solved, triumphantly and at great expense. It was a little black suede number, as soft and clinging as a glove, brief in all departments as though (Clara had said) a piece had been removed for every ten pounds over a hundred. Still, when I put it on I knew it had been worth every penny. It was a bad girl's dress. Edward would really disapprove.

I took a train, first class, and a taxi, and arrived at the Ebury House Hotel in Knightsbridge at about ten to eight. Tristan, Vanessa and Lew were waiting for me in the foyer. My publishers were immaculate, Tristan wearing his black tie and bum-freezer with the easy style of accustomedness, and Vanessa in a burgundy velvet cocktail dress with a couple of frills for a skirt. Lew had on a white tuxedo. He exemplified the difficulty of the person who has not got anything especially wrong but who,

318

in the company of those who have got everything absolutely right, simply cannot win.

They greeted me with cries of delight, astonished that I had made the journey unaided, and rained kisses on me. They then fell in round me like an armed guard and escorted me up the stairs to the pink and white salon where the pre-dinner reception was being held. While I had my picture taken for *Pub Talk* and the Betabise house journal, Tristan and Vanessa were sucked away from my side by gossiping colleagues, but Lew stayed close, smelling slightly of toothpaste, his hand guiding my elbow. I felt like a contestant on a game show, surrounded by dozens of wily compères.

'Are the others all here?' I asked through gritted smiles.

'Of course. The important thing for us is to mix and mingle, and be seen to be seen. Especially as you're so good at it.'

'Not that anything can affect the outcome at this stage,' I pointed out.

'No, but you must get across as a person who simply doesn't *need* to win,' explained Lew. 'Which shouldn't be difficult in that dress, Harriet,' he added. 'You look great.'

'Thank you, Lew.'

In truth, I was feeling good. The prospect of sex with Edward, of possibly bringing the acceptance speech into play, of all this benign publicity cancelling out that generated by *Considered Opinion*—all combined to make me sunny and tractable. I moved from group to group under Lew's supervision, beaming and nodding and making modest and intelligent remarks, while Lew watched my lips and endorsed my every word.

We'd worked the length of the room and washed up near the fireplace when I heard a familiar voice.

'Hallo, Harriet.'

'Pippa!'

She looked terrific, in the kind of way only the young and thin can attempt, let alone get away with. She wore navy woollen leggings and a garment that might have been a large sweater or a small dress, and which slipped off to one side to reveal her bra-less shoulder. Her face was bare, her hair artfully scrubby. At the end of the leggings were black and white baseball boots.

'You look wonderful,' she said.

'So do you.'

Pippa's large agent, a-rattle with tortoiseshell beads, came to her side like a chaperone scenting trouble.

'What's this? A mutual admiration society?'

'More or less,' said Pippa. 'Harriet, do you know Deirdre Wainwright?'

'How do you do.'

'Hi there, Dee,' said Lew.

'You two have met?'

'The network of agents, my dear,' said Deirdre.

'Isn't this a horrid situation?' said Pippa. 'I really don't want to be here. Shall we go for a Chinese?'

'You won't say that when you win,' put in Deirdre smartly.

'When?' said Lew. 'With all due respect to Pippa I think you should allow the rest of us an "if".'

'Yes, Deirdre,' said Pippa. 'You've no idea how embarrassing I find this.'

We were spared further embarrassment by the announcement of dinner and we all trooped out of the salon and back down the stairs to the dining-room. I noticed Coral Delgado hanging on to the bannisters, Roland Cuthbertson in a white tux that put poor Lew's in the shade. Bruno Barnard in tobacco-coloured corduroy and Erin Payne looking pale and sad. Perhaps, I thought, that was the right way to look, you were so much less likely to betray undignified disappointment. Whereas if, like me, you were a silly grin on legs, you stood every chance of having it publicly wiped off.

The authors and their minders had been thoughtfully scattered among the dozen or so round tables, and there was a representative of the Betabise organisation with each group. To Lew's dismay it was not he, but Tristan, who was paired with me. We sat opposite one another, with Rhiannon Parsons on Tristan's right. I could tell by the very angle of his head, and of hers, that he had her on toast.

The judges with Andy Fairclough (it sounded like a pop group), were right next to us and as we sat down I spotted Bernice, grinning and waggling her fingers at me in the least discreet way possible. How I'd missed her before was a mystery since she was dressed for the occasion in a plunging pink leather shift with a halter neck, which gave the impression that she was carrying her breasts slung round her neck in a nosebag.

'Yoo-hoo!' she mouthed. Andy Fairclough, who was sitting next to her, must have thought his birthday and Christmas had come all at once, his face was a study. When he realised whom she was signalling at he gave me a fleeting smile, and then turned to Bernice to address the serious business of what she did, where she came from, and whether she was married. Arundel, mercifully, sat at an oblique angle to both of us and appeared not to have noticed his wife's contortions. From time to time I could see his sharp profile dipping storklike into his wine glass. I could only pray that R.N Morrell, a genial old biddy, and the fey and wimpish Lawrence Bennett of Sallow and Windrush had managed to keep his more poisonous impulses under control.

I was seated between an elderly publishing knight for whom all awards dinners had long since blended into one bibulous haze, and the bright, prickly editor of a new literary magazine. Between the knight's amnesiac ramblings and the editor's disguised sniping there weren't many laughs to be had. The result was I drank rather more than was judicious, and when the coffee and liqueurs were brought round I even accepted a Drambuie.

I'd actually begun a second one by the time we'd had the comfort break, and when R.N. Morrell finally approached the lectern and clasped its corners for support I was feeling no pain.

The sparkling conversation—which had only been a time-filler anyway—died away and all faces turned towards R.N, shedding their false expressions of interest and assuming instead those of overmastering greed and ambition. Even Tristan, that *summa cum laude* graduate of the Shires School of Savoir Faire, made eye contact with me and flashed me a this-is-it look. There was a deep, deep silence, broken only by R.N's droning peroration and the bubblings and garglings of the sleeping knight. I began to appreciate how tight I was. Champagne, fine wines both red and white, and a tumblerful of Drambuie, sloshed about inside me forming a swill with the partially digested products of the Betabise Fine Foods Department which had composed our meal. I needed the loo, and the services of a mirror. I was not someone who sparkled when squiffy. In fact, I developed the red nose and rheumy eyes of a lush by about the second glass. Underpinning all these thoughts was the concern that I did not wish to be summoned to the lectern not looking my best.

I needn't have worried. When my name didn't appear in second or third place my hopes gave a final desperate leap. But it wasn't till well after Pippa had risen from her seat and was threading her way towards R.N that I realised I was that most dismal of creatures, an also-ran.

Anti-climax came without climax ever having happened. I was suffering from the female, literary equivalent of blue balls.

On the other hand, it was Pippa. Pippa who didn't blush or simper, who kept her head high and leapt up on to the platform in her baseball boots without using the steps. Pippa who would have no truck with hypocrisy or gushing. Pippa who received her fat cheque, her motherly kiss from R.N, her backslaps from peers and rivals, with considerable dignity and no false modesty. Watching her, I knew the prize had gone to just the right person. I felt no envy, just a drab, dull disappointment. I blew her a kiss as she was borne away to be interviewed, and there dawned the horrid prospect of renewed conversation. Tristan was at my side like the genie of the lamp.

'Bad *luck*, Harriet,' he said. 'You mustn't worry, these things are so subjective. To be shortlisted is the real prize. Everyone knows the final choice is often a compromise candidate.'

The magazine editor was all kindness now. It went to a typical competition book, he confided in me. 'Only just over a hundred pages long and obviously autobiographical.'

What a slimy little creep he was. 'Do you know,' I said, 'what a—'

'Harriet!' Vanessa arrived with an ashen-faced Lew in tow. 'Harriet, *what* a shame. I could honestly have wept. In fact I did weep.'

She obviously had not. 'So did I,' said Lew, kissing me. He obviously had. 'I'm afraid there's simply no justice.'

'All's fair in love and war,' I muttered. 'Excuse me, I need to pop out for a second.'

As I fled, I heard Tristan saying to whoever

324

would listen: 'She's quite simply our most versatile author.' God, but these people had stamina!

I burst into the Ladies like an axe-murderer on the run from the FBI. Deirdre Wainwright sailed past me, and Erin Payne and Debra Field exchanged commiserations in front of the mirror. I might have dipped out again till the coast was clear, but just then water gushed noisily and Bernice appeared.

She embraced me in a slippery, creaking embrace. 'Who cares about some bloody silly prize, anyway?'

I extricated myself. 'Exactly.'

Debra and Erin left the room and I dived into the loo.

'It definitely went to the right person,' I said over the partition. 'She's really nice.'

'Hm.' I could actually hear Bernice doing her mascara. 'No clothes sense.'

This was rich, coming from her. As I emerged from the loo it struck me that Bernice, in the pink leather, looked just like a gigantic, ambulant sex aid.

'I'll never speak to Arundel again,' she went on.

I sat down on a red dralon-coverd stool. 'Why not?'

'Because of what he's done to you, Harriet!'

'But you said he wouldn't hold a little thing like you and Gareth against me.'

'Cheeky. Perhaps not, but it made him look for a pretext to rubbish you. And you, like the sporting girl you are, gave him one.'

325

'What, for heaven's sake?'

'Considered Opinion.' Bernice turned from the mirror, smacking her newly-reddened lips. 'I realise now you were doomed as soon as that story appeared..'

'But that had nothing to do with books, or writing—or anything!' I protested incredulously.

'Perhaps not. But a great deal to do with publicity, Harriet. Something you've always been good at and of which Arundel strongly disapproves. You mark my words, he'll have processed that caper of yours to good effect. I remember now, he was really cheerful the moment he'd read about it.'

'Oh well,' I said, beginning to think of Edward. 'I wouldn't have won anyway.'

'Maybe not,' said Bernice, giving the leather shift a yank which nearly catapulted her breasts to freedom, 'but you wouldn't have been completely overlooked, either.'

'Never mind,' I said, linking my arm through hers as we made for the door, 'it's history now.'

I spent the next three-quarters of an hour standing in a corner with Vanessa, Tristan and Lew, all three of whom looked as though they were presiding over a laying-out. I myself was quite chipper, but the funereal metaphor was sharpened by the comings and goings of others who variously offered their sympathies, advised me to make the best of it, and praised the nobility of *Reap*. Bernice cruised the rest of the company, occasionally winking at me when I caught her eye.

It was not till I was just about to leave that I suddenly came face to face with Arundel.

'Good evening, Harriet. My commiserations.'

'Hallo, Arundel. Thank you.'

That was all we said. But as he walked away he gave me a smile of such chilly, poisonous complacency that I knew, without a shadow of doubt, that I had been nobbled.

I sought Bernice without further ado. 'Bernice!'

'I'm free.'

'You were right.'

'I always am. About what?'

'About Arundel.'

'Oh, that. You wouldn't believe me.'

'Well, I do now. I just met him.'

'Don't say he told you!'

'He didn't have to. It was written all over his face.'

'So what shall we do?'

'That's what I was going to ask you.'

'Come with me.'

Out in the car park Bernice unlocked the Jag and took something out of the glove compartment.

'What's that?'

She opened her hand. 'Swiss army knife, everything but colour telly. He always carries it.'

Even I blenched. 'But Bernice, you're not suggesting...'

'Not *him*, Harriet, the tyres!'

Oh, the glee with which I set about my task! While Bernice kept cave like a monster animated condom, I squatted down and slashed

327

and jabbed to my heart's content. I didn't just let the tyres down, I demolished them, and watched the pompous Jag subside, a useless lump of metal, on to the tarmac.

I'd more or less finished the last tyre when I heard Bernice squeak my name, and looked up to see a tall, dark figure standing over me.

'Arundel...?' I quavered.

'Edward,' came the reply. 'Harriet, you must come with me.'

I don't know exactly when it was I smelled a rat. It may have been when Edward insisted I vandalise my £150 micro-dress with his kitchen scissors...or when he ceremonially lit three dozen of his thick, white candles with a flaming taper and placed them all around the sides of the room...or when he put on the Ring Cycle at full volume as he got undressed...or when he tied my black tights around his forehead like a mature person's Rambo...or when he began to hum so loudly that the tendons in his neck stood out...

Whenever it was that my suspicions were first aroused, the crunch finally came when, as I lay like some punk-Cinders on the black satin bedspread, he reached up and took a cat o'nine tails from the wall.

It must be said that even as I screamed blue murder and put both feet through one knicker leg, I noticed that Edward had never looked more magnificent, all black and white, and gleaming with his fell purpose. Fergal had spoken no more than the truth when he'd

328

described Edward as hung like a jackass and now, as I pogoed for the bedroom door, his vengeful prick menaced me like a broadsword poised to strike.

'Edward!' I screamed. 'You're going too far!'

'No, Harriet,' he boomed. 'It is you who go too far. Always, always, too far!'

By slamming the door in his face I just managed to gain those vital seconds required to free my leg and get it through the proper aperture. But at once he was upon me. In the passageway we struggled. He was a big man, but I was no weakling, and he was considerably hampered by his mounting enthusiasm. Brünnhilde warbled and shrieked as we swayed about in the darkness. When, suddenly we bumped against the wall I felt the hard edge of something pressing on my temple—it was the photograph of Persephone. I freed a hand and scrabbled to get a hold of it.

'Now, Harriet!' growled Edward. *'Now...!'*

But I'd grasped the picture, and was able, just, to draw my arm back far enough to deliver a resounding smack to the back of his head. The glass shattered and flew in all directions. Edward let out a tremendous roar of pain and rage, but I must have stunned him slightly, for he let go of me. I got halfway to the front door before he was after me again, crunching over the glass in his Argyll socks like some tranced yogi.

I don't know what came over me. Perhaps being branded a wicked woman had finally taken effect on my personality, or perhaps the memory of a thousand professional fouls came to my aid. At any rate, with a maniac howl, I launched myself at him, caught him off guard and off balance and sent him hurtling back through the bedroom door.

Frantically I struggled with the various bolts and locks and finally burst out on to the landing, just as a lady with blue hair and a quilted dressing-gown came out of the door opposite and I saw, from the corner of my eye, the flames beginning to leap up in the bedroom...

'I'm sorry,' she said, 'but I must complain about the noise.'

The police were very understanding, really. The fire engines had reached Blantyre Mansions promptly and got the blaze under control before it had done too much damage and there had been no casualties, apart from Mr Lethbridge, who was going to be kept in hospital overnight for observation. No harm done this time, although, they added with confiding avuncular smiles, it might be as well if I quietened my social life down a bit.

They drove me in a panda car to the Ebury House Hotel to collect my coat and handbag. The receptionist appeared understandably relieved when I refused her suggestion of a room for the night, and even called me a mini-cab.

The driver was elderly, Asian, and inclined by temperament and circumstances to silence. I sat in the back and stared out of the window at the bright city streets, the dim, sleeping suburbs, the flat, unhelpful darkness of the countryside. But it was my life that flashed before my eyes.

Bernice, telephoning at three the following afternoon, woke me up. 'Hallo, can't talk—he thinks I did it! Christ, Harriet, the things I do for you, it's been the night of the long knives here while you were rolling in the hay with Lethbridge—I'm a bally martyr to friendship—shit, here he comes—!'

George brought the children home in the early evening. They said they'd had a wonderful time. They were even prepared to be gracious about me not winning.

'I shouldn't worry about them,' said George when they were out of the way. 'This boyfriend of hers sounds a responsible chap, and you know how important mobility is at that age. And Gareth confided in me—had a little fling with an older woman, it's all over now but it made him realise there's more to life than football. A perfectly healthy development, and the best possible way to learn about sex. Wish I knew who she was, I'd like to shake her by the hand.'

On Monday morning, Reg Legge was first to call. 'Your husband rang and gave me the bad news just now, Mrs Blair. I'm sorry you've changed your minds. Your Gareth had the makings of a class player. Good head on him. Still, if he's got that many new interests, good luck to him.'

Vanessa was next. 'The *on dit* has reached us,

Harriet! Sounds nasty, Tris and I do hope you're quite all right. I won't even ask what took you away to Blantyre Mansions without even saying goodbye—you always were a dark horse! But none of it's going to do *Reap* any harm, no harm at all...!'

I went to do some shopping at Betabise in Regis. Near the check-out, there was Colin, un-Bros-like in his brown overall, dismantling the shortlist display and filling it up with copies of *Slow Boat to Samarkand* by Pippa Llewellyn. 'Neminday,' he said. 'You can't win 'em all.'

Back at home I surprised Noleen in the garden with Declan. She was speaking to him, loudly and clearly. I could even hear her through the kitchen window. 'You listen to me, Cecil O'Connell,' she was saying. 'You ask for a raise, or you don't come near me for a week! *And* I'll tell her about you and that fat woman up the road!'

After lunch it was George. 'Harriet—I asked Era for a proof copy of this book of yours and I just got it today. That's me, isn't it, for Christ's sake? It's quite unforgivable. Everyone's going to know. What the hell am I going to tell the people at work? You and I have got some serious talking to do.'

I even had a unprecedented call from Fergal. 'Having a bit of a bash for Edward—the silly sod bloody nearly incinerated himself over the weekend. Burning subversive literature I shouldn't wonder. Do come if you can, lovey—and bring along any other agreeable women you happen to know as long as they're clean and take a broadmindeded attitude. I'm inviting that tight-arsed crowd off the wireless so we'll need a bit of light relief. Got to cheer the bugger up, and you're just the woman for the job.'

Around teatime Percy pushed a copy of a play through my letter box, and with it a note: 'Harriet—see what you make of this, I think it's rather droll, and it does have plenty of women. I'd particularly like you to look at Mrs Peasemould, the VAT inspector who comes in in Act Two. We all feel that after your last performance you're more than ready for good, solid character parts.'

It was my turn to make a call. 'Bernice? How sweet of you to take the rap for me. Look, some friends of mine are throwing a party, but sadly I can't go. They said bring a friend—could you deputise for me? I know you'd enjoy it, they're really lovely people. Yes, sure—the pink would be perfect.'

For the first time in twenty-four hours, I smiled. But not for long.

'We haven't met,' said the strange woman's voice. 'My name's Eleanor Mulholland. I simply must talk to you about the pony I bought from you for my daughter Lucy...'

The publishers hope that this book has given you enjoyable reading. Large Print Books are especially designed to be as easy to see and hold as possible. If you wish a complete list of our books, please ask at your local library or write directly to: Black Satin Romance, Magna House, Long Preston, North Yorkshire, BD23 4ND, England.

This Large Print Book for the Partially sighted, who cannot read normal print, is published under the auspices of

THE ULVERSCROFT FOUNDATION